D0181352

AN
OCEAN
AWAY

AN
OCEAN
AWAY

LISA HARRIS

NORTHEAST COLORADO BOOKMOBILE SVS
WRAY , CO 80758
(970) 332-4715
(800) 306-4715

summerside
PRESS™

3NECBS0090826U

Summerside Press™
Minneapolis 55438
www.summersidepress.com

An Ocean Away
© 2011 by Lisa Harris
ISBN 978-1-60936-107-5

All rights reserved. No part of this book may be reproduced in any form, except for brief quotations in printed reviews, without permission in writing from the publisher.

Scripture references are from the following sources: The Holy Bible, King James Version (KJV). The Holy Bible, New International Version®, niv®. Copyright © 1973, 1978, 1984 by Biblica, Inc.™ Used by permission of Zondervan. All rights reserved worldwide.

All characters are fictional. Any resemblances to actual people are purely coincidental.

Cover design by Lookout Design, Inc.
Interior design by Müllerhaus Publishing Group | www.mullerhaus.net

Summerside Press™ is an inspirational publisher offering fresh, irresistible books to uplift the heart and engage the mind.

Printed in USA.

DEDICATION

To Allen Avery, who taught me so much through his love
for the African people. You will forever be remembered.
1944–2010

The world and its desires pass away,
but the man who does the will of God lives forever.

I JOHN 2:17 NIV

NORTHERN RHODESIA, AFRICA

1921

CHAPTER ONE

Lizzie MacTavish froze as she watched the giant beast walk across the dusty path in front of her. She crouched in the thick folds of tall grass between Chuma and Esther, her two young African charges, holding her breath until she thought her lungs were going to burst.

The elephant lumbered toward them, close enough that Lizzie could see the infant hidden beneath the gray shadows of the mother's belly. Close enough to see its long eyelashes that kept out the dust from storms that regularly swept across the plains and the creases in its wrinkled skin, tinged with the brown mud from the African soil.

Finally, Lizzie took a gulp of air, breathing in the sweet scent of the *mufufuma* tree and its violet blossoms that mingled with the musky odor of the elephant. Overhead heavy clouds gathered, waiting for the first showers of the season to fall. October always brought a change in the activities of village life. The lazy days of winter, with its sharp winds and grass fires, had all but disappeared.

As winter merged into the rainy season, the grasslands presented an abundance of fragrant flowers that perfumed the morning with their sweet smell. Even the trees were laden with scented blooms, making up for the humid and sultry air. It was her favorite time of year, when men worked to cut the trees in the fields, and women planted the maize, sorghum, and millet in the fertile soil and harvested pumpkins and ripe forest fruits.

Esther tugged on the melon-colored fabric of Lizzie's skirt. "*Bama* will not be happy when she finds out we have wandered past the far pasture and toward the banks of the river."

Lizzie kept her voice to a low whisper. "Your mother will be busy for hours as she awaits the birth of yet another one of your sisters or brothers."

A grin spread across Chuma's face. "My father is praying for a son."

Lizzie frowned. A son, of course, would be preferred. Daughters were regarded simply as wealth, much like the cattle that were often valued above both wife and child. It was one of the tribal beliefs Lizzie disagreed with. Wasn't it the woman who stamped the corn, prepared the meals, and bore the children? Even the Holy Scripture said that men and women had been created equal in God's sight.

"*Ma*, it's coming closer." Esther, who was barely five, nudged Lizzie with her chocolaty brown elbow.

"Shh." A tremor shook the ground as the massive animal made its way past them, her long tail swatting away the constant barrage of flies.

At the moment, Lizzie felt no need to be concerned for their safety. From the time she could toddle across the swept African soil and out of her parents' thatched hut, she'd discovered wonderful things like termite hills and dragonflies in the open veld. When she was older, and her father wasn't busy trying to turn the natives from their wooden objects of worship to the one true God, he'd roamed the banks of the Zambezi River beside her. Here they'd explored the sun-cracked paths and tall grasses where wildebeest and buck roamed the plains that stretched out as far as the eye could see.

In five short months from now, the entire scene would be transformed into one solid expanse of water. The next cycle would bring the swollen river that would drain from the highlands into the flood plains. Then the tributaries could only be traversed by dugout canoes and waterfowl, like the Egyptian geese and the white-marked duck, which hid in the sandbanks as they preyed on the river's rich food supply.

Lizzie scratched the end of her nose, content with the unexpected lazy day she'd been offered. If the chief wouldn't allow her to aid in the delivery of his daughter-in-law Posha's third child, despite her nurse's training, then she would keep herself busy daydreaming beneath the endless African sky. Here, along the familiar shaded riverbank of the Zambezi, was the one place her foreign heart had found to belong.

The elephant flicked her trunk across a tusk then prodded at her off-spring. Lying on her stomach in the tall grass, Lizzie raised her head so she could see beyond the elephant and calf to the great Zambezi Valley where herds of zebra and antelope searched for food along the last of winter's barren land. The distant blue hills were lost in the heavy morning mist that rose from the river, but soon the sun would rise toward its zenith, melting the steamy vapors while the great plain shimmered in the afternoon heat.

Esther nudged Lizzie again. "*A-tu-ende.*"

"English, Esther. You will never learn if you don't practice." Lizzie eyed the plump girl with her soft clothing made from skin of a *lechwe* doe and softened her expression. "We will return home soon, but you know you won't be allowed to see your mother until the baby is born."

"Bama promised me that as soon as he's born I can hold him."

"And you will, but until the little one arrives we must wait," Lizzie insisted.

Chuma wasn't convinced. "Bama is strong. The baby will be born quickly."

Esther jutted out her lips and pointed to the lumbering elephant. "Look, the elephant is leaving, and I'm tired."

Lizzie pulled the young girl close with one arm and rubbed the dark tuft of hair on the top of her head. "The Bible says that the patient in spirit is better than the proud in spirit."

Chuma frowned, apparently as bored with the afternoon exertion as his younger sister was. "I'd much prefer the tale about how the hare made the hippopotamus and rhinoceros engage in a tug-of-war, or why the zebra has no horns."

Esther nodded. "You did promise us a story, Ma, and it will help to pass the time until we are able to see the baby."

Lizzie stood and shook off the pieces of grass stuck to her skirt. "All right then. If I promised a story, then a story it will be."

With the elephant moving away, the young siblings followed Lizzie along the winding path toward the village as she assumed her role story-teller. Their tribe had no written literature, but from an early age she'd been captivated by the oral stories. While her father taught her the biblical accounts of David and Goliath, and Moses' crossing of the Red Sea, she'd sat by the fire night after night, listening to the tribe's folktales in their native tongue. They were passed down from generation to generation, and she'd never grown weary of the repetition, practicing until she could reproduce the stories herself with all the gestures and eloquence of a skillful narrator.

Lizzie cleared her throat and took the children's hands in hers before beginning her story. "There came a certain day, when the animals were all gathered together across the vast African plain. There were elephants, warthogs, zebra, buffalo, and every other animal you could think of, all assembled together. Now the time came for the animals to select horns for themselves, so the animals said, 'Let's choose our horns.' And they did. They all ran toward the horns, the elephants, warthogs, zebra, buffalo, and every other animal you could think of, to make their selection."

Esther squeezed Lizzie's hand. "What about the kudu?"

"Even the kudu."

"And the reedbuck?" Chuma asked.

"Yes, even the reedbuck." Lizzie skipped over a broken limb in the path and smiled. No matter how many times the children heard the tale, they still asked the same questions. "So all the animals ran to select their horns. But the herd of zebra remained behind."

An eerie trumpeting sounded behind them. Lizzie stopped. She smelled the foul scent of the male elephant before she saw his massive torso. Ears flared back, he ran toward the female and her young. A wave of fear coursed through Lizzie's body as she squeezed the children's hands. She'd heard stories of the rare occasion when rogue males attacked female elephants—and killed any humans in their path.

A tar-like secretion trickled down the side of its head as the animal stopped and bent down to dig its tusks into the ground. The female, sensing the danger for her and her calf, turned, wavered momentarily, then headed straight toward the three of them.

"Chuma..." Lizzie's voice caught in her throat.

She scanned the low-lying valley behind and the border of the forested bush before them, searching for a safe place to hide. A guinea fowl fluttered into a nearby shrub, flapping its wings in alarm.

Transfixed by the vagrant animal, the children didn't move. Lizzie pulled on their arms and started running toward the trees. "Hurry, we've got to run."

With its young beside her, the mother continued to dart toward them. Lizzie's heart beat like the pounding rhythm of a village drum as she forced them to keep moving. Esther tripped on a rock and stumbled to the ground, compelling Lizzie to pick up the screaming child. Blood oozed from her knee, but there was no time to examine the wound.

The elephants drew closer. Lizzie grabbed Chuma's hand and, balancing Esther in her arms, turned north along the riverbank.

It seemed a lifetime before they managed to cross the shallow valley and make their way up the hill. Lizzie stopped beside a gnarled fig tree and looked back. The male had given up its chase and now thundered off in the opposite direction, allowing the mother and her young to escape in peace.

Chuma struggled to catch his breath. "If I had my bow and poisoned arrows, I'd go after that elephant."

Lizzie set Esther on the ground beside her. "You can't kill such a mighty beast with a poisoned arrow."

"I would take one of *Tata's* hippo spears," Esther announced, as she sat to examine her scraped knee.

Chuma fiddled with the plaited grass bracelets on his arm and frowned. "Father would no sooner let you carry one of his barbed war spears than he would suck the seeds of a baobab fruit."

"Stop arguing." Lizzie retied the ribbons of her straw hat beneath her chin. "There's nothing to worry about anymore. Let's go home and see if you have a new brother or sister."

The suggestion worked, for Chuma started walking toward the village beside Esther, who quickly forgot about her injury as she followed her brother down the beaten path.

"*Ndawala, ndawala, kwiwe-e, kwiwe-eyè.* I threw a spear, threw a spear, in the east, in the east…." Chuma sang, pulling back a thick reed behind his head like a spear. "You still haven't told us the rest of the story. Why doesn't the zebra have horns?"

"Yes, do tell us," Esther pleaded.

Lizzie flicked an ant off her arm. "Let's see, where was I?"

"You had just told us that all the zebra had remained behind," Chuma informed her.

Esther stopped and dug her toes into the dirt. "But why?"

Lizzie took the young girl's hand. "Because they were too busy grazing, so when the zebra finally reached the place where the horns were being chosen, they found that the others had taken them all. And much to the zebra's surprise, the only things left were a mane, long ears, stripes, and a big mouth."

Esther giggled and pushed out her lower lip.

"The royal eland laughed at the zebra. 'See what has happened because of your love of grazing,' he said. 'We have finished the horns, even the little ones have horns, but you…' One of the graceful reedbuck held his own horns high and laughed as well. 'Look at you—only a bit of color, ears, and drooping lips were all you could take.' And their friends condemned them, telling the zebra that they were gluttons, and that their eating had deprived them of their horns."

Chuma walked beside Lizzie, shaking his head. "The poor zebra."

"The zebra were indeed sad because they had no horns," Lizzie said. "And to this day, the zebra is considered a glutton, for it seems that he, above all other animals, spends all his time eating."

Esther clapped her hands together. "Tell us another story, Lizzie."

Lizzie's heart warmed at the child's enthusiasm. "First, you must tell me how the zebra really got its stripes."

Chuma kicked a pebble across the path with his big toe. "It was

Creator God, the God who formed the heavens and the earth with His own hands and who chose the pattern and size for each one of His creatures."

"And who made you?"

"The same Creator God who made everything from the smallest flea, to our beautiful cattle, to the mighty banks of the great Zambezi."

Lizzie smiled at the answer, but knew all too well that few people in the young boy's tribe, save Chuma and his family, had accepted the truth of the Creator God as described in the Holy Scriptures.

"You're exactly right, Chuma—"

"Don't move."

Lizzie stopped abruptly, turning from the children to the source of the deep, male voice, startled when she saw the man's fair complexion, mirroring the color of her own skin. It was the one thing that had always separated her from the tribe. The man stood six feet ahead of them, where the path merged with another that led to the river, a rifle poised in his hand.

Between them was a black mamba.

Her gaze dropped to the hissing sound, and she watched the olive-colored snake out of the corner of her eye. It was at the edge of the path, poised to strike.

Her muscles tensed as she squeezed Esther's hand and took a step backward. She wasn't sure who she should fear the most—the snake or the stranger with a gun pointed in her direction.

CHAPTER TWO

Lizzie watched, speechless, as the man lifted the rifle to his shoulder and took aim at the reptile before squeezing the trigger. The shot echoed across the quiet morning and silenced the hissing of the snake. He tossed the still moving form into the brush.

She drew the children closer to her side. "There was no need to kill it."

"It might have bitten you."

"I've heard of very few times when a snake attacked a person if left alone."

His eyes widened. "Then perhaps you aren't well informed. Just one week ago, I watched a man die after being bitten by a puff adder. And let me tell you, his demise was far from pleasant."

She studied the stranger dressed in tailored pants and a khaki shirt. The clothes were worn but surprisingly clean. What stood out, though, were his eyes. They were a piercing color that reminded her of the iridescent blue of the glossy starling that perched in the branches of the acacia trees.

But she wasn't sure she should trust him. Except for those from the mission whose goal was to bring God's salvation to the people, most white men came to exploit the people, the land, or the animals.

Pushing her shoulders back, Lizzie tilted her chin. "It isn't often we see Europeans wandering through the bush."

"I'm an American, and I'm looking for someone." He set the end of the rifle on the ground and caught her gaze. "Maybe you can help me."

She cocked her head and eyed him suspiciously. "Who is it that you're looking for?"

"A woman named Lizzie MacTavish."

She put her hand to her throat, clutched her mother's gold locket between her fingers. "I'm Lizzie MacTavish."

A smile spread across his tanned face. "Miss MacTavish, I've come to take you back to New York."

The moment he spoke, Andrew Styles knew he'd made a mistake. In the excitement of finding the object of his quest, he'd thrown away all sense of decorum. And as one who had made it his lifetime ambition to study human nature, he of all people should know that in the African bush etiquette required proper rituals of greeting. Miss Mac-Tavish had spent the majority of her existence among the natives and no doubt had become a part of their culture. One never came right out and announced the purpose of one's visit. Conversation must follow a certain course, no matter how urgent the message.

"I'm sorry. I shouldn't have been so forthright with my news." He gripped the stock of his rifle and worked to come up with a new approach. "I've been traveling for weeks, and to find you is a relief. Your aunt and uncle told me about the splendid work you are doing among the natives, but…"

He stopped in mid-sentence, watching as her brown eyes narrowed and her lips curved into a tense frown. Flattery wasn't going to work in this situation. And he wasn't sure what approach would. While the skirt that reached to her ankles seemed completely unsuitable for the bush, she appeared to be at home in her surroundings without looking like the prude female he'd expected. She also managed to convey her American roots with her upswept hairstyle and tailored blouse—not unlike one of Charles Dana Gibson's *Gibson Girls* from a decade past. Andrew hadn't expected her to be so self-assured, poised, and... beautiful.

She tilted her wide-brimmed hat to block the sun. "Why would my aunt and uncle send you all this way to take me back to New York?"

"Your aunt and uncle didn't send me."

"I don't understand."

"I came because of your grandfather."

"My grandfather?" The expression on her face softened. "Is he all right?"

He blew out a sharp breath. As happy as he was to find Lizzie Mac-Tavish, this was the moment he'd dreaded as he'd crossed the Atlantic and then the rugged bush of southern Africa. "I'm sorry to have to be the one to tell you this, but your grandfather recently passed away after a short illness."

Miss MacTavish's chin dipped. "What happened?"

"The doctors believe his heart gave out." He waited a few moments, while the children stood patiently beside her, before breaking the silence. "I understand you were close."

"Did you know him?" She looked up and he caught the glistening of tears in her eyes before she turned and started walking toward the village nestled against the forest in the distance.

"No, though I wish I had." He caught up to her while the children followed silently close behind them. "From what I've heard, he was quite the explorer."

She pushed back a strand of her blond hair that had fallen loose against her shoulder then readjusted the pink ribbons that secured her hat beneath her chin, the pain in her expression obvious. "When I lived in New York, I spent as much time with him as possible. He was an amazing man who traveled extensively throughout Europe, and once from Alaska to South America."

"He was from Ireland?"

"Yes, and that was where he met my grandmother. He proposed three days after they met and eventually brought her to New York after they married." She stared across the veld at a herd of zebra grazing in the distance, seemingly lost for a moment in memories from the past. "The stories he could tell would keep me riveted for hours on end. We used to sit in his library in front of this grand fireplace that took up one entire wall and he would talk about..."

She stopped and shook her head. "I'm sorry. I realize you did not come all this way to hear me ramble about some old man you didn't even know."

"Quite the contrary. I regret never having met the man, as I am sure I would have found his stories fascinating as well."

The smile he'd hoped to evoke didn't appear. Instead her eyes darkened and her brow furrowed. "What I don't understand is why you would travel all this distance to tell me about my grandfather. I'm sure you have far more important things to do, and a telegram, or even a letter, would have been far simpler."

"Perhaps, but your grandfather was not only an extremely wealthy man, but very explicit on how he wanted his will to be carried out in the event of his death."

"Knowing my grandfather, that doesn't surprise me, but neither does it explain why I'm needed back in New York. While he didn't agree with my decision to continue my parents' work, he knew how important it is to me. And how hard I've worked to prove myself to the people here. If I were to leave now, much of the progress I have made would be lost." She clasped the hand of the little girl beside her as if searching for moral support. "Surely his solicitors can carry out the details of his will without my being there."

"There are…" Andrew paused, wishing for a moment he could disappear amongst the tall grasses of the open savannah surrounding them. But putting off the inevitable would change nothing in the end. "There are further conditions to the will."

She stopped walking and caught his gaze. "What do you mean, further conditions?"

"As I have told you, in order to execute the will, his solicitors need you to return to New York."

"But why? What else is stipulated in the will?"

Andrew searched for words that would soften the blow of what was to come. "As you have already said, your grandfather didn't like the idea of your living alone in such a remote location. Which means that while your grandfather cared deeply for you, he was also extremely worried for your safety."

"What does that have to do with my returning to New York?"

Andrew blew out a deep breath. "The will stipulates that you return to New York and live there for one year before you are allowed to collect your inheritance."

"For one year?" Lizzie's mouth gaped open. "Surely you are not serious."

"That was your grandfather's stipulation."

"No." Lizzie bustled down the dirt trail, her two wards in tow. "My grandfather might not have agreed with my living here, but he would never have demanded something like this."

"You can read the will for yourself. I brought a copy, written in his own hand."

She shook her head. "And what would be his reason for requiring this of me?"

"I can only tell you what his solicitors told me." Andrew hurried to catch up. "He felt that a year back home would give you the opportunity to reevaluate the wisdom in your decision to continue your work here. But that doesn't mean you'd have to return permanently. After one year you could come back to Africa…with your inheritance."

"So he believed if I stayed there long enough I'd eventually forget my life here?"

"Perhaps it was more than that. Perhaps he believed it was time you took a well-deserved furlough. Or that time in New York would better afford the opportunity for you to find a husband." Andrew caught the tint of blush that swept across her cheeks at his words, looked askance, and cleared his throat. "Whatever his reasoning, he clearly believed that this time away would be best for you. You would receive a generous monthly allowance at first, then after one year, his entire estate would go to you—minus a moderate monthly stipend for your uncle."

Lizzie's jaw tensed. "What happens if I don't return?"

"The inheritance would then go to your uncle." He pulled his leather bag off his back. "I have a letter from your grandfather's solicitors that will explain everything as well as coffee and beads for the chief, sweets for the children, and for you, dresses, a traveling costume, and other gifts—"

Lizzie pressed her fingertips against her temples and shook her head. "I don't require new clothes or gifts."

Anger laced her terse words. Any hopes of a warm welcome had disappeared. He shoved aside the sliver of worry that she wouldn't return with him. Given time to adjust to the idea, he had no doubt that she would jump at the chance to collect her inheritance. A year living in New York was a small sacrifice to ensure the financial security of her work and mission. Whether she ended up staying or not would be up to her.

Andrew cleared his throat. "Please know that while I understand your hesitation, your grandfather's will is very clear. You must return with me in order to receive the money. Surely twelve months is short compared to an inheritance that could be used to help the people here for many years to come."

She grabbed a stray lock of her curly hair and tucked it under the brim of her hat before turning to leave. "I am sorry for the trouble you have gone to, Mr..."

"Styles. Andrew Styles."

"...Mr. Styles. While my grandfather's money would certainly be a financial blessing, I'm not sure I can consider leaving for such a long period of time. I've worked too hard to find my place among the people to simply walk away."

The veins in his neck pulsed as she pushed past him. He couldn't afford to not take her back. "But I'm not leaving without you."

"Then you misunderstood me." She turned around, her eyes flashing. "God has called me to work among these people. I will pray about my decision, but if I'm not convinced that my returning is a part of God's plan then even an inheritance from my grandfather can't entice me to return. You have to understand that this is not a decision I can make quickly."

He pressed his lips together, knowing that further debate between them at the moment would do little to help his cause.

"I'm sure the chief will be pleased to welcome you into the village for food and a place to sleep." She nodded at the two children with her, addressing them in English. "Let's go. This man has obviously been wandering through the plains in the heat for far too long."

The little girl put her hand to her face and giggled. "Or perhaps he was stung by a scorpion and is hallucinating."

He watched as Lizzie MacTavish stormed down the path with the two children dressed in animal skins in tow, their brown skin glistening beneath the midday sun—a sharp contrast to her fairness. For the first time since he left America, he began to harbor second thoughts about his arrangement to bring the young woman home. He had believed the plan to be foolproof. Surely he could make her realize that returning to New York was the wisest option. He might not have expected her to put up a fight, but one thing was certain. This was one fight he intended to win.

CHAPTER THREE

Andrew sat on a three-legged stool outside the chief's hut beside his two African guides. For what he was waiting, he wasn't sure. No doubt it was an act of politeness to leave him sitting here to settle in comfortably until he was greeted in the traditional manner. Normally, he would welcome the chance to collect himself and catch his breath, but today it left him with a sense of irritation.

After Miss MacTavish's initial outburst, she hadn't spoken a word to him the entire way back to the village, but while the young woman's reaction had taken him off guard, he would be prepared now. Maybe he was the foolish one, expecting her to be grateful that he'd come to rescue her from the hands of these uneducated savages like an acclaimed hero. He flicked away a mosquito that buzzed in his ear. There was only one problem. To her, these people weren't savages. They were a part of her.

He stared across the open space in the center of the village to the cattle hold. Like other villages he'd visited on his previous trips through the Dark Continent, at least three dozen huts were built in a circular pattern around the edges of the large space, the chief's being the primary structure behind where he sat. Beyond the huts were the cattle pens that held their prized animals, and beyond them, the vast Zambezi Valley.

Andrew wiped beads of perspiration from his brow with the back of his hand. Though winter wasn't yet officially over, the sun beat down on the cracked dirt, and in the distance, the yellowed earth seemed to palpitate in the afternoon heat. Soon the evening shadows would cover the plain and the distant hills, painting them the gray and bluish hues he'd noted the night before and bringing with them a refreshing coolness.

An old woman appeared out of the plastered doorway beside him and handed each of the three visitors a cup of water. He took a sip of the cool drink, tired of waiting. Five minutes later, Miss MacTavish approached from the west with an old man she introduced as the chief.

"*Wabonwa*." The chief sat in front of them and greeted them.

"He says you are seen," Miss MacTavish translated.

Andrew nodded as he noted the chief's leopard skin loincloth, rows of ivory bangles on his forearms, and missing front teeth. "Please tell him he is seen."

She turned to the chief. "*Ndaabonwa. Wabonwa aze.*"

With Miss MacTavish as his translator, Andrew asked the traditional questions about the man's wife, children, and cattle.

His two guides snickered beside him.

Andrew leaned forward and stared at Miss MacTavish. "What did you tell him?"

"That you had heard of the great beauty of the chief's cattle and wanted to see if the reports were true. And that there was one in particular that had been ornamented with bells that had caught your attention. You might be willing to make an offer for the beast."

"I'm not interested in catt—" He stopped short as he caught the gleam in her eye. He hadn't expected her to be full of wit and jest. "So have you told him the real reason I'm here?"

She dipped her head. "I also told him you arrived with a message from my family."

"And have you informed him that it is important you return home?"

"I have informed *you* that a decision like this cannot be made quickly."

Andrew signaled one of the guides, who opened his packs and began laying out their contents on the ground. "Please tell the chief I have gifts for him and his family."

Miss MacTavish raised her brows. "One must be careful when attempting to bribe a man as powerful in the community as the chief."

Ignoring her comment, Andrew handed an open sack of coffee to the chief, who received it with both hands and a broad, toothless grin.

"Receiving a gift with both hands implies that the receiver appreciates the magnitude of the gift," Miss MacTavish informed him. "The chief is pleased with what you have brought."

Andrew pulled out a sealed envelope from his front pocket and handed it to her, hoping she would now feel the same. "I also have a letter from your aunt and uncle."

She took it from him—with one hand—and stuffed it into her skirt pocket.

His brow narrowed at her reaction. "Aren't you going to read it?"

"Later."

The chief rose, speaking to Miss MacTavish before he left.

Andrew set his pack beside him on the ground. "Why is he leaving?"

"A more serious matter has to be dealt with, so he cannot stay. There is a dispute between one of the men here and another from a neighboring village. It is up to the chiefs to hear both sides and give a judgment." Miss MacTavish sat back down on her stool. "They will bring you food now, and since it's not fitting for a guest of the village to eat alone, the chief has chosen me to join you, despite my objections."

A table was brought out and two pots set in front of the four of them. After washing his hands in the offered bowl of water, Andrew dipped his fingers into the thick porridge, then into the sauce with its bits of meat. It was time to make peace between them.

"I'm afraid I was given the wrong impression of you by your aunt and uncle."

"And what impression would that be?"

"That you would welcome the opportunity to return to America."

Miss MacTavish shook her head, blinking rapidly. "You don't know anything about me. I was raised in a hut on the other side of the veld and learned these people's language from the time I could walk. I can retell their traditional stories as well as anyone in the village. Nothing makes me feel more at home than roaming the banks of the Zambezi or joining the women while they pound the corn."

She stood, dumping her stool over in the process, and started pacing. "But my father and mother also never let me forget where I came from. My father made certain that I learned from the greatest minds. Philosophy from Aristotle's writings, literature from Shakespeare, and poetry from John Milton and Robert Louis Stevenson. My mother taught me how to sew and make biscuits and pancakes, and pies from wild fruits. I'm here because God has called me to be a light to these people."

"That might well be true, but your grandfather wasn't the only one worried about your well-being. Your aunt and uncle are concerned as well." He chose his words carefully as she paced in front of him. "I don't think your aunt ever felt right about allowing you to return to Africa as a single missionary after the deaths of your parents."

"I am twenty-five years old." Frustration tinged her voice. "And it's not as if I traveled here alone or returned without any knowledge of the language or people, or their sicknesses for that matter."

"You make a valid point, though as I said, both your aunt and your uncle do not see it that way."

"I'm sure you know that living here always brings with it the threat of danger. Inter-tribal conflict, the ongoing risk of malaria, and other life-threatening diseases, such as typhoid, known to plague both the Africans and the white settlers." She dismissed him with a wave of her hand. "And you should also know that none of those dangers have ever discouraged me from living here."

Andrew searched for a response that would tone down her anger toward him, but came up empty. Why was it that everything he said sparked discord with her?

She righted the stool and sat down again, speaking before he'd had time to formulate his words. "How is she?"

"Your aunt?"

Miss MacTavish nodded.

"She's not been well lately. She took the death of your grandfather quite hard and has been ill."

Miss MacTavish leaned forward. "What is wrong with her?"

"I'm not sure. I was told that after your grandfather's death, her health began deteriorating. By the time I set sail to come here, the doctors had yet to diagnose what was wrong. She had become weak to the point that it is now necessary for her to use a wheelchair. It's been several months since she's performed for an audience."

Miss MacTavish shook her head. "Music and performing are my aunt's life. I can't imagine her not playing and singing." He caught the flash of guilt in her expression. "The way you describe her almost makes it sound as if she has given up on life."

"I could not answer that. I didn't know her before, except to hear her sing at one of her performances, so I have nothing to compare how she is today with how she used to be. I found her warm and quite charming, though there was always sadness in her eyes, as if she were looking for something, but had yet to find it." He caught her gaze, not above adding an extra layer of guilt. "She wants you to come home. Needs you to come home."

"I just don't know how I could leave here for so long." Her fingers toyed with the folds of her skirt as she stared across the compound. "There is so much work to do."

Andrew took another bite of his porridge and watched her expression. She hadn't said no this time. Perhaps he was making progress. With a long journey ahead of him, he wasn't looking forward to staying here any longer than necessary. But with thoughts of continued funding ever present in the back of his mind—a motivation he wasn't going to share with the woman—he clearly had no choice. And in the meantime, he'd find every way possible to convince Miss MacTavish to return to America with him as quickly as possible.

CHAPTER FOUR

Lizzie pounded the long wooden pestle, measuring almost as high as her own five feet five inches, into the large mortar with every ounce of strength she could muster. Porridge would eventually be made by adding the resulting flour to a pot of boiling water and stirring until the spoon stood up straight. But today she had little interest in the corn she was slowly grinding.

Instead, her mind went over the correspondence she had received from her uncle. She'd read the letter so many times in the fading light the evening before that she had memorized it.

I can only hope that this letter finds you in a timely man ner. By now you have heard of your grandfather's death and the stipulations of his will. Besides the loss of your grandfather, your aunt Ella is not doing well I am afraid that trying to keep up her busy performance schedule while caring for your grandfather during the weeks leading up to his death has taken a significant toll on her health. And to add to that, we continue to worry about the conditions you are living in. We are able to give you everything you need, including family. Please, come home. You belong here, not living with a band of savages....

"*Pe! Pe! Pe!*" Lizzie pounded harder, the tribal expression venting her frustration over misguided words.

These people weren't savages. But this was something her aunt and uncle would never understand. They equated happiness with material things, education, and social status, and couldn't begin to understand her hesitancy in returning.

She'd been eighteen when both of her parents had died within a few short days of each other during a typhoid epidemic. After their deaths, the decision was made for her to return to New York to live with her father's older brother and his wife. While her aunt and uncle were well-off and had given her everything she needed physically, it hadn't taken her long to realize that she didn't require wealth to be happy. Three years later, after finishing her nurse's training, she'd returned home to Northern Rhodesia.

A stab of guilt coursed through her like the raging Zambezi River as she continued pounding. It wasn't as if she didn't appreciate what her father's family had done for her. They had taken her in as a young girl who'd lost her parents and her country in only a few weeks' time. But neither was she ready to leave the place God had called her to for such a long period of time.

"Good morning."

Lizzie started at the sound of Mr. Styles's voice. While she spent some of her time teaching English to those interested, it was rare that she heard the unaccented tones of her mother tongue.

She leaned against the smooth edge of the wooden pole and eyed him thoughtfully. He wore the same tailored pants and khaki shirt, but this morning he'd donned a tan vaquero hat that made him look like a cowboy. His unshaven jawline gave him a rugged look, and the morning sunlight made his eyes appear an even brighter blue, if that was possible. All things she shouldn't notice about him. But it didn't matter anyway. None of it changed the way she felt about his reasons for being here.

She turned her attention back to pounding the flour. "Did you sleep well?"

"Despite the constant buzzing of the mosquitoes, I suppose I can't complain. Do you think the chief would be willing to share some of the coffee I presented to him?"

She dropped her gaze to focus on a black beetle that poked its way across the ground. "It is always wise not to throw your gift into the fire."

"Meaning?"

"Don't throw away your chance to pacify one in power, because it might not come again."

"Wise advice for someone so young."

She couldn't help but look up at him, not sure if he was making fun of her or giving her a superfluous compliment. "I know I can find you some sour milk. It's especially good on porridge." She watched his nose wrinkle at the suggestion, and she pressed her lips together to stop the smile from spreading across her face. "Breakfast will be served soon."

He sat on a tree stump and watched her. She started pounding the corn again, no longer able to handle the intensity of his gaze. "What is it?"

"Watching you reminds me of the similarities between the different African countries. I've spent time exploring throughout the regions of both North and West Africa and while they have their own unique qualities, so much, on the surface anyway, remains the same."

Mesmerized by the sound of his soothing voice, she continued her work. She didn't want to be drawn to this man whose only goal at the moment was to convince her to return to America with him, but at the same time she couldn't dismiss her intrigue any more than a zebra could grow horns.

"What is similar?"

He rested his elbows against his thighs. "Smoke rising from outdoor kitchens where women prepare the morning meal. The aroma of onions and tomatoes drifting in the breeze. Children laughing and playing on the dusty ground." He stood and walked toward her, stopping only a few feet from where she worked. "In West Africa they make a staple called *fufu*. Two women pound the cooked pieces of manioc, rotating the mixture with their hands as the pale yellow and white pieces of the root blend together, never missing a beat. They continue in perfect rhythm, picking up the tempo as they go."

Listening to the rhythm of her own pounding, she looked at him. For a moment she couldn't speak. It was as if time hovered between them, waiting for one of them to speak before it continued on to the next second.

The chirp of a cicada cried out, announcing the coming rains and drawing her back to reality. Wiping her hands on her skirt, she shook her head. These sudden romantic inclinations were ridiculous. Had it really been that long since she'd seen a man so—so handsome? The very thought was preposterous. Clearly she'd forgotten the reason for his arrival at the village. He was here to take her home.

She cleared her throat, making a decision as she set down the pole. "I want to show you something."

Andrew followed her as she carried the mortar to one of the nearby huts and gave instructions to a young girl in her native tongue. Miss

MacTavish walked with both grace and purpose. Back held erect, hips swaying softly as her bare feet padded against the hard earth… he hadn't been prepared for this. The woman was not only beautiful but could hold her own in a conversation. And with a charming sense of wit as well. The thought made him smile.

White patches of mist rose along the edges of the village but were already beginning to dissipate as the sun made its way above the horizon. They headed out of the village, which was quieter than normal, he was sure, because the majority of the occupants had left to work in the field.

A mangy dog staggered past them, gaunt and half-starved. An animal treated, no doubt, with far less affection than their prized cattle. Outside the edge of the village, he studied a group of girls carrying clay pots filled with water on their heads, their hair twisted and powdered with some sort of ash and paste. If he wasn't in a hurry to get Miss MacTavish home to her family, he'd have welcomed the time to stay and study these people.

Miss MacTavish stopped at the edge of the bluff. Below them the veld, Africa's never-ending grassland, was covered with a carpet of purple, pink, and white.

She stood facing the panoramic view, her hands behind her back and the wind gently tugging on the loose strands of her hair that brushed against her face. "They call it the wonder month. While the weather is unpleasantly humid this time of year, the stunning array of flora makes up for it."

"It's beautiful." He pulled his Kodak camera from his bag, unfolded it, and took a photo of the colorful scene in front of him.

"You're a photographer."

"I like to think so." He slid the camera back into his bag. For the moment, he was intrigued more by what she was thinking than nature's display. "Why did you want to show this to me?"

Her gaze across the plain never wavered. "I want you to understand why leaving here is not a decision I can make overnight. These people are not a bunch of heathen savages. This is their world and they survive on God's bounty." She finally looked at him. "They have close-knit families where the parents dote on the children and care for their well-being as best they can."

He didn't miss the contented expression on her face. She turned to follow the ridge of the bluff, but her explanation did little to convince him of the logic behind her continued presence here.

"But why do *you* stay?" he asked. "Don't you dream of marriage and having a family like every other young woman your age?"

He waited, but she didn't answer. Something stirred within him, but he couldn't identify what. All he knew was that he felt a deep sense of urgency to understand why she had returned to what most of the world referred to as the Dark Continent when she'd been offered everything she could have ever wanted in New York.

He studied her expression. "I've gone to school and studied human nature firsthand on explorations from Senegal to Gabon, but I'm surprised that you would even consider giving up your grandfather's vast fortune for this."

"I haven't made my decision yet." She turned her face to him, her brow raised. "And I know I can't save the world. All I want to do is make a difference. I want them to realize that their Creator God, the One they believe created this world but now has gone away and left them to manage on their own, doesn't live far from them."

"But will that really make a difference? What about the fact that over half their children will die before they reach their first birthday?" He stopped and dug the heels of his boots into the ground, working to control his deep-rooted irritation. "These people don't need stories of a giant fish that swallowed an errant man of God, or how a warrior marched around a city wall and watched it collapse as the trumpets cried out. They've plenty of fables of their own. If you insist on coming in and changing the world they've lived in for thousands of years, teach the mothers better hygienic rules, how to boil their water, and how to keep their huts clean from vermin."

"I am doing that as well." Her voice rose both in volume and emotion as she spoke. "Before I returned, I studied nursing so I could help them take better care of the physical issues facing their families."

"And they let you?"

"I'm slowly being allowed to do more and more things." She started walking again. "Though there are still some who aren't convinced that women, in particular, are capable of holding knowledge that would surpass their own medical practitioners."

The rattling call of a kingfisher called out in the distance as it flew parallel to the reed-fringed waterway. The yellow sun continued on its course toward the west, another sign of his delay. He hadn't expected to come in and simply sweep her away, but her indecision still frustrated him.

"We should go back now." She turned toward the village. "I have work to do."

"While I work to find a way to convince you to return with me."

"You who are so clever—"

"Another African proverb?"

She laughed. "A riddle. You think you are clever, but you can't tie water up in a bundle or catch hold of a shadow."

No he couldn't. And he had a feeling he wasn't going to be able to tame the fair-haired beauty who stood beside him either.

CHAPTER FIVE

Lizzie looked up from the newly tilled soil that crumbled beneath her hoe to the white clouds forming along the distant horizon. Today she would finish clearing her small plot of land. Tomorrow she would begin sowing the fertile ground, leaving the tiny seed to wait for the rains that would in turn nudge the green shoots to appear. She wiped away the beads of sweat on her forehead and smiled at the image of rows and rows of millet, sweet potatoes, beans, peanuts, and pumpkins that would soon lie beneath the afternoon's golden sunlight.

Here, days were not marked off by dates on one's social calendar. Instead, planting season was welcomed by the appearance of the Pleiades in the east after sunset and before summer rainclouds dropped their heavy showers across the vast grasslands. Life was a never-ending cycle of planting and harvesting, summer and winter, life and death, and the fruitful rewards that came with working the soil.

Gripping the handle of the iron hoe, she cut the broad blade into the final patch of ground still needing to be cleared and thought of the solicitors' request and her aunt's illness. If she left now, she'd never see those rows of sweet potatoes and pumpkins, watch the plains fill with water when the rains came, or see Posha's baby take her first step. She'd miss sitting beneath the blanket of stars at night and telling stories of God's power when He saved the Israelites from the Egyptians or Daniel from the mouths of the lions.

She closed her eyes and for a moment pictured herself standing on a street corner in Manhattan. Sidewalks were crowded with hundreds of people as automobiles rushed past on congested streets—

The familiar squeals of Chuma and Esther tugged Lizzie from her memories and back to the African veld. She opened her eyes as the children appeared at the top of the slight rise that overlooked pockets of women, amidst charred stumps of trees, also preparing the land for the coming planting season. Beyond them, a long line of hills, tinted blue in the afternoon light, stretched out to meet the thick forests.

Lizzie paused, holding up a hand to block the sun, and leaving the decision for another day. "Has the baby come?"

Esther's frown deepened against her chubby cheeks and emphasized her solemn expression. "It will come soon, but for now we are not allowed near the shelter to be with Bama, and Tata is with the chief discussing important things."

Lizzie's brow furrowed. "Is anything wrong?"

Chuma shrugged. "Tata does not speak to children of such important matters."

Esther gripped her corncob doll against her chest. "Which is why Chuma wishes to take his bow and arrow into the bush and prove he is a man instead of simply minding the cattle, but I want you to tell us another story."

Lizzie caught the irritation in Chuma's expression at his sister's words, but it was the worry in Esther's eyes that prompted her to kneel down in front of the young girl and take her hand. "Are you worried about your mother?"

Esther's chin quivered. "What if Bama dies?"

Lizzie closed her eyes, trying to suppress the memory of the infant who at the last full moon had been quietly buried outside the family hut with only the mother allowed to openly mourn her loss.

She opened her eyes and gazed into the young girl's face. "We must not stop praying that God will protect both Bama and the baby. Remember the story of David and the giant?"

"Goliath?"

Lizzie nodded then brushed away the pool of tears that had collected in the corners of Esther's eyes. "He protected David from the giant who wanted to kill him. And that same Creator God who made the heavens above us and the tiny seeds we will soon plant in the ground cares for you and your Bama very much."

Esther's timid smile reappeared. "Then will you tell us that story again?" Lizzie looked to Chuma, who was busy poking at a trail of tiny ants in the newly tilled ground. "What if the two of you pile up the remaining grass that is still to be dried and burned while I finish tilling the ground, and I will tell you the story?"

Lizzie picked up her hoe while Chuma and Esther began working. "The people of the Creator God had a problem. They weren't getting along with their neighbors."

"Like Tata and Mawela from the other village."

"Yes, but they were also very afraid."

"Why?" Esther stopped working, clearly more interested in the story than clearing the dead grass.

"Because the Philistines had many giants living in their land, and one of the biggest giants was named Goliath."

"How tall was Goliath?" Chuma asked.

"He was as tall as the tallest grain bin and carried a spear that was much, much longer than Tata's hippo spears." Lizzie's hoe hit a root, and she reached down to throw it away. "Everyday, Goliath would stand in front of God's people and shout—"

"Miss MacTavish!"

Lizzie jumped at the sound of the booming male voice. Turning, she peeked up from beneath the wide brim of her hat. Mr. Styles stood at the edge of her land, camera in hand and his well-chiseled features hidden by the growing shadows that still lingered in the afternoon sunlight.

He plodded across the newly tilled land. "I've been looking for you, though I see you've been busy. I had no idea that you were so industrious."

Lizzie pressed her hand against her heart. "Mr. Styles. Must you always sneak up and startle me like a scheming black mamba?"

His smile only broadened. "I assure you, I had no intention of startling you, Miss MacTavish, nor is my bite venomous."

Lizzie exhaled sharply. "Then why must you follow me everywhere I go?"

"How else can I convince you to return with me?"

She ignored his blatant plea and went back to her work. "Can't you see it is planting season? The ground must be hoed, and the grass and rubbish thrown into piles so the ground can be sown before the first rains appear."

He folded his arms across his chest and grinned. "It is not a quarrelsome man but a leopard that thrives on fighting."

Lizzie's frown deepened. "Meaning?"

"That you are not the only one who has collected a few proverbs. There is no profit in our being quarrelsome."

"Perhaps not." Lizzie leaned against the end of the hoe and caught his gaze. "But neither does the road pass on your head."

Mr. Styles's left brow quirked. "Meaning?"

"That it is quite possible for me to decide my way without consulting you."

She let out a low humph. She'd believed that her temporary escape to the field after the noonday meal would rid her of Mr. Styles's unending discourse and constant barrage of questions. Apparently she'd been wrong. But her decision would not be made in haste, and no matter how charming he most likely appeared to young women on the other side of the Atlantic, his charisma and attempts to shower her with gifts would not work on her.

She looked up again and tried to size up his tall, lanky stature. His soft hands suggested he preferred talking to physical labor. And while he might have traveled throughout this great continent, from her observations, he seemed to know little of the ways of her people.

"Has the baby come?" Esther addressed Mr. Styles in English, pulling Lizzie from her thoughts.

"That I do not know, but I was asked to pass on a message." He turned to address Chuma. "Your...tata...is looking for you. He said if I saw you, I was to remind you that you were to be out herding the cattle."

Lizzie's brow furrowed. "Chuma? Is that true?"

The boy's gaze dipped. "I was on my way."

Esther turned to Lizzie. "If I go with him, you will finish the story later?"

"Of course."

Chuma picked up the bow and arrow he'd set down, then grabbed his sister's hand. Lizzie watched the two ebony-skinned children scramble through the sparse bush toward the pasture where the prized cattle fed before returning to their pens in the village at dusk.

Mr. Styles plopped down on a small mound of dirt she still needed to smooth out before planting. "So, you are a storyteller?"

"Yes…no." Her words fumbled from her lips.

"Which is it?"

She sighed. How could a man in need of so much conversation travel for days on end with no company other than the vast African sky and a couple guides for company? Here, there was little time for such idleness while the men cut trees in the fields so the women could plant the crops before the dry soil was moistened by the coming rains. It wasn't until the sun sank beneath the horizon and night appeared that time could be given to such merriment.

Lizzie brushed a patch of dirt from her skirt. "The children seem to enjoy my stories."

"Then perhaps I should have come earlier since I have so little to do."

She dug the end of her hoe into the dirt, feeling self-conscious at his interest. "I could come up with a job suitable for your talents."

He glanced at the piles of grass now drying in the late morning sun, as if manual labor was beneath him. "And what job would that be?"

She nodded to a group of black-billed francolins searching for food at the edge of her field and filling the afternoon breeze with their occasional *krraae-krraae*. "Soon I will need someone to guard my field from the antics of these bothersome fowl. They are plentiful this year and surprisingly clever."

"Clever?"

"They are waiting to scratch up the grain before it has a chance to sprout."

His smile was back. "That does sound like a problem."

"No more difficult than the monkeys and bush pigs that try to steal the young plants while no one is watching."

Mr. Styles rubbed his scraggly beard. "Now, I do believe you mock me, Miss MacTavish, in offering me such a trivial job. But that won't deter me from finishing what I came here to do."

She looked up at him then turned back to her hoe and the remaining untilled ground. As far as she was concerned, she was safer exploring the surrounding forests that teemed with insects and vipers than enduring the persistence of Mr. Styles.

"Is this where you were born?" he asked.

She arched her back and pointed toward the river. "At that time, the village, which they move every few years, was located up the river. They gave my parents a small piece of land in the village to build a hut and a second place for crops. When I returned after their deaths, they gave me a place to live and allowed me to cultivate this piece of land."

She held her hand across her forehead in order to block the sun whose yellow and gold rays now brushed their vibrant strokes of color across the distant hills. The familiar smells of blossoms, forest fruits, and newly tilled dirt filled the air. He might not understand, but this was her home.

Lizzie weighed the situation. If conversation could not be avoided, perhaps she could find a way to use it to her advantage. "Tell me what has happened over the past few years. I receive little news this far into the bush."

"What would you like to know?"

She felt her shoulders relax slightly as she dug into the last small section of earth. "It doesn't matter. Politics, books, fashion, sports. The last piece of news I received was sometime last year when the veld-fires had begun, and the men had gone off hunting."

"Let's see." Mr. Styles pressed his palms into the dirt and leaned back. "The Olympics were held in Belgium last summer, and the United States was the unofficial team champion. The Cleveland Indians beat the Brooklyn Dodgers in the last World Series, and the U.S. recently negotiated peace with Germany."

As much as the man's persistence might irritate her, it was impossible to curb her interest. "What else?"

"President Harding was the first president to travel by car in an inaugural parade, and"—Mr. Styles paused, seemingly for effect—"the first mail plane flew from New York to California."

"From New York to California?" Lizzie stamped her hoe against the soft earth. "How is that possible? I saw a plane once and it looked to be pieced together with nothing more than canvas and wire. To fly across the entire country is—is preposterous."

Mr. Styles laughed, then reached up and touched the side of his jaw. "Granted, they did have to fly from field to field as they made their way across the country, but they made it all the way to California. And I'm sure it is but the first of many continental flights."

"It's funny." Lizzie wiped her forehead with the back of her hand. "Part of me expects things to never change, because here, little changes from year to year. There are seasons for planting and harvesting, and a set time for rain, winter and summer. Sometimes I forget that life there is so—so different."

"Progress is slower here."

Lizzie finished the last small patch then dropped her hoe to the ground before sitting down beside him on the mound of dirt. While she would always feel that this land and its people ran in her blood, she couldn't dismiss the strong connection she had with her parents' homeland.

"What about fashion?"

"Fashion?" Mr. Styles laughed. "I was led to understand that you are not interested in such things."

"I'm not. I'm simply…" She scrambled for an excuse. "…curious. That is all."

"Women's fashion is hardly a part of my expertise. My brother, Charlie, has a sister-in-law you should be talking to. The last time I saw her the hem of her skirt had shortened quite a bit, and she was wearing some kind of rolled stocking. But from what I've heard, she's always been the rebellious type and a bit ahead of the times."

"I see." Lizzie felt her cheeks flame at the scandalous image his words invoked. How had her innocent questions brought them to such an intimate topic as women's underclothing?

She turned her blushing face away from him then stilled as she caught movement from the corner of her eye. An old slave woman skirted the edge of the plot without looking their direction. Wrinkled skin hung on her boney stature, making the woman appear twice her probable age. Lizzie bid the old woman good afternoon—something rarely done to a woman of her status who held no rights. The woman clasped her twisted hands together and let a faint smile pull at her lips before she vanished into the edges of the forest.

The image of Mr. Styles's sister vanished along with the village slave. Manhattan suddenly seemed very far away. Modesty here might follow a different set of rules, with the women wearing skirts made from skins, beads, and nothing above the waist—something her father had never been able to get them to change. She would always insist on wearing long skirts and high necklines. And certainly never anything as scandalous as short skirts and rolled stockings!

She stared off into the distance where the sun had begun its descent behind the hills. "You have yet to tell me what keeps you returning to this vast continent. Scientific knowledge or perhaps fame and celebrity?"

Mr. Styles reached up and pressed his fingers against his jaw again. "Both, I suppose. I've written dozens of newspaper articles about my previous expeditions, and one day plan to write a book about my travels, complete with photographs."

"The life of an explorer must be exciting, fraught with danger and wild animals."

"Not all of it is so romantic, though I have had my share of adventures. And could probably tell a few stories myself." His hand touched the side of his jaw again.

"Is something wrong, Mr. Styles?"

"It's nothing." He shook his head. "My tooth has been sore for several days."

"I have something that can help." Her offer slipped out before she weighed the consequences. She might find Mr. Styles's anecdotes interesting, but she had no intentions of forgetting his true purpose of being here.

"You have a dentist here?" Mr. Style's brow lowered, his skepticism clear.

Lizzie simply smiled. "No, but something just as good."

CHAPTER SIX

Andrew followed Miss MacTavish back inside the circular enclosure of the village without any further explanation of her intentions. For all he knew, she could be taking him to the local medicine man to have the tooth extracted, something he was quite certain she would enjoy witnessing. And something that made his blood run cold.

He stopped beside one of the huts that over time had deteriorated to watch the familiar scene unfold around him. Women carrying hoes were returning from the fields in time to stoke their fires and prepare the evening meal. Others repaired baskets and stamped corn while the cattle filed into the enclosure amidst a thick cloud of dust and the rhythmic beating of a drum.

Andrew drew in a deep breath of the smoke-filled air from cooking fires that mingled with the pungent scent of cattle manure and decaying fish. He might not know everything about the customs of this culture, but there was one method of tribal markings, the knocking out of the upper teeth in order to resemble their cattle, he'd once witnessed firsthand.

A small boy had sat down between the legs of one of the elders who gripped his head. Then, with an iron chisel he'd proceeded to break out the front tooth, root and all, for to be a child with all one's teeth was to be the laughingstock of the village. Which guaranteed that once his teeth had been removed, there were several more children in line waiting their turn.

Andrew pressed his fingers against his jaw. No amount of pain was worth going through what he had seen that day.

"Mr. Styles?"

"Yes?" He looked up too quickly, shooting a jolt of pain up the side of his face.

"Are you coming?"

For a brief moment, he studied her subtle curves, the tilt of her head beneath her wide straw hat, then stopped at her face to search for any traces of amusement—which was ridiculous. This woman was a missionary, an unselfish pioneer who had come to bring light to the world of the heathens. She obviously took no joy in seeing other people's suffering.

Unless—

"Mr. Styles?" A hint of exasperation flickered behind her eyes. "Is there a problem?"

"A problem? Of course not. Just—just the painful tooth."

"Which is why we need to take care of it."

He followed her into a small dirt yard that surrounded a hut with its unplastered mud walls and thatched roof. "You have yet to tell me by what means you plan to do this."

"Sit down."

He stumbled onto one of the wooden stools in front of a hut while she grabbed a handful of something and dumped it into a black pot. "What is that?"

"The root of the Lutende bush. After soaking it in water and warming it on the fire, you put it in your mouth. I have been told that the taste is far from pleasant, but it will rid you of your toothache."

"So no pulling of the tooth?"

Miss MacTavish set the pot on a pile of stones atop a smoldering fire. "You think it should be pulled—"

"No!" He gave her a half-hearted laugh. "Your remedy sounds fine."

"Do I detect a note of fear in your voice?" Miss MacTavish glanced up at him beneath those long, dark lashes. "Children here are not allowed to even wince when their front teeth are pulled as it would show them to be cowards."

Andrew squirmed. "So I understand."

She went back to stirring the mixture. "I could describe many tribal remedies that would make the extraction of a tooth seem mild."

"That is quite all right. And I agree with your assessment that the…Lutende bush is a good place to start."

He watched her bite the tip of her tongue as she concentrated on her task. Before his arrival, he'd imagined her homely, quiet, and certainly not one to ignore the wishes of her grandfather. But instead, Lizzie MacTavish was passionate, beautiful…and made the seemingly simple task he'd agreed upon complicated.

He cleared his throat. "May I ask you a question?"

She crouched in front of the fire and continued stirring. "Does it have anything to do with your determination to make me leave?"

"In part." He smiled at her forthrightness. "You've made it quite clear that you are torn by the thought of leaving, but I have to admit that I am still puzzled by your reasoning. I can't imagine anyone who would even consider trading a country home, electricity, piped-in water, and telephone, a large inheritance for this"—he pointed to the hut behind her—"this structure that barely keeps out the elements."

Her frown deepened. "While money is a necessity, there are things in life more important than the comforts of wealth."

"Perhaps, but you are a single woman, alone in this environment. You have to get lonely."

She pointed with her long wooden spoon toward a group of children playing at the edge of the yard. Beyond them, women prepared the evening meal, while the men smoked and talked outside their huts. "I'm hardly alone, nor do I see what my being a woman has to do with anything."

"I didn't mean—"

"I could name women explorers who arrived here long before me. Have you never heard of Isabella Eberhardt, or Mary Kingsley, and the list of women who went out as single missionaries like Mary Slessor to Calibar—"

"Yes, but they are still in the minority—"

"In this clearly male-dominated profession of explorers and missionaries. Is that what you mean?"

Andrew clenched his jaw together then groaned as the jolt of pain intensified. He was not being paid enough for this.

Miss MacTavish stood. "Are you ready?"

His earlier hesitation surfaced. "You are sure this will work?"

"These people might not see the difference between medicine and the magic done by the witch doctor, but I have found that many of their medicinal remedies work well."

"So you have tried this cure?"

"Just yesterday, on a boy who came to me with a toothache. It worked splendidly. Now open your mouth and show me where it hurts."

He pointed while eying the mixture. "How long do I have to—"

"It's hot." She shoved the soaked root into his mouth, stopping him from protesting further. "You will need to keep it there until it grows cold."

Lizzie sat on the three-legged stool near the fire, pleased she'd found a way to quiet Mr. Styles. For a man, he talked as much as a group of women. It was one of the things she had disliked most about living in New York. What Bette Young had worn to dinner the night before, or where the Boytons were planning to go for their summer holiday seemed to her a frivolous waste of time. Her work in the hospital had been one thing that had brought with it a deep sense of fulfillment, but even that hadn't squelched her desire to return to the one place she felt at home.

The familiar lean form of Chuma's father, Kakoba, with his coal-black skin and missing front teeth appeared in front of them, interrupting her present train of thought. She stood to greet him, but her smile quickly faded as she caught the visible fear in his cloudy dark eyes. "What is wrong?"

"Posha has just given me another son."

"There is a problem with the child?"

"No. The child is fine. The problem lies with Chuma and Esther. They are gone."

"Gone?" She shook her head, somehow hoping that the slight gesture would help to clarify the situation. "I was just with them not too long ago and they were headed out to watch the cattle. Of course, you know how Chuma thinks of himself as a man, often losing track of time." She searched for a probable explanation of their disappearance. "He is probably out in the veld right now with his bow and arrow, pretending to track down an elephant, and Esther—"

"You do not understand. They have not run off. They have been taken."

Mr. Styles's warnings of the danger of the African bush whirred around her like a swarm of bees being smoked out from the hollow of a tree. "Taken by whom?"

"By Mawela."

The deep-rooted rivalry between the two clans was no secret among the villagers, though few were bold enough to talk about what had begun the feud. And then, despite the animosity between the tribes, Kakoba's sister, Kacha, had fallen in love and married the rival chief's son, Mawela.

Lizzie struggled to understand. "Why would Mawela do such a thing?"

"Kacha was sick for five days with fever. This afternoon she died, and Mawela is blaming our family." Kakoba pressed his hands together in front of him. "They have taken my children and two others until payment can be made for Kacha's death or a substitute wife given to replace her."

"How do you know this?"

"One of the herdsmen taken with Chuma and Esther was able to escape and return to the village. He heard their captors say that the children would not be released unless the fines were paid. And if we don't pay, they plan to sell them as slaves to compensate for Kacha's death."

"So they will be enslaved for the death of your sister even though you had nothing to do with it...." Her stomach heaved. "They can't do that."

"They already have."

"Where have they taken them?"

"They are most likely headed to their village. And after that…"

Lizzie's temples pounded. He needn't say more. Even though the trading of slaves was strictly forbidden by the British authorities, slaves were looked upon as less valuable than prized cattle and often traded for hoes and salt, and they were still commonly traded from master to master. And at times, even freemen were known to be seized and sold.

But not this time. She would not let this happen with Chuma and Esther.

Mr. Styles spit the compress from his mouth and rubbed his jaw. "What's going on?"

Lizzie ignored his pleas for her to explain. Her mind, still unwilling to accept the implication of Kakoba's words, was too frazzled to attempt a translation.

She focused instead on Kakoba. "Can the chief not make a judgment on your behalf due to the fact that you are being wrongfully accused?"

"It is possible, but such an action might take too long." The man's nose flared. "If the price is not paid to redeem them, I may never see them again."

She knew he was right. She'd heard stories of those who'd been taken away with nothing more than an accusation resembling the truth.

Mr. Styles gripped her arm, his face markedly pale. "Tell me what has happened."

"It's Chuma and Esther," she said, switching to English. "They, along with two other children, have been taken as slaves."

Mr. Styles's eyes widened. "But the British government doesn't recognize slavery—"

She pulled away from his grip. "It doesn't matter what a foreign government allows or disallows. These people have their own set of laws and rules and not all of them strictly follow the ways of colonization. Surely you have learned that in all of your travels."

"I am no stranger to ancient customs of exchanging cattle and ivory for young boys or the Arab slave traders who traveled long distances to capture slaves, but today's government holds a very strong position against this and has made marked progress in stopping such crimes."

"I realize that, but there is not time to have the authorities intervene. By the time someone arrived, it could be too late."

Lizzie squeezed her eyes shut. Unmarried women who were slaves were often treated as prostitutes, while the older women, like the one she'd seen this afternoon, spent their days in the fields. Not every man and woman lived out such a fate, but even if treated kindly, they were still slaves with no rights. And no child should have to experience being ripped away like this from their mother.

The burning scent of the Lutende bush permeated her senses. She quickly yanked the pot from the fire, dumping some of the contents in the process. Standing here would get them nowhere. "We must go after them."

"Wait." Kakoba dropped his gaze. "There is something else you must know."

"What?"

Kakoba hesitated with his response. "Some still blame you for my sister leaving in the first place as you were the one who encouraged her friendship with Mawela. They also say that you have angered the ancestors in the process. I felt I should warn you."

"But that is nonsense." A wave of anger spread through her. Throwing blame on another was as common as the pesky tsetse fly in this country. "Your family blames me for your sister leaving, and now her husband's family blames you for her death. You and I both know that none of this is true."

"You know I burned my amulets in front of your father and the Creator God, but even I have to acknowledge that since your return the rains have scattered, the crops suffered, and then the death of Beliya's child—"

"You blame these things on me as well?"

"I am just repeating what some say."

Even for one like Kakoba whose family had accepted Jesus as their Lord and Savior, it was difficult not to put blame on someone else for his problems.

Kakoba caught her gaze. "I am asking you to come with me to find them. You are friends with my sister's family. Perhaps you will have some influence on getting my children back."

Lizzie shook her head. "What influence can I have when I am the one being blamed for your sister leaving in the first place?"

"I will leave the decision in your hands, but I cannot wait."

Lizzie knew what she must do. "I will come with you."

Mr. Styles moved in front of her. "What are you going to do?"

"I'm going with Kakoba to find his children."

"This isn't your fight."

"Isn't it? These are my people. What happens to their children, to all of them, affects me. And besides that, they blame me in part for what has happened, which means I need to help make things right."

Mr. Styles's brow furrowed. "Why do they blame you?"

Lizzie clinched her hands at her sides, wishing she could erase the painful incident from her memory. "A month ago I helped with a delivery where the child was born breech. The mother is lucky to still be alive. There was nothing I could do to save the child."

"That's the real reason you aren't allowed at Posha's delivery."

"Yes."

"And you believe that finding Chuma and Esther will help absolve you?"

She didn't know what she believed anymore. "Maybe."

Mr. Styles's face appeared pale in the lingering twilight. No doubt his tooth, without the effects of the medicine, still hurt.

"You must stay here. You can use some more of the medicine from the pot."

"I think you need to stay as well."

Lizzie shook her head. "Kakoba's sister was a friend, and I knew her husband's family. If the children are with Mawela's family, I might be able to influence the chief to have them sent home."

"And if you can't?"

"We will find them." Her stomach tightened. If they were too late, and they'd already been sold to yet another neighboring tribe, finding them could prove to be impossible. But she wasn't ready to quit now. "And convince Mawela's family to let the children go."

"I'm coming as well."

"You can't come with us."

"Why not? In case you forgot, I am an explorer, and I'm certainly not just going to sit here waiting."

"Fine." She grabbed a small bag from inside the hut then reappeared. "But I will not allow these children to pay the price for something they didn't do."

CHAPTER SEVEN

Andrew followed Kakoba and the other men as they trudged across the seemingly endless savannah with its tall grasses blowing in the evening breeze. He wondered if his plan to return to New York with Miss Mac-Tavish was about to experience another unfortunate delay. She hurried beside him across the sandy soil, determination woven into her every step. But he too felt that same sense of determination. He had agreed to take 30 percent of his fee as a down payment and the remainder when he returned, but only because he'd been certain he'd have no problems convincing her that her place was now in New York.

He'd been wrong.

Which he had yet to understand. Every woman he knew would have given anything to live the life available to Lizzie. He glanced at her, but all he could see was the darkened silhouette of her slender form. He had no idea whether their presence would help or hinder the situation, but nothing, it seemed, would deter this young woman once her mind had settled upon something. She had said little since their departure from the village beyond, other than commenting on the humid night air. He was certain her mind was busy formulating a plan that would ensure the children's redemption if the hoes and bags of salt, brought by the men, proved insufficient.

A streak of lightning flashed in the distance, a sign that the impending rains would soon sweep across the plains. There was nothing to obstruct their view of the display, save an occasional tree with its massive limbs standing guard like a ghostly sentry. The distant mountains, lying against the edges of the flatlands to their south, were barely visible in the pale moonlight.

He'd once traveled this route when the sun-cracked plains had been swallowed by floodwaters from the swollen Kafue River. Men had stood in their dugout canoes, continuously searching for fish along the windy waterways until the flats dried out after the rainy season had finally passed. Tonight it was the brilliant panoply of stars that brought back memories of sleeping beneath the same black covering of sky, while listening to the constant beating of drums in the background.

A lion roared in the distance, breaking the stillness of the night and reminding him that danger didn't lie solely with the men who had taken the children. He stared across the darkened flatlands in search of the carnivore, but there was no way to see what—or how many—were out there. During the day, one could see the antelope, zebra, and other animals grazing on the earth's bounty. Such an abundance of food meant an abundance of lions, cheetah, and wild dogs that habitually preyed upon the food source.

"What happens when we find them?" Andrew broke the uneasy silence that had settled between them, curious about how this tribe would try to settle the issue.

She turned to look at him. "Are you asking because of the book you want to write or simply as one worried about the children's welfare?"

He smiled at her forthrightness. One could never question where one stood with the woman. "Both I suppose. I find human nature fascinating."

"There is nothing fascinating about the traffic of human flesh. People are often taken as slaves because of crimes they've committed, then end up being traded from master to master, stripping them of any rights they might have. It's also not unheard of for a person to be seized as a slave as they are walking through the forest or to their field."

"What happens to them?"

"In either case, it is often possible to redeem the slave for a price."

"And the price is paid in hoes and salt?"

"Or cattle. It depends on the worth of the slave."

Her chin dipped, making him wish again that he could read her expression. But he knew all too well that these children were not simply village children who had disappeared into the night. They were as close to her as family. He thought of her aunt and uncle back in New York. Perhaps far closer than family.

"It is possible," she continued, "that the chief will speak in favor of the children and order those who have taken them to give them back to their families."

"And if they refuse to give them back?"

"That is not an option we can accept."

Her boldness impressed him. How else could a single woman have survived in such a harsh environment on her own for so long?

Andrew's stomach growled, reminding him that he'd had nothing to eat since some porridge and sauce at noon. And while he didn't mind the rather bland taste, after days of eating the same fare, he was beginning to long for some of his sister-in-law's roast beef and mashed potatoes.

He dug into his bag and pulled out two wrapped chocolate bars. "I brought something for you. I had actually planned to give it to you after dinner, but since we both missed our chance to eat… It's called a Baby Ruth."

She took the offered gift without slowing her pace. "It's called a what?"

"A Baby Ruth."

Lightning flashed in the distance, illuminating her surprised expression for a brief moment. "I do not understand. What is a Baby Ruth?"

"It's a chocolate bar named after President Cleveland's daughter."

"Why would anyone name candy after someone's daughter?"

"I don't know." Andrew chuckled at her logic. "I never thought about why. That is simply what it's called."

"Strange."

"Forget the name and just try it. It's chocolate and peanuts. If nothing else, it will give you some energy after missing dinner."

Miss MacTavish peeled open the wrapper. "You brought this with you all the way from New York?"

"It's not exactly an item you can pick up between here and Livingston. Besides, I thought you would appreciate it more than the chief would."

She took a tentative bite. "My uncle owns a candy factory, but I don't remember the last time I had a piece of chocolate. It's—it's quite good."

"Last year the company ordered biplanes to drop the candy with little parachutes as an advertising gimmick. Apparently it worked. Americans can't get enough of them."

"A gimmick?" Her pace slowed. "Like bribing me with chocolate?"

"Consider it a gift and nothing else."

"So this has nothing to do with convincing me to return to New York with you."

"It's a candy bar, Miss MacTavish, nothing more. And somehow, I hardly think that chocolate will turn out to be the motivating factor in convincing you to return with me."

He ripped open his own candy bar and finished it off in three bites. She could be as irritating as a mosquito bite. But while his intentions were, for the most part, sincere, he had never been one to pass up an opportunity. Especially when she was the one who had brought up the subject. They could only stay at this impasse for so long, because he needed to get back to New York. And he wasn't going to return without her.

He considered his words carefully. "I had dinner with your aunt and uncle the night before I left New York. Their cook prepared the most delicious chicken a la king."

His stomach growled at the memory. The half-stale candy bar had done little to ease his hunger.

Miss MacTavish still nibbled on her candy bar. "How well do you know them?"

"Your uncle, as you probably know, has a great interest in exploration and other cultures. We met last fall when I lectured to a group in the city. He was the one who recommended me to your grandfather's solicitors."

"I'm not surprised that subject interested him. He has an extensive library where I fell asleep many evenings sitting in his large leather chair."

Andrew smiled, picturing her curled up with a thick-spined book. "Your uncle was most gracious in letting me have access to his books. I think, if he didn't have a business to run, or perhaps if he were twenty years younger, he would have joined me on this trip."

"He always was a bit of a dreamer."

Andrew swallowed hard. And a gambler and womanizer, but those descriptions he'd keep to himself. They came to the top of a small rise, where finally, in the distance, he could see the flickering of orange flames from cooking fires in a village.

He took another peek at her profile. Perhaps he was making progress after all. Adding a layer of guilt to the situation could only manage to push things in his favor. "Your aunt mentioned that they had never had children and how she thought of you like the daughter she'd never had."

"I find that hard to believe as I spent very little time with my aunt."

"Apparently it was enough." Andrew caught the hesitation in her voice. "You sound surprised."

"I just...I suppose I didn't realize she felt that way."

Lizzie quickened her pace to catch up to the men who'd lengthened the distance between them, now that the village was in sight. Irritation swept over her. Mr. Styles's presence had brought with him such a jumbled mixture of emotion. Perhaps she'd been the one who had expected too much. Her aunt and uncle had given her everything she'd needed physically, and no one could have expected them to have filled the hole left in her heart by the death of her parents.

She drew in a deep breath of the night air. Its scent was laced with the unpleasant odor of the Kigelia tree's deep maroon flowers, and she wished she could go back in time to when her parents were still alive, when she'd been naïve enough to believe that life would go on forever without changing like the rhythmic flow of the seasons.

She couldn't begin to count the number of nights she'd sneaked out onto the veld to lie down and watch the stars fill the nighttime sky. While those in the village paid little attention to the pattern of the stars, she still remembered lying beneath them beside her father and listening to him talk about the constellations.

He'd taught her to recognize when Venus made her appearance in the sky, and when the Pleiades signaled the time of cultivation, but the most spectacular had been when they watched Halley's Comet pass by in 1910. No amount of longing would bring those days back, but neither would she ever forget those memories buried deep within her heart.

She took the last bite of the candy bar Mr. Styles had given her, then shoved the empty wrapper into the small bag she carried. The familiar chirrups of the cicadas played in the distance, competing with the rest of the nightly symphony of insects and the subtle growls of animals, but for the moment, her mind returned to the bustling streets of New York City.

She had spent little time in her aunt and uncle's plush residence.

Instead she'd lived at the hospital, where most of her time was occupied attending to patients during the intensive three-year program. Her aunt and uncle had been pleased with her choice of schooling, but had expected her to remain in New York once her studies were finished. She'd never intended to stay.

It hadn't taken her long to realize that the streets of Manhattan were as foreign to her as the African bush was to her aunt's cultured friends.

"Miss MacTavish, I apologize if I upset you by talking about your aunt."

Lizzie drew in a short breath and tried to erase the lingering frustration she'd brought with her across the Atlantic. "It is not your fault. You must think me cold."

"Why would you say that?"

"Because despite what I think about my grandfather's inheritance, my aunt's illness should have me on the next ship to New York."

He paused for a moment. "May I be quite frank with you, Miss MacTavish?"

"I'm quite certain there is nothing much I can do to stop you, so by all means, please say what's on your mind."

"I have been quite surprised at your hesitation to return with me and have wondered in particular why not only the wishes of your grandfather, but the ill health of your aunt is not motivation enough."

Lizzie wondered if there was a hint of criticism in his words. "I will always be grateful for everything my aunt and uncle did for me while I lived in New York, but the people here need me."

"As their savior?"

"Their savior?" She stomped across a patch of sandy soil and felt her temper flare. "That is where you are wrong. They do not need me as their savior. But if God has called me here, as I believe He has, then I need to stay and do what I can."

"Even after what Kakoba said to you tonight?"

Lightning flashed again, illuminating the mountains in the distance. No matter how hard she tried, she'd been unable to dismiss the significance of Kakoba's words.

"When he told me there were those who blamed me in part for the disappearance of his children, his words reminded me of how..." Lizzie pressed her lips closed, surprised at how close she'd been to revealing the truth. She shook her head. She did not owe Mr. Styles, or anyone else for that matter, an explanation of why she couldn't leave. "It is nothing."

"From the sound of your voice I do not believe it is nothing." There was a note of sympathy in his voice. "I'll make a deal with you."

"A deal?" She hesitated.

"I'm beginning to wonder if I have a choice. If I await your decision, we might both die here on this fertile ground before ever getting back to New York. You tell me the truth about your reluctance to return, and I will promise not to pressure you into leaving."

She studied his profile, wondering why she should trust a man whose sole reason for being here was to take her home. Her uncle had clearly trusted him with her well-being, but for all she knew Mr. Styles's motivation in being here was purely financial.

"Are they paying you well to bring me back?"

His gaze dipped. "Well, enough to fund my next exploration."

"Then why would you promise not to pressure me into leaving?"

"Because I'm curious, I suppose. I've spent years trying to better understand human nature, and you are different from anyone I've met before. I want to understand your need to stay when common sense in general, and a waiting fortune in particular, would have most people already having packed their bags and aboard the next ship."

"The situation is complicated."

"Look ahead of us. There is nothing more than sand and soil and brush. Even with the faint flickering lights of the village on the horizon, we still have time before we reach it."

Lizzie felt her shoulders relax slightly. Perhaps it was due to the darkness that hid his expression or the ease of speaking her parents' native tongue that compelled her to answer his question. Perhaps it was because he, like herself, was different. Or perhaps it was simply because she'd held in emotions for so long that needed to be expressed.

"There were other reasons for my returning than my faith." She might not trust his motives, but there was definitely something cathartic about speaking aloud about her loss. "When I returned to New York after my parents died, life was different. I could discuss philosophy and literature but didn't understand how to truly communicate with those around me. Women were tall and graceful like the great white egret, the men witty and knowledgeable, but for myself…I was the outsider."

She'd attended parties in her uncle's house and afternoon tea with her aunt's friends, who had spoken about Africa as the land of the heathens and savages in a way that had left her nauseated. Perhaps they hadn't meant to, but neither had they made any effort to understand their differences or to welcome her into their circle of friends for who she was.

"But are you not an outsider here?"

She considered his question. "It is different, because here I am expected to be an outsider. Everyone who sees me notices that my skin is pale, that my hair is too fair, and that I dress like a European.

"But in New York, I was supposed to be a part of society, and yet as hard as I tried, I never was able to fit in. I am not naïve enough to believe that I will one day completely fit in here either, but at least most accept me for who I am. Which means that to me these are my people."

"Perhaps you're not the only one who feels like an outsider."

His statement piqued her curiosity. "You speak of yourself?"

"I speak of anyone who wishes to be something he is not. The one who never completely fits into the world he was brought into and dreams of breaking free of the stigma that forces him to stay where he is."

"And is that what compels you to explore? To see and become something bigger and better?"

"Partially, I suppose. My mother's father explored the world and returned home with tales of savages, cannibals, and adventure that would make your skin crawl. Yet from an early age, I admired him and wanted to be like him."

"So it runs in your blood, this obsession to explore."

"I believe that would be an accurate statement."

The flickering of orange in the distance was now directly ahead, and they were silent again as they approached the village. While Mr. Styles assumedly pondered her response, Lizzie questioned why she'd spoken so freely to him. Maybe it didn't matter. Her confession changed nothing between them. They still had opposing ambitions, and she would not forget hers.

At the entrance to the village, they were greeted as if they had been expected. Kakoba immediately asked for the chief, and a few minutes later, they were ushered to the chief's hut and asked to sit down outside the entrance.

Mr. Styles sat beside her on one of the stools. "What happens now?"

She leaned back against the thatched structure behind her and tried to shake the fatigue settling over her body. "We wait."

CHAPTER EIGHT

Lizzie's head smacked against the wooden post behind her, jarring her awake. Darkness hovered like a heavy blanket, and they had yet to speak to the chief regarding the missing children.

She leaned forward in an effort to stretch her stiff muscles. Kakoba and the other men sat with them in front of the chief's hut, alert despite the late hour.

Mr. Styles nudged her with his elbow. "Are you awake?"

"Yes. I—I must have dozed."

Lizzie drew in a deep breath, still trying to clear her head. She'd slept little the night before as she'd read and reread her uncle's letter along with the one from her grandfather's solicitors while weighing the validity of their requests. Another night with little sleep had left her exhausted.

"You snore."

"I do not."

Mr. Styles laughed, but his smile quickly faded. "When do you think they are coming to talk with us?"

"I don't know. I certainly did not think it would take this long."

The irritations from the long journey and lack of sleep multiplied. Sitting here would do nothing to find Chuma and Esther and the other children, and she knew the children must be terrified. Direct accusations that the delay was insulting might be taboo, but it also seemed pointless to sit here while nothing was being done to rectify the situation.

As if he'd read her mind, an old man, dressed in the skin of a leopard, stepped out from the large hut behind them and sat on an empty wooden stool across from them. Lizzie squirmed as the long-winded greetings began. Even in the face of tragedy, tradition triumphed.

Kakoba, like herself, tired quickly of the formalities. "I'm here for my children."

The chief rubbed the stubble on his chin. "I am fully aware of my son's claim against you."

Kakoba's nostrils flared. "Where are my children?"

"They are safe." The chief held up a gnarled hand, his placid expression appearing that he spoke of something no more urgent than the weather. "I have made sure of that."

"So they are here?"

"Due to a matter I find most unfortunate."

"A matter that has nothing to do with my children."

"On the contrary. It has everything to do with your children, as they are a part of your clan."

"Your son's claims regarding my sister's death are false. I cared deeply for her welfare, and while I might not have agreed with her decision to marry your son, I held no animosity toward her or Mawela. I had nothing to do with her death."

"That is not what my son tells me. He claims you were here five days ago and had a fierce argument with her. The next day she fell ill, and now she is dead. I see no other way to interpret what happened. We both know that for a price, the death of anyone can be bought by a visit to a sorcerer."

"I no longer practice those ways, as I said, nor did I have anything to do with her death." Kakoba proceeded to pile the hoes and salt before the chief then offered one of the bags to him with both hands. "But I am prepared to pay if that is your judgment. We brought hoes and salt. Allow us to redeem the children and have this matter settled and put behind us."

"I don't see it as quite so simple." The chief nodded for Kakoba to drop the bag he held with the rest of the pile. "They are four strong children. They would bring quite a good price if I decided to sell them."

"You cannot do that." Kakoba's voice rose. "My daughter is six. She is no use for planting or harvesting."

"There are other uses for girls beside field work."

Lizzie felt her stomach roil. Her father had continuously preached about the evils of such practices, but his insistence had brought about little change. She could not let this happen to Esther.

Mr. Styles pressed his shoulder against Lizzie. "What are they saying?"

"The chief has accused Kakoba of having a death curse placed upon his daughter-in-law."

"Does he have proof?"

"Rarely is proof the issue in situations like this one. They will continue going through the typical negotiations, but the chief seems certain that the elders will agree that Mawela is due more than a few hoes and bags of salt—perhaps they will even award him the lives of the children."

"Can they do that? Even though Kakoba had nothing to do with his sister's death?"

"To you it might not seem fair, but it is not uncommon for people to be given as slaves to compensate for the death of others. If the two men cannot resolve the issue between them here, there will more than likely be a formal meeting with the elders."

"What if Mawela took the children because he knew there were foreigners in Kakoba's tribe who could afford to pay handsomely to see the children returned?"

The thought sent chills down her spine. In her eagerness to make things right, had she actually made things worse?

Lizzie shoved aside her fears and sent up another prayer for the children's safety. "I have faith that he will eventually relent and let the children go."

She turned back to watch Kakoba. The muscles in his jaw tensed as he stood erect in front of the chief. "Let me talk to your son, since he is the one who has made this claim against me."

"I am sorry, but he's not here."

"When is he due to return?"

"I do not know."

"You know that we are offering a fair price to redeem the children. Far more than they are worth, and it will save us from going to the authorities. Let us have them and we will leave. There is no reason for our villages to continue fighting each other."

"You are wrong. The claims against you are worth far more than a handful of salt and a few hoes." The chief moved forward and leaned against his cane. "And it would seem that we have the advantage, for we have your children. So while you might believe this to be a fair price, I do not."

Kakoba took a step forward. "I am tired of the games you play. What I offer is fair. I want my children brought to me now."

The chief tossed the bag of salt in front of Kakoba. "In addition to the hoes and salt you brought us, I require three of your cattle to replace the life of my son's wife."

Kakoba dropped back onto the wooden stool in front of the chief. "What we have offered you is more than fair considering you have no proof of the claims being brought against me."

"Without the cattle, I'm afraid I will have to give permission for the children to be sold."

"We did not bring cattle. We assumed—"

"You assumed wrong."

Lizzie caught the desperation in Kakoba's voice. Cattle were prized above the children themselves and often used in negotiations, but if Kakoba left to retrieve the cattle, there was no guarantee that the children would be here on his return.

The chief stood. "I apologize that you had to come all this way for nothing."

"Wait." Lizzie held up her hand. No life was to be so easily brushed away. "We have no intention of leaving without the children."

The chief sat back down. "Excuse me?"

Lizzie knelt in front of the chief and caught his gaze. "As you know, I grew up across the great flood plains not far from where your people live and knew your son's wife well." Lizzie glanced briefly at Kakoba, who nodded slightly at her to continue. "I have watched the Zambezi swell when the rains come and the veld burn in the heat of the summer. I have planted pumpkin and maize and helped with the harvest, and I have lain in the tall grasses and watched the elephants rumble across the earth."

"I knew your father well." The chief studied her for a moment, as if contemplating his response. "He was a good man, and while I might not have always agreed with his ways, I did respect how he tried to help our people."

Lizzie drew in a deep breath. "As you knew, my father was a good man. I too know that Kakoba is a good man. While the rift between these villages is strong, Kakoba is not one to take revenge into his own hand. He, like my father, follows the ways of the Creator God."

The chief's toothless smile broadened. "Surely even those who follow your God fall from time to time and give in to temptation."

"That might be true, but I know that Kakoba had nothing to do with Kacha's death. Neither do I believe that a life of slavery is befitting anyone, let alone a small child who has done nothing to deserve such a sentence."

The chief rubbed his hand across his wrinkled forehead as if considering her pleas. "Elegantly said, but I believe I still have the advantage, as I am the one who holds the children."

Lizzie continued her ongoing prayer for wisdom in what to say and for peace for her jumbled nerves. "We both know that there are many sicknesses that can kill a strong man in less time than it took for Kacha to die. What evidence does your son have that she did not simply die of natural causes?"

"What evidence do you have that she did?"

Lizzie bit back a barbed response. A sharp answer would do nothing for their situation. But neither was she willing to drop the matter. "Out of respect for my father's name, I am asking that you put aside your animosity toward Kakoba's family and reconsider your judgment." Lizzie stood and caught the chief's gaze again. "We do not plan to leave here without the children in our company."

"You are persistent."

"As it is said, one can only eat an elephant one bite at a time."

"What else of value might you have to add to the hoes and salt?"

"I have nothing but my words. And the knowledge that it is you and Kakoba's father who hold the key to ending this—not your son Mawela or Kakoba."

"And what do you know about Kakoba's father and myself?"

Lizzie swallowed hard. She'd come too far to quit now. "I know that once, many years ago, you fought over who would win the heart of one woman. She is dead, but the animosity that runs between you is still strong."

The chief stood and bridged the short distance between them. Lizzie held her breath, certain she'd rather face the rogue elephant than the wrath of the chief.

"You have spirit and courage. I respect that."

Relief swept through her. "Thank you."

"What about your necklace? It would make a fine gift for one of my wives."

"I…" Lizzie looked down at the necklace her mother had given her for her sixteenth birthday.

The chief fingered the locket, close enough that she could smell the beer on his breath. "You give me the jewelry instead of the cattle, and I will let the children go."

Without hesitating, Lizzie unclasped the locket from her neck and handed it to him.

The chief smiled then turned to one of his men. "Get the children."

CHAPTER NINE

Lizzie hurried from the village between Chuma and Esther, the young girl's hands firmly gripping both hers and her father's. While she'd noted the relief in Kakoba's eyes, she also hadn't missed the glint of fear that remained. If Mawela returned, it was possible he might try to convince the chief that the price they'd paid to redeem the children was not enough to cover the death of his wife. And with tensions still high among the small party who'd accompanied them to the village, she knew that next time, their reaction would not be to compliantly hand over a handful of hoes and salt.

They hurried across the edges of the open plain, close to the thick forest, where it would be harder to see them in the moonlight if pursued. Kakoba clearly wasn't taking any chances of losing his children a second time. The chief's judgment might stand as law, but it wasn't uncommon for a child, or an adult for that matter, to simply disappear at the hand of an enemy. And Mawela had already made it clear that he did not intend to play by the rules.

Kakoba's breathing sounded labored beside her as the flickering orange flames from the village vanished behind them. "I owe you the lives of my children."

"You owe me nothing. I am just grateful that God heard our prayers and answered them by giving us back your children."

"I am still worried about Mawela. The fact that he was not there makes me believe this is not over as far as he is concerned."

Lizzie picked up Esther, who was struggling to keep up. "He will listen to his father, mourn the loss of his wife, then find another to take her place as all men do."

"Perhaps, but I know Mawela. He has a tendency to drink too much, and his temper rivals any man I know. When he his angry, there is no way to reason with him."

"But the problem, as you know, is greater than the death of your sister or Mawela's accusations that you are the one who killed her." She knew she had overstepped her position as an outsider in the village, but until the situation was resolved, the rift between the clans would only continue to deepen.

"None of it will be over until your father and his father put behind them the feud that began before you were born." She continued to weigh each word carefully. "Sita is dead and nothing anyone does will bring her back, yet year after year I hear talk of the bitter enmity between your villages. Of how your father stole Mawela's father's wife, and so he retaliated by burning down your village. As a follower of the Creator God, you need to be the one who convinces your father to put a stop to this, or this hatred will trickle down through yet another generation."

Kakoba shook his head. "*Mulikani ki yena sila.*"

"Your friend has become your enemy?"

"And I fear that it would be easier to tame a wild dog than have them change their ways. Both my father and Mawela's father are stubborn."

"And they have passed their stubbornness on to their children."

"You speak boldly." Kakoba clicked his tongue. "But perhaps you are right. It is time for the elders to meet and put an end to the discord."

Andrew rubbed his neck, wishing now for the concoction Miss Mac-Tavish had prepared for him earlier. After weeks of sailing the Atlantic, followed by the journey through the African bush to find Miss Mac-Tavish, his body longed for a week's sleep—not another night trek across the savannah and its oppressive climate.

He quickened his pace to catch up with Miss MacTavish, who walked near the front of the group with Esther asleep against her shoulder. Perhaps conversation would distract him from the ache that had intensified in his jawline.

She glanced briefly at him. "Is your tooth still bothering you?"

He touched the side of his cheek then winced. "Only slightly."

"Once we return to the village it would be wise for you to try the medicine once again."

"Yes ma'am." He smiled at the now familiar determination in her voice, matched only by the fortitude in her step and the tilt of her chin. "Kakoba must be grateful."

"He is."

"I might not have understood the words you said to the chief, but I didn't miss the passion in your voice."

"It wasn't my passion that changed the chief's mind."

"I'm not sure I would agree with that, especially since the necklace couldn't have been worth even one oxen in his eyes."

"True, but the necklace was what allowed him to appear the victor without losing respect."

The moon went behind another cloud, making him thankful for the lanterns the men had brought. "Was the necklace valuable?"

"Only to me."

She gave no further explanation, leaving the relative quiet of the savannah to hover between them.

"Was it a gift?" he finally asked.

"My mother gave it to me on my sixteenth birthday, two years before she died." Her lips were pressed tightly together, her gaze straight ahead, as if the mention of the necklace had opened up a chest full of memories. "It was a wedding gift given to her mother by my grandfather before they sailed to the United States from Ireland."

"It sounds to me as if my family isn't the only one with the spirit of adventure in their blood." When she didn't respond, he continued. "You miss her, don't you?"

"Very much."

While it seemed to be true that any thoughts of returning to New York had been forgotten due to the children's abduction, it was clear to him that family was an important part of who she was. No matter which side of the Atlantic they resided on.

And while he still might feel slightly guilty for playing on her emotions as they approached the village earlier, he also knew that understanding her better would help to give him an advantage in his situation. In order to take the upper hand and be able to talk some sense into her, he needed to make her more sympathetic toward him. For he still had no plans of leaving without her. Neither was he planning on staying long.

"What about your parents?" she asked. "Are they still alive?"

He glanced at her, surprised she'd decided to continue the conversation. "I never knew my mother. She died when I was three. My father spent most of his time working or drinking, while my grandparents, his parents, took care of my brother and me the best they could."

"I'm sorry you never knew your mother. Sometimes I still see my mother walking across the veld in the distance even after all these years. Then I have to stop and realize that she isn't coming back." She repositioned Esther on her hip as they mounted a small ridge that over-looked the open savannah. "What about your father? Is he still alive?"

"He died in an automobile accident a few years ago in the Lower East Side of Manhattan. I was traveling with the doughboys across the Atlantic to the frontlines when I got the message that he'd been killed."

"You were in the war?"

"I was a correspondent."

"I remember reading the daily news from overseas and thinking about those who were losing fathers, brothers, sons." Her voice carried a wistful tone. "I had just lost my parents and felt like I understood a small part of what they must be experiencing."

"It must get lonely without them here."

"Sometimes. I don't believe I will ever completely get over the loss of my mother or my father." Her fingers touched the empty hollow of her neck.

Guilt resurfaced, and Andrew swallowed hard. Not that he was responsible for what had happened tonight, but his presence and his constant barrage of questions regarding her return had to weigh heavily on her mind. "You didn't have to give him the necklace. I saw the way you negotiated for their release. I believe he was ready to do whatever you said."

"Like what? Trade them for some of your Baby Ruth bars?" Her laugh rang loud, but hollow. "It doesn't matter. The children are safe. That is why we came."

Esther turned her head, moaned, then snuggled back into Miss MacTavish…Lizzie's shoulder.

Andrew cleared his throat. "May I call you Lizzie? Miss MacTavish —and Mr. Styles for that matter—seem so…formal."

She paused before answering, making him uncertain as to what she thought about his request. "I suppose that would be all right."

"Then I'm glad you are in agreement with my suggestion. I find the use of surnames at times far too laborious." He stepped over a small mound of dirt, wondering how much farther until they reached the village. Each step jarred his head, adding to the pulsating pain in his tooth. Apparently even conversation wasn't enough of a distraction. But the pain didn't stop him from asking another question. "What happens next? Do you really believe that the animosity that runs between these two villages is going to end with a few hoes and bags of salt, or even a necklace?"

"Not completely. But for now, Chuma and Esther can return home to their mother, and we can pray that this situation is behind us."

A flash of movement in the tall grasses caught Andrew's attention. A tawny lioness crouched in the moonlight, every muscle taut and steady as she waited near the fringes of a small herd of zebra.

"Ma?" Esther's eyes were open.

Lizzie looked in the direction Esther pointed. "What is it?"

"There's a lion stalking the herd." Andrew answered for her.

Lizzie stopped and set the young girl on the ground. "Chuma, Esther, get down and don't move. She is too busy to worry about us right now, but if she catches our scent, that could change."

The men in the party had also spotted the animal and quickly extinguished their lanterns before raising their spears, poised to react if the lioness changed her course and came toward them. Andrew crouched down beside Lizzie, fully aware of the danger the lion posed for both the herd and their party. He'd seen the jagged scars left on the bodies of men who had slain one of the animals, and had heard stories of not-so-lucky herdsmen mauled and killed from an encounter with the beast.

Andrew's heart pounded, his muscles frozen. In the light of day he would have taken a sequence of photos of the lioness. Tonight he checked the perimeter of the zebra herd by the light of the moon to see if the feline was alone or if she'd brought the other females of her pride to hunt with her.

A second female appeared, crouched low as she circled the herd on the far side. This was certainly not the first time he had come face to face with danger on his treks throughout the continent, and he knew enough to take precautions to ensure it wasn't his last. He wouldn't be like one daring white sportsman he knew who'd hunted across the continent like it was a game and then later met his fate in the jaws of a lion.

With a sudden burst of speed, the lioness on the left made her move. Andrew watched, amazed at the power and speed of the cat as she lunged for her prey. One zebra hesitated for a moment, confused as to which direction it should run. While the herd scattered, the lioness took advantage of the hesitation and pounced, followed by the second lioness that helped drag the animal to its death. In a matter of seconds, the kill was complete.

Beside him, Esther's small body trembled as she buried her face in Lizzie's skirts. She stroked the young girl's head. "What you saw is God's plan for the animals. The lion must eat the zebra, just like we must eat the bush pig and the antelope to survive. It is how life continues."

With the lions busy eating, they started walking again. Chuma held up a long shaft of grass behind his head and charged toward an imaginary enemy.

"If I remember correctly," Andrew began, "the young David you spoke of earlier did more than slay the giant, Goliath."

Chuma turned around, his spear still high in the air. Andrew had Lizzie and Chuma's attention.

"What else did he kill?" Chuma asked.

"He killed a lion."

"And a bear," Lizzie added.

"What happened?" Esther's voice was laced with curiosity.

"I believe Mr. Styles is quite capable of telling the story. Are you not?"

"I think it might be best for me to save my storytelling skills, lacking as they are, for another day."

"Then will you tell us, Ma? Please?"

"I believe the children are right." Andrew smiled. "We all know that you are far more capable of telling the story than I am."

"Because I am a better storyteller, or because it has been so long since you've opened the Good Book?"

A twinge of guilt surfaced at Lizzie's question, but Andrew brushed it away. "I suppose I will have to admit that there is a portion of truth behind both statements."

Lizzie's laugh seemed to chisel away at the wall she'd erected between them. "One day David was out in the pasture watching his sheep, just like when you, Esther, are out helping your brother watch your cattle. And David was the youngest of his brothers and not near as important as them."

"Young like me?"

"Yes, but you are very important."

"One day, David saw a lion sneak into the pen, ready to eat one of his sheep. Filled with courage and strength from God, he killed the lion with his bare hands."

"Even Chuma couldn't do that."

"Anything is possible when the Lord is our strength. Isn't that true, Mr. Styles?"

"Andrew, remember?"

"Isn't that true…Andrew?"

Andrew cleared his throat. "I suppose there is some truth in that statement."

"Who is our source of strength?" Lizzie addressed the children again.

Esther, who was now fully awake, skipped beside Lizzie in the moonlight. "The Creator God."

The shadow of the village finally came into view, with a few flickerings of orange dancing in the moonlight from fires still burning. Andrew glanced at Lizzie's shadowy profile beside him, suddenly sorry the night was almost over. Somehow she'd managed to find the courage to stand up to the chief, which had enabled them to return with the children. Even if it had cost her personally.

Ten minutes later they entered the village that still lay sleeping. Nothing seemed to have changed since they left. The cattle were in their pens and only one of the dogs roamed the entrance.

A scream shattered the silence.

Andrew's senses heightened. "What was that?"

A woman ran up to Kakoba, her hands moving as fast as her words.

Lizzie turned to Andrew to translate. "Kacha's husband, Mawela, arrived a few minutes ago. He's claiming that any fine paid by Kakoba won't be enough. He intends to take Kakoba's wife as his own."

CHAPTER TEN

Lizzie rushed through the entrance of the village on the heels of Kakoba and the other men, terrified by what had been said. Thick smoke from a large pile of ash smoldering in the cattle pens to protect the herd from mosquitoes filled the air with its pungent odor. The normal bustle of activity had stopped hours ago when the covering of night had spread across the village, but a few staggered from their sleep and into the darkness to see what was going on. Lizzie ignored their startled glances. If what they'd been told was true, the lives of Posha and her newborn baby were in danger.

Lizzie stopped at the edge of Kakoba's compound and drew in a sharp breath. Mawela stood in front of the family's hut, one beefy arm wrapped around Posha. He held the sharp tip of a battle-axe against her throat. From inside the darkness of the hut, the baby cried.

Esther screamed and started running toward her mother, but Lizzie grabbed her and gathered her tightly in her arms, pressing the young girl's face against her skirt so she couldn't see what was happening.

Torches began to light up the darkness as curious villagers began forming a circle around the edge of the compound.

Mawela didn't seem to notice. Instead, beneath the flickering glow of the torchlight, he kept his gaze focused on Kakoba.

Mawela spewed out an insult then spit, "I have been waiting for you."

The veins in Kakoba's neck bulged. "I was out looking for my children you took from me. And even though I am innocent of my sister's death, I spoke to your father and redeemed my children."

"Then my father is a fool. A pile of hoes or salt or cattle will do nothing to make up for Kacha's death." Mawela shook his head. "You never wanted me to marry her, did you? You always believed I wasn't good enough for her."

"Even if what you say was true, why would I kill my sister to hurt you? How can you think that I do not mourn her death as much as you do?"

Andrew spoke to her above the growing chaos around them. "What is going on?"

"Apparently the taking of the children and paying of the ransom was not enough. Kacha's husband is still demanding his revenge on the family over his wife's death."

"And all this stems from a woman two chiefs fought over years ago who is now dead?"

"People have murdered for far less than this. It's not uncommon for blame to be placed on someone for a natural death."

Like her being blamed for the death of Beliya's child. The reminder pricked against her pounding heart, but tonight wasn't about her. Now it was about saving Posha from this drunken man.

Kakoba started walking slowly toward Mawela. "This matter is over. I have paid the fine your father pronounced, which means there is no need for further retaliation. Taking my wife or killing me will only add another hole in the clan and not fix anything."

Kakoba circled the small yard then stopped to grab a spear leaning against a tree. Lizzie handed Esther to one of the women standing beside her, who whisked the young girl away.

Mawala gripped Posha tighter. "Put the weapon down or I will kill her."

Despite her trembling hands, Lizzie knew she must stop Kakoba from making the situation worse. "Don't harm him. You will only make things worse."

"Why?" Kakoba took another step forward. "Talk will not end this situation tonight. It will not stop until someone's blood is shed."

"And then another and another. Is that what you want?" Lizzie turned to Mawela. "Is that what both of you want?"

Posha whimpered in Mawela's arms and cried out to her husband.

"What is it that your Bible says?" Mawela's words were slurred, his eyes glassy, and he was clearly drunk. "An eye for an eye. A tooth for a tooth."

"It does not mean you have the right to take revenge on an innocent man. If you let my wife go, I will let you go unharmed and will forget what happened here tonight. The same as I promised your father. We have let this go on between our clans for far too long. And it is time we convince our fathers of the same thing before this evil spreads further."

Mawela stumbled and almost dropped his battle-axe, but didn't loosen his grip on Posha. "I will never forget. Don't you see? I have nothing to lose. My wife is gone, along with the unborn child she carried."

Kakoba had started moving forward as Mawela spoke but stopped at the man's last statement. "I didn't know she carried your child."

"And would that knowledge have made a difference? Would that have stopped you from putting a curse on her so that her death would bring me pain?"

Lizzie stood at the front of the crowd, not knowing whether it was wiser to stay quiet or get involved. Mawela clearly felt he had nothing to lose. And Posha's eyes told Lizzie she knew it as well.

"I would never harm my sister, and if you weren't drunk, you might see that. This must stop before someone gets hurt."

Mawela laughed. "Before someone gets hurt? It's far too late for that. I lost my wife and child, and you are going to pay."

Lizzie's heart pounded in her throat as she watched the two men crouch low and face each other. She'd watched mimic fights at festivals or funerals, where dozens of men had lined up then rushed forward while throwing their darts into the air at their foes. But this was no game to entertain an audience. It was a fight to the death. There would be no need for the one who lost tonight to fake his own death as he would in a mock fight. His blood would be spilt across the dark soil.

With one hand still grasping Posha, Mawela lunged toward Kakoba. He staggered slightly, allowing Kakoba to evade him.

Mawela shouted in defiance and prepared to make his next move. The crowd surrounding them continued to grow, none of them willing to break up the match.

"We've got to stop them," Andrew said.

Lizzie turned to Andrew. "How? If you step into the middle of this, Mawela will not hesitate to kill Posha—or you for that matter."

"Then you must convince Kakoba to stop. Surely his actions are only making things worse."

"And you think I do not realize that? But what would you have him do? His wife's life is at stake, along with his own honor. I'm not certain anyone would be able to convince either man to back down at this point. Kakoba was not the one who initiated the fight. And he will not be the one who backs down from the fight."

"Where is the chief? Surely he could put a stop to this."

Lizzie scanned the growing throng, but there was no sign of the chief. The metal blade of Mawela's weapon glistened in the light of the torches.

Mawela waved his battle-axe in the air. "All I have to do is slit her throat and you will begin to feel what I am feeling."

"And then what will happen?" Kakoba's father, the chief, emerged from the crowd. "If you kill her, I will see to it that you are taken to the authorities on charges of murder. There are other ways of handling this situation."

"Like the way you handled things with my father?" Mawela's words were slurred. "There is a price for stealing one's wife."

"I did not steal your father's wife. She came to me quite willingly. Kakoba, drop your spear. Mawela, give me yours and let Posha go. Let this end now."

"You play me for the fool. Don't come any closer, because I will kill her."

Mawela took another step backward then faltered as he tripped over the cooking fire that still smoldered, loosening his hold on Posha. Kakoba took advantage of the momentary distraction, but Mawela was too fast. His fist met the edge of Kakoba's jaw. Unable to keep his balance, Kakoba fell to the ground.

Lizzie moved to help but stopped at the sound of crackling flames. Bright orange embers flew upward then were caught by the wind. Several of the sparks from the cooking fire had landed on the straw roof. Cries went up from the crowd as thatch, straw, and dry wood, caught in the path of the flames, were devoured by the orange glow as it spread like a dynamite fuse across the roof. Within a matter of seconds, the roof of the hut was a blaze of flames and smoke.

Lizzie's heart pounded. The baby!

Without pausing to think, Lizzie gripped the sides of her skirt and rushed toward the hut. Thick smoke burned her eyes and throat. Blackness engulfed her. Even in the daytime, the windowless huts were lit only by the light entering the narrow doorway. In the darkness of night, with thick smoke surrounding her, seeing anything had became impossible.

She squeezed her eyes shut for a moment and tried to calm the panic rising inside her as the long wooden poles, bark, and thatch burned above her. She pictured the layout of the room. To the left was a clay fireplace and firewood, to the right, a platform holding clay pots. Suspended from the roof along the edges of the hut were bundles of medicines, baskets, and gourds full of milk. In the far corner, past a rack of spears, was a bed made from sticks and covered with skins. Lizzie crossed the hard clay floor. The baby had to be on the bed.

She stopped when her knee hit the edge of the platform. The newborn was bundled in the center of the bed whimpering. Snatching the baby into her arms, she headed toward the exit. Before she had taken three steps, a large burning piece of thatch fell to the ground, blocking the faint outline of the door. Lizzie pressed the baby close to her pounding heart and prayed for a miracle.

For the first time in as long as he could remember, Andrew found himself praying. Flames engulfed Kakoba's hut as he ran after Lizzie. The glowing blaze crackled, spreading flames across the dry thatch before jumping to the next roof. If the fire wasn't put out quickly, the devastation would be tremendous.

He'd seen the results of a fire that had swept through a village once before. In a matter of minutes, dozens of huts had been reduced to nothing more than smoldering piles of ashes. Four people had died that night. He couldn't let that same fate happen to Lizzie or anyone else living here.

Standing in the threshold, his eyes worked to adjust to the hazy darkness. Embers crackled above him, and orange sparks dropped like rain from the burning thatch. His lungs gasped for air and his eyes burned from the thick smoke.

"Lizzie!"

He tripped over a clay pot and heard it smash into the wall.

Where was she?

He called for her again. This time she cried out from the other side of the room. A large pile of thatch had fallen from the roof and now burned on the dirt floor between them.

"Lizzie! Follow my voice."

He reached out his hand as her shadow finally emerged in the darkness. Another piece of thatch crashed onto the dirt floor beside them. She stumbled, her arms gripping the wailing infant. He pulled her toward him in an effort to protect her from the falling debris.

He felt her body heave in his arms. "I—can't—breathe."

"Stay low. We're going to get out of here."

Andrew ripped off the sleeve of his shirt and pressed it against her mouth and nose. The heat of the fire intensified, singeing the hairs on his arm. Smoke surrounded them, making the blackness of night even blacker. All he could see were the flickering of flames and the heavy smoke. If the rest of the ceiling collapsed before they escaped, they'd never get out alive.

Lights from several torches appeared in the doorway. Kakoba crossed the threshold, shouting as he took the baby from Lizzie's arms and led them outside. Andrew felt Lizzie fall against his chest as the hut collapsed behind him. Sparks popped and another hut burst into flames.

Andrew drew her away from what was left of the burning hut then stopped, bent over, with his hands pressed against his thighs as he sucked in the fresh air.

Lizzie's lungs burned as she sat in the dirt, trying to draw in a deep breath. By now, the village had erupted into a state of panic. Those who had slept through the fight between Kakoba and Mawela had been drawn from their huts by the smell of smoke. Villagers rushed past her, trying to put out the fires that had quickly spread beyond Kakoba's compound. Already she could see a dozen thatched roofs blazing in the darkness.

Someone brought her water to drink, but her hand shook as she tried to bring it to her lips. A hand grasped hers and helped to steady the cup. She looked up and tried to focus on the figure.

Her eyes burned. "Andrew?"

"Drink it slowly."

She coughed, then forced down a sip of water as he knelt beside her and guided her hands. "Are you all right?"

In the light of the moon, she studied his face, blackened by soot, his dark eyebrows singed, and his shirt smelling of smoke.

"Kakoba is okay?"

"Yes, and so is Posha. Kakoba was able to get up and stop Mawela. He was so drunk, he finally passed out cold."

"I—I couldn't find my way out of the room." Her voice cracked and the panic she'd felt just a few minutes ago returned. "It shouldn't have been difficult in such a small space, but I couldn't see anything. I couldn't find the door, and it was hot...so hot."

"It's okay now. It's over."

"It's not over." Her throat ached at the effort to speak, but the hissing sound of the fire that seemed forever imprinted in her mind wouldn't leave. Nor could she dismiss the startling reality that Kakoba, and only God knew how many others, had just lost everything they had.

"Trust me, Lizzie. Everything is going to be all right now. You saved the baby's life, and the men are working now to stop the fire."

"But it's not over." Panic swept over her as she searched the crowded compound for the children. "Not only has Kakoba lost everything, but what about Chuma and Esther? Nothing is settled. If Mawela takes them again—"

"Don't worry about that. For now, they are fine."

"And Posha? You're sure she is fine."

"Yes." He helped her take another sip. "Drink some more water then take several deep, slow breaths and don't worry about anything else right now besides breathing."

Lizzie shook her head. She had to see with her own eyes that the children and Posha were okay. "I want to see them."

Andrew hesitated. His lips pulled into a solemn frown before he finally nodded and pointed to the other side of the compound. Lizzie rose to her feet and smoothed down the singed folds of her skirt. Even in the dark covering of night, the fire's destruction was apparent as she made her way across the compound, now empty as the villagers fought to stop the spread of the fire. Kakoba's hut lay in a smoldering heap of ashes with nothing left to save.

Lizzie turned her attention to Kakoba, who sat huddled with his wife and children on the edge of the yard, away from any danger of the fire.

Lizzie knelt down beside Posha. "Are you all right?"

Posha's ebony cheeks were streaked with tears as she looked up from the newborn that lay sucking at her breast. "You risked your life... and saved my baby."

Lizzie grasped her hand and squeezed it. "I'm sorry for all that has happened. I can't imagine how frightening it must have been. And for your home..."

"My children are all here. Kakoba is alive.... That is all that matters for now."

Kakoba nodded. "There will most likely be a counsel to determine the cause of Kacha's death, but for now Posha is right. We are together, and we are alive."

Lizzie moved to stand up then stopped. There was a large blood-stain on the shoulder of Posha's shirt. "You've been injured?"

Her hand reached for the mark. "No... It was not me."

"Are you sure?" Lizzie's voice cracked as she quickly checked Posha's shoulder for any sign of an injury, since it was possible that shock had numbed her response. Posha shook her head. Nothing.

"Kakoba?"

"My jaw will be sore, but I am fine. Mawela did not touch me with his weapon."

"Lizzie? Come here, please."

Her attention snapped to the other side of the compound at the sound of Andrew's voice. She hurried over to where Andrew crouched. Moonlight spilled over the scene, revealing what he had found. Her stomach heaved. Mawela's body lay still beside a pool of blood collecting beneath him, soaking the African soil.

CHAPTER ELEVEN

Lizzie dropped to her knees beside Mawela and listened for his breath. There was no movement from his chest. No reaction to her presence. Only the eerie, startled look of his glassy eyes staring back at her. "He is dead."

Kakoba crouched beside her, his hands pressed against the sides of his head. "How did it come to this? My sister, her unborn child, and now her husband. The man might have incensed me and dishonored my wife, but I never wished for his death."

Andrew helped Kakoba to his feet. "None of this is your fault. Just be thankful that Posha and your infant are safe. And that Esther and Chuma have been returned. There will be much work involved to reconstruct your home, but Mawela and his lies will never harm you again."

Lizzie moved away from the body. Around them, darkness tried to hide the horror of what had happened, but both the body lying in front of her and the heavy scent of smoke filling her lungs from smoldering huts told her otherwise. The other villagers worked to stop the fire from spreading throughout the entire village, but her mind couldn't erase the darkened form of Mawela's lifeless body.

Lizzie caught Kakoba's gaze. With a people whose superstitions ran deep, the shedding of blood meant consequences that came both from the physical and spiritual world. An act of murder, especially when against a family member, could result in the retaliation by the ghost of the victim. It was a belief even Kakoba struggled to dismiss as untrue.

Lizzie wiped a streak of blood from her hand onto her skirt. In the distance, the orange glow of the fires seemed to have diminished to a thick smoldering smoke. "He died falling against his battle-axe."

Kakoba shook his head. "They will still blame me."

"Why?" Andrew didn't look convinced. "He was holding his battle-axe in his hand when he fell. There is no doubt."

"His people will see it different." Kakoba's hands shook as he pulled his arm back behind his head as if he was demonstrating what had happened. "They will say that I am to blame for his death, even though I never held any intention of harming him."

Andrew stepped in beside Lizzie. "We all saw Mawela start the fight. All Kakoba did was defend himself. Mawela was the one too drunk to stand up. There will not be anyone who tries to question Kakoba's innocence."

"That is not how everyone will see the situation. They will see that Kakoba had plenty of motivation. When Mawela's father arrives he will not simply take our word for what happened."

Lizzie pressed her lips together. They had little time left to discuss the matter before the others in the village returned from putting out the last of the fires and discovered that Mawela was dead.

Kakoba shook his head. "Lizzie is right. The men from Mawela's village will only look at the situation one way when they find their brother's blood spilt across the ground. They will say that I took his life in revenge of the ransom he demanded when he took my children. They will say I killed him out of anger instead of waiting for the elders to meet and make a judgment."

Lizzie let out a soft sigh. "Thus the feud between your families continues."

Andrew shook his head, apparently still not completely convinced. Or perhaps not wanting to be convinced. "There are many witnesses who saw that your hand had nothing to do with his death."

"No." Kakoba pressed his hands in front of him. "I will be blamed for his death."

Lizzie weighed the situation, knowing Kakoba was right. The baby cried in Posha's arms while Esther and Chuma lay fast asleep against her legs. Any relief she'd tried to find in the situation vanished and was replaced by a heavy discouragement.

Hadn't she come here to bring the good news of peace? Like her father, she'd shared how Christ had displayed His power on the cross when He destroyed the power of the numerous divinities that held them captive with His resurrection. In turn, that meant that revenge, offerings to those same divinities, and even slavery had no place in one's life.

But instead of embracing the message she shared, many continued following their traditional beliefs, and at times, even those who claimed to follow the Creator God turned back to their old gods for protection when things went wrong. A shiver ran up her spine despite the humid air. The British had better success in squelching the constant raids that had once plagued the region—better than she ever would in changing the stubborn hearts of those she worked with.

The chief and several of the men arrived in the compound, spears in hand and anger written across their faces.

"Where is he?"

"Mawela?"

"Is he not the one responsible for what happened here tonight?" the chief spat. "He is no different from his father, whose ears are as long as a Kudu's. Over half of the village was burned down in the fire. Many have lost their huts, their grain and milk, and over a dozen cattle died when the corral caught fire."

Kakoba went to his father. "The one you speak of is dead."

"How?"

Kakoba pushed his shoulders back and held his head high. "We do not know. We thought at first that he had fallen on his battle-axe in his drunken stupor, but there is no sign of his weapon."

The chief thrust his spear into the ground in front of him. "There is little left of the village, and a runner has confirmed that men from Mawela's village are coming."

"What if they demand more than cattle and hoes? What if they accuse me of murdering him?"

"I will not allow that. We have a right to demand payment after what Mawela has done to our village. Such an act will be considered far worse than murder."

"But I am still worried about my wife and children."

The chief looked to Lizzie then back to his son. "I must speak to you. In private."

Lizzie watched the two men move to the far side of the compound then drop down onto a wooden stool that had somehow escaped the fire. Clearly the chief did not want her to hear whatever he had to say to his son. Exhaustion overcame her but did nothing to take away the sting of the situation.

Andrew squatted beside her. He was certain she wanted to see how extensive the damage from the fire had been, and the coming daylight would allow them to do just that. But for the moment, he was more worried about her. "What do you think they are discussing?"

"I'm sure they're trying to decide the best way to respond to what has happened tonight."

He sat on the ground, the muscles in his arms and legs aching from the long night with little rest. And as the sun began its ascent, its light revealed there would be little rest on the horizon for either of them. "Even if you are right, I don't believe that the chief, or the authorities for that matter, will allow revenge in this situation. If a man is attacked, doesn't he have the right to defend himself?"

"Yes, but in this situation, I fear that anything we say won't stop Malewa's clansmen from coming and demanding payment for the loss of life."

"Life for a life?"

"They won't necessarily demand a life. In their culture, if his friends had been here, they could have killed Kakoba and it would not have been called a crime. But more typically, revenge is taken through demands of property. The matter will be brought before the chief, who will award damages to his family."

"So once again, Kakoba is to blame for what has happened." Andrew stood and folded his arms across his chest.

"There is much involved in the death of a person."

"Like?"

"There are others to be reckoned with, from the communal god of the family, to Mawela's ghost."

Andrew dug his heel into the ground. "I was right when I told you it was not safe for you to be here. And especially now with this situation. I can take you to Livingston, then on to New York where people don't blame others for illnesses, or send raiding parties to avenge a clansmen's death. You'll be safe there. You'll be with family—"

"How can I leave now?"

He was irritated at her stubbornness. "I promised your uncle I would return with you."

Lizzie's eyes widened. "Perhaps you shouldn't have made a promise you weren't sure you could keep."

"Maybe not, but why risk your life for these people? I know how quickly the news about Mawela's death will travel. When men from his village show up with spears, intent on avenging Mawela's death, your life could be in danger."

"I have told you that I am considering my grandfather's wishes, but until then, I suggest you decide what you are going to do. Because I have no intention of leaving anytime soon."

"You are the most difficult woman I have ever met."

"Save your complaints for another day. The safety of these people is my primary concern, and if I can help, then I must stay."

Andrew paused, then decided on another approach. "What if staying isn't what is best? What if the women and children left the village for a while? Even you have to admit it would be safer if they are not here when Mawela's avengers arrive."

"Where would they go?"

"I don't know. Perhaps up the river where I've heard there is a mission. They could receive temporary shelter, along with food and clothing."

"I know the Carruths well who run the mission station, and they are good people who wouldn't hesitate to help." Lizzie shook her head, for some reason still unconvinced by his reasoning. "But the rains are coming and many of the crops have just been planted. If they leave, all their hard work will have been in vain. Temporary shelters can be built and those who didn't lose their possessions will share with those in need."

"But what if they demand more than Kakoba can pay or take the children and his wife in exchange for what happened?"

She hesitated. "I don't know."

He sensed her resolve was beginning to crumble, and he decided to press on. Because whatever the true source of his motivation, even she had to admit he had a valid point. "If they left, it would only be temporary. Just until the situation with Mawela's family is settled and until huts can be built again."

"Even if what you say is right, the chief will not agree."

"Perhaps not." He caught her gaze, determined to convince her. "But I don't believe they are safe here, and I don't think you do either. Not until this matter is settled. Think about it, Lizzie. Even you said that this situation reaches far past the death of Mawela's wife. The grudge between the villages runs deep and a few sparks is all it's going to take to start another raging fire."

She shook her head. "Is this another ploy to get me to leave with you?"

"Forget about that for a moment and tell them. Tell them I can take them to Livingston. Tell them that Posha and the children will be safe there until the matter of Mawela's death is settled."

Lizzie pressed her fingers against her pounding temples and tried to work through the consequences of the villagers leaving. Posha would need help, which meant that she would need to go as well. "We do not know that they will come after Posha and the children."

"Just like no one expected Mawela to come for Posha?" His voice rose. "If nothing else, give them an option."

Her mind swirled as she tried to contemplate the consequences of leaving...and of staying. "Why does it matter to you? I thought your only goal was to convince me to leave."

"Something—something happened tonight, as I watched them lose everything they had, that made me see these people for something more than—"

"Than what?" The lines around his eyes had softened, but she wasn't convinced of his sincerity. "A group of savages?"

"You can question my motives for being here all you want, but Kakoba doesn't deserve to pay the price for what happened here tonight. Tell him."

Lizzie turned away. Maybe she had misjudged him.

Kakoba stormed toward his wife. Apparently the discussion with his father had been heated.

She stopped him midway. "Mr. Styles is offering to take Posha and the family to Livingston until you are certain they are safe. I told him that it is not practical, but—"

"Livingston?" Kakoba spun around to face them.

Andrew took a step forward. "You need a place for them to go that is safe. We could take your family and anyone else who wants to go with us until we are certain that it is safe to return."

Lizzie coughed, still trying to clear the smoke from her lungs. "As much as I hate to admit it, he might be right. Not only do we risk conflict from Mawela's people, the village is gone and many of these people have nowhere to stay."

"My father is going to insist Mawela's father pay for what his son did."

"And then what? We demand cattle for the burning of the village and they demand cattle for the death of Mawela. When does it ever end?"

Kakoba paused for a long moment, then nodded. "I will ask my father to give the villagers a choice whether they want to stay or leave."

Lizzie switched from English to Kakoba's native tongue. "If he agrees, let Mr. Styles lead the group, but I will stay behind. I was able to talk to the chief and redeem Esther and Chuma. Perhaps I can help in this situation as well."

Kakoba dropped his gaze.

"What is it?"

"I think it would be wise if you left as well."

"Why?"

"I told you earlier that some blamed you for Kacha marrying Mawela. There are others who—who are blaming you for the fire."

"What? No!" Desperation seeped through the channels of her heart. "You must tell them that has nothing to do with me. This all stems back to your father and Mawela's father and their fight over one woman—"

"Right now that doesn't matter."

"And you really believe that things are worse today because I'm here?"

"It does not matter what I think. I am sorry."

Kakoba turned away, but she was far from finished. "The rains would have been late whether I had been here or not. Just like I have nothing to do with your crops failing, or when your children are sick—"

"I understand what you are saying, but you know well of the superstition that runs deep among my people. They look for someone to blame when things go wrong. The burning down of a village is worse than killing a man. Just like Mawela's family will blame me for what has happened tonight, your presence will continue to divide until this matter is settled."

"And because Mawela is dead, I too must pay the price? No. If that is the truth, then things will not change. The next time a child dies or the crops fail, or a lion kills one of your cattle, then I will be blamed because I angered your gods."

"Be careful how you speak. While I am on your side, there are others who for now say nothing because they respected your father and what he did for the people. But that can change."

"So I have to leave."

"I think it would be best."

"And not come back. Is that what you are saying?"

"You have always been an honored guest among my people. Given time, those who doubt will once again see things the way I do."

An honored guest? Lizzie felt her lungs constrict. This was her home. The place she'd grown up...

Kakoba moved to speak to his father, once again in private, then returned after a moment to address Andrew. "My father agrees with your proposition."

"What about Posha?" Lizzie glanced at the young mother who had fallen asleep beside her children.

"She will be fine. She is strong enough to travel."

Andrew picked up the bag he'd dropped on the ground when he arrived. "How much time do we have?"

"We must leave before the others arrive. I will tell everyone to take what they need and leave immediately. Because it is not a question of if they will come...but when."

CHAPTER TWELVE

Lizzie hesitated on the edge of the village as dawn broke across the veld. Golden rays of sunlight had painted the adjacent forest of winterthorn trees a warm orange. In front of her, a group of elephants lumbered through the tall grass on their way toward the river where hornbills cried out their drum-like call to welcome another day.

She turned back around to face the scene she wanted to avoid. Lit now by the light of the glowing dawn, the devastation seemed to multiply across the smoldering compounds that had been destroyed during the night. Most had lost everything they had, though they could be thankful that no one had died in the fires.

Rebuilding would come slowly. The women would need to gather the tall grass from the savannah while the men cut poles in the forest to make up the framework for their huts. It would take time to replace what had been lost, from the gourds full of milk that had once hung from their roofs, to the grain that had been stored in clay containers.

She watched the men, women, and children file out of the village, carrying nothing more than the food they'd been offered by neighbors who had been spared from the ravaging tongues of the fire. Seventeen had decided to go upriver with Andrew and his guides to both seek arbitration from the authorities and get help from the mission until the situation settled down and it was deemed safe to return.

Lizzie turned again, then let her gaze stop at the far corner of the village. Gray smoke still rose from the place she once called her home. Gone were the thick walls of clay and the carefully laid thatch. And while her earthly possessions had been few, there had been a trunk full of her father's books, a few faded photos, and letters from her grandfather and close friend Sarah.

She turned once more away from the scene to a herd of zebra grazing in the distance. Strange how they seemed unaware of what had happened the night before during the lion attack—or that another one could strike again at any moment. They were content to spend their days grazing amongst the sweet grass and the season's colorful spread of flowers and take what life gave them without complaint.

Consider the lilies of the field...

Lizzie swallowed the emotion threatening to overflow. It was a verse she'd heard her father use dozens of times. The lilies of the field, the zebras of the plain, and the birds along the banks of the river didn't toil, and yet God cared for them. Guilt mingled with a deep sadness. As much as her father had believed in that verse and the God who had spoken those words, there were still moments like these when reality pulled on the frayed edges of her faith and made her question the mind of the Creator God about whom she'd worked so hard to teach.

Andrews's words and those of her grandfather's solicitors played repetitively in the back of her mind alongside her father's. Perhaps they were right. Perhaps it was time for her to return to New York and fulfill the last wishes of her grandfather. Maybe God was using the destruction in the village to nudge her forward. Her father had always told her how God works in mysterious ways. She could use the money she'd inherited to send more missionaries who would bring the message of the Creator God to unreached places....

But other words of her father's competed with the demands of her grandfather. Earthly treasures, he'd reminded her often, had a habit of corrupting moral character. A life of piety with God was far better than riches without His presence.

Her father's compelling words weren't the only reason she wanted to stay. She'd worked hard to not only prove herself to Kakoba's people, but to make this life—and this land—her own. Which meant that while a hut might never compare to her aunt's lavish townhouse, this land was hers.

Leaving now would mean she would not be here to help rebuild. Things here would never be the same again. No matter what happened. No matter what she did.

"Are you about ready to go?"

She looked up at the now familiar face of Andrew with his vaquero hat and lopsided smile and tried to suppress the frustration longing to escape in the form of biting words. But none of this was his fault. "I suppose."

"I've been looking for you. I thought you might be down at your hut."

"There is nothing left."

"I know. And I'm sorry."

"Most of what I had can be replaced." And for what couldn't be, she would keep them safe in the recesses of her memory. She pushed back the tears. "The people here are not sentimental. They live from day to day, ensuring they have enough food to eat for the day and that their families are safe. Beyond that they have no need for frivolous things."

"It's okay." Andrew's eyes darkened. "There is nothing wrong with a pretty dress, a new pair of shoes, and a shelf full of books, or the physical memories of your parents."

She wiped her eyes and forced a smile. "What about you? Did you lose anything?"

"Everything that I didn't have with me last night."

"Including your camera?"

He patted the bag slung across his shoulder. "For some reason I brought it with me, along with most of my notes. I can recreate what I lost."

"I am sorry."

"A notebook of handwritten notes seems unimportant compared to those here who have lost everything. And the chief is smiling because he still has the gifts I gave him."

This time, the smile she gave him was genuine. "I don't suppose you talked him out of some of the coffee?"

"As I recall, someone advised me against taking back gifts already offered." He shook his head. "I know this can't be easy for you. Losing your home and now having to leave."

"It isn't the first time." She pointed across the veld toward the river to the familiar spot she'd visited often in the past four years. "I buried my parents beneath the shade of a mahogany tree. I thought they would like it."

"I'm sure they would."

"I think what is hardest for me to deal with this time is the belief that I am somehow at fault for at least some of this situation. That hurts more than the loss of my possessions." Tears surfaced, but this time she refused to let them fall. "I have worked hard to earn my trust with them, and I'm not sure it is something I can gain back, no matter what I do."

Andrew shifted his weight to his other foot. From the pained expression on his face, he clearly felt uncomfortable dealing with a woman's emotions. His gaze dipped for a moment before he looked up again. "Are you going to be okay?"

"I will be." She didn't want to make him feel uncomfortable, but talking through the situation was beginning to clear her head. And in a small way, helping to ease the feelings of loss. "Things change suddenly, don't they? Two days ago, all I was thinking about was planting my field, telling stories of David and Goliath to the children, and practicing English with Kakoba and his children."

"And now?"

"I'm having to face the fact that the chief has ordered me to leave and I have no home to return to. And then, of course, there is the issue of my grandfather's will. I thought I was strong, but I can't help but wonder why God would take me away from here. And now…I might not have a choice."

"I can't answer that for you. You're the one who is supposed to have the answers when it comes to such spiritual matters."

"At the moment I seem to have far more questions than answers. So much of what happened in these past few hours seems so unnecessary A man is dead, half the village burned down, and now we are running away like we are guilty of something…. Like I am guilty of something."

"My grandmother always used to tell me that it doesn't matter what anyone else says about you as long as you stay true to who you are."

Something startled the zebra, and they ran in unison toward the river until they were nothing more than small dots along the horizon. "Wise words, I suppose."

"Somehow, no matter what has happened here today, I am quite certain that one day soon you will be returning."

"I wish I felt as confident as you sound."

Andrew turned around as those who had decided to leave with his guides made their way up the narrow escarpment to where they stood. "Maybe you haven't lost everything after all. They trust you enough to come with you."

"Maybe."

Or maybe they simply felt they had no choice.

She studied the familiar faces of the men, women, and children who now joined them on the ridge. These were the ones who had befriended her, taken her in when her parents had died, and then again when she returned three years later. Perhaps Andrew was correct. Perhaps she hadn't lost everything.

Kakoba and his family joined them, following close behind as they set off toward the river.

Esther carried her corncob doll in her arms and struggled to keep up with the procession. "I don't want to go. I want to sleep."

Lizzie reached down and picked her up.

Kakoba glanced at Lizzie. "You spoil her."

"Sometimes that is a good thing." She turned back to Esther. "We will look at this as an adventure. We get to take a canoe down the Zambezi River."

Chuma bobbed up and down beside her. "And I brought my bow and arrows so I can defend my mother and sister."

Esther snuggled into her shoulder, and a small wave of peace brushed over her heart as they hurried toward the river. No matter how terrible the situation, God was still in control.

Posha walked ahead of them, her sleeping newborn baby securely tied to her back with a worn piece of cloth. Andrew kept up with his two guides, who were leading the group. A part of Lizzie wanted to believe that they had been too hasty in reaching their decision to leave the village, but while her heart longed to stay, her head knew they'd made the right choice. Years of discord between the two villages would not be settled quickly, even if the British authorities stepped in.

Exhaustion swept through her as Kakoba caught up to her and matched her pace.

"With all that happened tonight, I have yet to tell you thank you for what you did for me and my family. The way you talked to the chief, then how you saved my son from the fire. My wife and I are both grateful to you."

"It is only through God's strength that my words were coherent and that your child now lives. My only regret is that there are those among your people who blame me for what happened."

"You must believe that I am not one of them. And in fact, I am quite certain that there are more who do not blame you for what happened than those who want to use you as the scapegoat for this deep-seated hatred that runs through my people."

"And your father. Do you think the day will come when he no longer blames my presence for what happened?"

"When you told me that my father is stubborn, you were correct. But I do believe that one day he will be forced to see that it was not your presence that is to blame for what happened, but instead, the longtime bitterness that has spread like the roots of the giant fig tree."

"Then I will continue to pray you are right."

"There is something else I wanted to tell you. I have spoken to your friend and the guides, but do not say anything to the others yet."

"What is it?"

"I believe someone is following us."

Fear that had settled in her stomach in the early hours of the morning resurfaced. "How is that possible? Surely Mawela's men have not had time to put a raiding party together."

"If he did, we have women and small children, which means they will move far faster than we do."

"What do you think they plan to do?"

"I don't know, except that they will not want to catch the attention of the authorities. Raiding parties have, for the most part, long since disappeared, and fighting is now limited to mimicking the act at funerals. But I fear even that won't stop them from trying to avenge Mawela's death."

"Which means?"

"At this point, I do not know."

"Surely they are not foolish enough to take justice into their own hands as Mawela did. The British authorities will not tolerate such insolence."

"All I can do is pray that I am wrong."

Lizzie plunged forward despite the fact that her body cried out for sleep. Beads of sweat gathered at her temple with the exertion, as even in the early morning hours the temperature had begun to rise. But safety would only be found if they hurried, putting distance between themselves and those wanting to avenge Mawela's life.

The terrain had slowly changed from the open savannah to the thicker brush edging the Zambezi River where soon they would make their next stage of the trip down the long waterway. Running through six countries, the mighty river made its way from the heart of Africa through the great Victoria Falls and eventually flowed into the Indian Ocean.

One of the guides signaled from the front of the group. Posha and her children, along with the other women who had joined them, stopped at the water's edge and began to fill the three waiting narrow pirogues belonging to some of the villagers.

Lizzie stopped at the top of a steep bank that overlooked the river's glassy surface where a scattering of dugout canoes traveled across the waters of the great river in the golden light of dawn. She blew out a sharp breath as memories of gliding down the river past banks teeming with life flooded over her. On the far side of the bank, hippos, an animal able to evoke the greatest sense of fear in her, basked in the morning sun alongside ten-foot-long crocodiles, while a panoply of birds— turquoise and black kingfishers, blue-green bee eaters, lilac-breasted rollers—filled the morning breeze with their unique calls.

Andrew called to her from the river's edge below. "Are you coming?"

Lizzie pushed away the memories, held up her skirt, and scooted down the embankment to join the others. Halfway down, her foot slipped on the sandy soil. Trying to regain her balance, she dug her boot into the ground but couldn't stop herself from stumbling the rest of the way down.

He caught her at the bottom of the embankment. Lizzie looked up into those bright blue eyes staring back at her in the morning sunshine and felt his grip tighten around her waist.

"Thank you." She struggled to catch her breath, irritated that he had such a dizzying effect on her. "The ground is slippery."

"Your carriage awaits, my lady."

His smile only managed to add to the flurry of unwanted butterflies inside her.

Fatigue washed over her. She couldn't think. He stared at her, waiting for her to move, but her legs wouldn't work. It had to be the extreme weariness she felt that caused her heart to race and her palms to sweat.

He looked at her and smiled. "Are you all right?"

"Of course."

She forced her feet to obey, pulled away from his grip, and headed for the canoe. Had he just laughed at her? Grabbing the side of the dugout, she steadied herself. Stepping into this canoe put her one step closer to crossing the Atlantic. But she was not going to allow herself to forget why Andrew Styles had made the long journey to find her.

CHAPTER THIRTEEN

Andrew plopped down in the dugout facing Lizzie, amused by the sudden shyness that had enveloped her. Something had passed between them as he'd held her against him for that brief moment in order to steady her. It was a look he'd seen in a woman's expression before. Interest…attraction…

He stopped his wandering thoughts as reality seeped in. He clearly hadn't gotten enough sleep last night and had been dreaming. Lizzie MacTavish held no interest in him as a man and, in fact, had made it quite clear that the sooner he was gone the better.

Their guide dipped his long pole into the water and guided the boat down the narrow channel of the river. Andrew pulled out his camera and turned his attention to a huge crocodile slipping into the water from the sandbanks where it had been lying in the morning sun. He had a number of contacts back home who were always looking for photographs for various newspapers and magazines. Americans loved a close-up look at the mysterious Dark Continent.

She motioned to a large fish eagle. Its black, brown, and white plumage spread out like a fan as it glided across the water. Andrew snapped the photo. In one precise, calculated move, the bird grasped a fish in its sharp talons and returned to the riverbank.

"I've watched that same scene dozens of times, yet I'm still amazed at their strength." She looked up at him with those big eyes that had managed to melt the irritation she'd inflicted on him during their first encounter. The same eyes that had him thinking those ridiculous—romantic—thoughts. "What do you plan to do with the photos?"

"I'll be happy if half of what I take is usable. Some of those will probably end up in magazines or newspapers, but I do have a publisher interested in my writings who might be willing to include the photos with them in a book."

The corners of her lips curved slightly. Not a true smile, perhaps, but the thought clearly intrigued her. "I've never met a real author before."

"I wouldn't say I'm an author...yet." Neither would he admit how captivating she looked floating down the water through the maze of sandy islands and channels that fringed the edges of the river. While fatigue marked her expression after the long night, the constant sense of determination in her eyes had yet to waver.

"A journalist then?" she asked.

"After eighteen months behind the frontlines, I'll claim that title."

Esther scooted carefully onto Lizzie's lap from behind, then settled down, seemingly content to let the gentle rocking of the narrow dugout lull her to sleep.

Lizzie ran her finger along the child's ebony cheek. "Tell me about the book you want to write. I'm sure the places you've visited in all your travels have given you plenty of ideas."

"There does always seem to be a story trying to take root in my mind."

"My father talked about writing down his experiences." A dreamy look settled across her face as she looked past him to the banks of the river. "I think living in the bush must have been satisfaction enough, though, because he never took the time. Instead of writing about his adventures, he read to me Lewis and Clark's amazing *Journals*, John

Wesley Powell's *Exploration of the Colorado River,* and even Richard Henry Dana's *Two Years Before the Mast,* that chronicles his life as a sailor almost a century ago."

"I'm not planning to write simply a travel journal chronicling the people and places I have visited."

"What do you mean?"

Andrew hesitated then pulled the leather book from his bag. While he'd written dozens of nonfiction articles for dozens of newspaper, the book he planned to write included a rugged hero, lost treasure, and a beautiful woman.

"I'm writing an adventure novel set against the backdrop of the Sahara." He unwrapped the plastic covering that kept the book waterproof, exposing its aged, brown cover. "I've been inspired by this— my grandfather's journal."

"Your grandfather?"

"You would have loved the stories he used to tell me about his adventures throughout Africa. How Nomads massacred half of the expedition team he was on and others went crazy from fever, but he managed to escape through the desert dressed as an Arab on a camel." Andrew chuckled at the memory of his grandfather's animated countenance as he described the daring adventure in vivid detail. "While he insisted otherwise, I've always been convinced that half of what he said wasn't true."

Lizzie laughed. "And I think my father would have liked your grandfather. He always loved a good embellished story."

"He would have loved to be here right now. Floating down the river in a dugout canoe, taking photographs of the exquisite wildlife, which, unfortunately, he wasn't able to do back then."

"Tell me about him. Why did he come to Africa?"

"My grandfather was an adventurer." Andrew caught himself unconsciously rubbing his sore jaw and pulled his hand away. "He had read the published volumes about René-Auguste Cailliés's travels through Mali in the early 1800s and decided that he too wanted to explore some of the continent's vast wilderness that had yet to be discovered. Unlike many of the European explorers of that day, he decided to follow Caillié's example and spent three years studying Arabic and reading everything he could find.

"He knew how, in the past hundred years or so, many explorers had either died of illness or been attacked and killed by ruling African leaders. He was determined he wasn't going to have his life end in such a horrid fate. During his time with the exhibition, he wrote about everything he experienced—their foods, camels, and clothes. He even worked to classify the vegetation in one remote area."

"And did he survive the trip?"

Andrew closed the book and started wrapping it back in the plastic. "Yes, but after his return, he couldn't shake his overwhelming desire to return to the interior. Nine years after his first expedition, my grandfather left on his second...and never returned home. I was twelve years old when we received the news of his death."

"I'm sorry."

"A friend of his who had gone with him on both expeditions was there at his deathbed. Several months later, after crossing a large portion of northern Africa by foot and almost dying himself from a bout with malaria, he arrived at my father's house in New York. He carried with him this journal that my grandfather had kept during the three months of their travels before he fell ill."

"He reminds me of my father in a way." Lizzie's chin dipped.

"Nothing anyone could say or do would have ever convinced him to leave. Even in those last days, when he was so sick with fever, he might have had a chance to survive with the proper medical help if he'd left."

It was something she would never know.

Lizzie drew Esther closer to her. Often she'd wondered what it was that made both men and women risk dying to try to conquer this vast continent. What was the desire that kept them here, and if they did leave, what forced them to return? She'd seen it in her father and mother. A desire that went beyond adventure, romance, and even religion. It was as if the continent had reached out, grabbed them, and refused to let go.

"Lizzie?" Andrew's voice cut through her thoughts.

"It's nothing. I'm just feeling a bit nostalgic, I suppose, with thoughts of leaving, and thoughts of my parents…" Lizzie stopped mid sentence.

She heard the hippos before she saw them.

Grunting and snorting, they appeared as the three pirogues took a narrow bend in the river. There were at least twenty of them, lying on the edges of the muddy banks, leaving little room for them to pass.

Her heart quickened as dark memories engulfed her. The constant chattering from the canoes stopped. The only sound breaking the eerie silence that hung in the humid morning air was the hippos' agitated grunts and their guide who tapped on the side of the pirogue with his paddle to warn the animals of their approach.

She'd seen it happen before. A hippo, charging for deeper water, had smacked into the bottom of a canoe and flipped it over. Lizzie swallowed hard, fought the memories. Common sense told her that nothing was going to happen, but she knew that all it had taken was one aggressive animal, and a woman and child had lost their lives that day.

The two other dugouts slid quietly ahead of them through the hippo-infested stretch of river to safety without incident. The giant animals harrumphed and snorted, carefully watching their passage.

Another hippo appeared to the left with a large scar across his shoulders. Lizzie's guide maneuvered to the right, but the massive bull still blocked their exit.

Lizzie's muscles froze. Their boat sat in the water, with only the current moving them forward. There was nowhere to go. Downstream, the bull stood guard. Upstream two hippos surfaced behind them then disappeared. She studied the glassy surface, searching the water for the telltale bubbles beneath. If they emerged from beneath…

Nothing.

The guides shouted back and forth, giving advice on how to get past. The bull submerged beneath the water, disappearing from view. Lizzie sucked in a breath. One of the guides yelled. She looked in the direction he pointed to the pod of hippos lying along the shore, several with their mouths wide open. The rogue bull had joined the herd.

Her heart still pounded as they took the next bend, leaving the hippos—and for the moment, the threat of danger—behind.

Lizzie gripped the edges of the boat, her knuckles still white. "They terrify me."

Andrew nodded his agreement. "They are intimidating to be sure, but your fear of them does surprise me."

"Surprise you?"

"In the short time I've known you, I've seen you encounter a snake, stand up to an angry chief, and rescue a baby from a blazing fire. I didn't think Lizzie MacTavish was capable of fear."

"You are wrong." She eyed his expression, certain he was teasing her. "Nothing has seemed routine since the moment I met you, and I'm hardly fearless."

"To be honest, my heart is still pounding from the experience as well. And if I understand correctly, you have every reason to fear them. I've heard of them charging people both in the water and on the land. They are an animal to be feared." He cocked his head, eyeing her closely. "I'm assuming something happened to instill this fear?"

A shiver crept up her spine. "I was twelve, maybe thirteen, years old. It wasn't uncommon for me to go on short trips with my father up the Zambezi to other villages."

She closed her eyes, and for a moment the fear she'd carried with her all these years was almost replaced by the constant strength her father had possessed. They would drift down the river in narrow dugout boats, and he would open up to her the wonders of life along the Zambezi.

"He knew everything about the birds and animals that depended on the river, from the great buffalo to the smallest butterfly. I could have listened to him talk for hours."

"He must have been an incredible man."

"He was." She smiled, knowing if she breathed in deep enough, she could still smell the dust from a herd of five hundred buffalo and see the colorful butterflies flitting in the wind. "There was one time, though, that I will never be able to erase from my mind. On that particular day, the river had filled from the rains farther north, draining into the watercourses where they then spill over onto the plains.

"We floated past a huge pod of hippos that stretched out across the wide river, sunning themselves in the noonday heat. We'd seen them sleeping and playing along that very stretch of river dozens of times, and with my father beside me I never thought much about the possible danger of those animals."

"What happened?"

"As always, there were several other boats out. Some were fishermen, and a larger boat filled with people was crossing the river. I remember thinking how peaceful the river was. A moment later one of the hippos rammed a smaller boat, literally shredding it to pieces."

"It must have been terrifying."

"It was. One of the women fell into the water. They managed to pull her out, but by then it was too late. She and the child strapped to her back were lost to the river. I remember the ride back home that day. I watched every shadow, every bend in the river, certain that we'd be its next victims."

He tilted his hat to shade his face from the rising sun. "It obviously didn't stop you from traveling on the river."

"There is no way to avoid it. But every time I float down this mighty river, I'm reminded of who is stronger." She cocked her head and smiled, thankful that for now, the danger had passed. "Perhaps you can add such a scene to your adventure book."

"Perhaps I will."

Their guide dug his paddle into the water and turned toward one of the islands in the center of the river behind the other canoes.

"What's going on?"

Lizzie called to Kakoba, who sat near the front of the canoe before answering. A sliver of fear had returned. "They still believe we are being tracked. We will stop here to let the women and children rest, while the men backtrack and see if it is true."

CHAPTER FOURTEEN

Something brushed against Lizzie's nose. She shook her head then swatted it away with the back of her fingers. She was floating through the maze of channels down the Zambezi with her father. He pointed to a kingfisher and they both watched as it perched on a long, swaying reed above the water with its tail pointed downward. The boat floated silently past until, with a sudden splash, the bird dropped to the surface, then came up with a tadpole in its mouth.

Something buzzed, this time in Lizzie's ear. She swatted at the offender.

"Ma?"

Lizzie opened her eyes. Esther hovered over her, pulling her from her dreams.

Wiping away the beads of sweat from her forehead, Lizzie studied the young girl's face and the thick tuft of hair that circled the top of her head. "You are supposed to be asleep."

Esther plopped down beside her. "I'm not sleepy anymore."

Lizzie rolled over onto her elbow and gazed out across the sandy terrain where some of the women and children slept on the ground. Several of the men, including Andrew, had stayed behind to guard the party from any hippos or crocodiles...or whoever was tracking them.

Lizzie yawned. "Are the men back yet?"

Esther shook her head.

"Is your mother sleeping?"

"Yes, and she has told me not to disturb her and the baby."

"That's a good idea. She's tired."

Three other girls sat down beside Esther. "We would like to listen to a story."

"A story?" Lizzie blew out a soft sigh, still trying to wake up. While sleeping along the river had helped, her brain still felt muddled. An hour or two wasn't enough to make up for a missed night's sleep.

"Please?"

Lizzie sat up and drew her legs toward her. "All right. How about the story about how the hornbill got his horn?"

The children grinned, their faces eager for the distraction from the hot afternoon. Andrew strode toward them and sat down on a fallen log directly behind the girls. The fact that he couldn't understand their conversation didn't seem to bother him at all.

Lizzie cleared her throat, then, ignoring Andrew's amused look, she began the story. "There was a small bird of little importance called the Tomtit that used to fly the banks of the Zambezi. Now, most of the animals that lived along the river, the elephants, hippos, crocodiles, and birds that gathered there daily for food, were not impressed with the Tomtit. His feathers were a dull brown, his eyes black, and in fact, there was nothing interesting about him except for one thing."

Esther leaned forward as her brother sat down beside her. "What was that?"

"He had a very large and very beautiful beak."

One of the little girls grabbed onto the folds of Lizzie's skirt. "What color was it?"

"It was yellow and orange and, sadly, was the only beautiful thing about the Tomtit. But there was one bird, the Hornbill, who was jealous of the Tomtit."

Chuma shook his head. "Why would he be jealous of such a homely bird?"

"Because the Hornbill did not have such a fine bill as the Tomtit. In fact, among all the birds that roamed the waters of the Zambezi, the Hornbill was the only bird who didn't have a fine long bill."

Esther giggled and stuck out her lips as far as she could like a bill.

"Now the Hornbill himself," Lizzie continued, "had bright eyes and beautiful black and gray feathers that all the animals envied. When he soared above the waters, they glistened in the sunlight, they were so fine."

"But the Hornbill was still unhappy?"

"He was unhappy, because he wanted the bill of the Tomtit." Lizzie nodded at her audience. "So because the Hornbill was so jealous of the Tomtit, he came to him one day and asked the Tomtit if he could try on his beak."

Chuma jumped to his feet and began mimicking the movements of the bird. He began preening his feathers and jumping on the ground with one hand above his head, representing the plume, and his other hand in front of his face, representing his beak.

The children roared with laughter.

"And did he let the Hornbill try on his beak?" one of them asked.

"He did. Because the Tomtit, being such an ordinary bird, could not believe that the Hornbill, who was such a fine bird, might want to try on his beak. So that is exactly what they did. They exchanged beaks. The Hornbill took the Tomtit's big, beautiful beak, and the Tomtit took the Hornbill's tiny beak."

Esther's eyes widened. "Then what happened?"

"The Hornbill loved the Tomtit's beak so much that he decided to keep it."

The children's eyes widened as Chuma sat back down beside them.

"But the Tomtit's beak was the only beautiful thing he had," Esther said.

"And now he was left with nothing." Lizzie rubbed the top of Esther's head and tried to ignore the amused grin marking Andrew's expression. "Can one of you guess what the moral of this tale is?"

When no one answered, she continued. "The Bible says that it is pride, like the Tomtit's; who thought his beak was better than all the others, that leads to destruction."

Andrew listened to the words that slipped from Lizzie's mouth like they were her mother tongue. Whatever the story she had told, it had completely captured the children's attention. It was impossible not to envy her. He'd learned a smattering of French and Portuguese to aid him in his travels, but had always counted on the help of a translator. To not have to do that would give him a tremendous advantage, but Northern Rhodesia alone boasted dozens of languages. Across the continent the number of different languages could in turn be multiplied by hundreds.

Her gift with the language and storytelling wasn't the only thing that impressed him. He could almost see why she didn't want to leave this place. Even with the problems facing them, it was clear she fit into this society in her own unique way, and that she was happy.

Her smile broadened as Esther whispered something into her ear. Lizzie nodded then laughed before catching Andrew's gaze. He felt the tips of his ears redden as all the children turned to him.

"The women are awake now, which means the children would like to play a game. They want to know if you would join them."

"What kind of game?"

"A simple child's game." Two of the children took Lizzie's hands. "Come. It will be fun."

Andrew stood, unable to remember the last time he'd played a game with a group of children. But he wasn't sure he had a choice. Before he could protest, two of the boys grabbed his hands and pulled him toward the others.

They began singing, with Lizzie's high, clear voice leading the chorus, as they stood in one long line that snaked across the large open space. The boy at the front of the line started running in a circular motion, weaving in and around small shrubs and bushes while the rest of them struggled to keep up.

Lizzie shouted above the children's singing. "The point is to not lose hold of the person beside you while the leader runs and pulls the group along."

As the children's singing continued, the pace quickened Two children fell and were dropped from the line. Andrew struggled to keep up.

A moment later, he tripped over a stump, fell backward, and landed smack dab in a pile of mud near the river's edge. He groaned and tried to sit up. He was far too old for this.

The children stopped their singing and gathered around him. Once he assured them he hadn't broken anything, they began laughing.

Which was worse.

Lizzie moved to stand over him. "I don't think I've ever seen you quite so...indisposed, Mr. Styles."

He groaned again. "You can call me Andrew, remember?"

Her smile broadened. "Andrew."

"And I'm certain that my fall wasn't that entertaining."

"Trust me, it was." She reached out her hand and helped him up.

He held on to her fingers after he was back on his feet, and for a brief moment forgot about the children still standing around them. Those mesmerizing eyes and soft skin... He was uncertain how it had happened, but this woman had somehow managed to worm her way straight into his heart.

Which never should have happened. He let go of her hand and rubbed his jaw. The ache was back.

Concern filled her eyes. "Are you all right?"

"Yes." He took a step back and reminded himself why he was here. There was much more at stake here than his foolish heart falling for a beautiful woman.

Chuma stepped away from the group, shouting something as he pointed upriver. Andrew moved toward the bank, thankful for the distraction. Kakoba and the other men were returning.

The children's jovial mood vanished. The men's return was all they needed to remind them that this was no ordinary trip down the river to visit friends and family.

Lizzie joined Kakoba and the other men along the river. Andrew stood back while they animatedly discussed the situation. Women and children had lined up on the bank, awaiting the men's decision. For a moment, he questioned his own.

What had he been thinking when he'd offered his guides to lead them back to the nearest mission? He had no guarantees that they'd even take them in, or that their leaving would solve the problem. If anything happened to them along the river, he would be the one to blame.

Lizzie joined him a moment later.

"Did they find anyone?" he asked.

She shook her head. "Kakoba is still convinced someone is following us, but they were unable to find out who."

"Which must mean that whoever it is doesn't want to be found." He shook his head. "What I would like to know is why. If they wanted revenge, as much as I hate to imagine such a horror, a river ambush wouldn't be that difficult."

"Then let's pray that's not what they are planning."

He jutted his chin toward the men who were still discussing something among themselves. Kakoba said something to the group then headed for the water's edge.

"What did he say now?"

"It is time for us to continue our journey."

Darkness began to settle over the waters of the Zambezi, bringing with it a welcome cool breeze after the sweltering heat of the day. Lizzie rubbed the back of her neck and tried to ease the headache that had strengthened over the past few hours. Despite the tension over the situation and Kakoba's belief that they were being tracked, she'd found herself enjoying Andrew's company—the reason she'd managed to slip into a different boat when they left the island.

If she let herself, she could almost forget he was here to take her back to New York. Instead, she could imagine him as the hero from one of the books her father used to read to her. Stories of Mary Kingsley fending off crocodiles with nothing more than a paddle, Joshua Slocum's amazing sail round the world, Isabella Bird's ventures through the Rockies before the turn of the century, or even one of the heroes from her father's stack of dime novels she'd managed to sneak and read in the veld away from her mother's watchful eyes.

Each book in her father's collection she had read and reread at least a dozen times, savoring them like a delectable piece of chocolate. Heroes were always bigger than life, and always rescued the girl.

Except she didn't want to be rescued.

It was a reminder she couldn't afford to forget. Andrew Styles's sole motivation to convince her to return was the hefty sum of money promised to him by her grandfather's solicitors. Which meant that any romantic inclinations she'd imagined on his part had nothing to do with her and everything to do with fulfilling his side of the bargain.

In a few hours they would be at the mission, where he would try to convince her that with all that had happened it was safer for her to return to New York, adding, of course, that after some time had passed and things had settled down in the village, she would be able to return to her people.

But just because he was handsome and her heart sometimes fluttered in his presence, such whimsical daydreams of romance could never become a part of the equation.

She turned to look at Andrew's pirogue skimming the water behind them. His vaquero hat was tipped over his face to block the sun, his arms folded across his chest, and his chin dipped as if he were sleeping.

She shoved the image away and returned to thoughts of her grandfather's solicitors' will. She'd had little time to think about her own future, but there was one thing she did know. If she returned, it would have nothing to do with Andrew.

She would be doing it for her grandfather, and him only.

Lizzie tried to stretch her legs without disturbing Esther, who lay sound asleep in the soft folds of her skirt. She felt anxious to reach the mission. Mrs. Carruth would be there, a jolly, matronly woman who would pray with her and help her make her decision.

The boat rocked beneath them.

Lizzie gripped the edge of the boat and searched the bank for signs of another pod of hippos. Deep ripples reflected on the water in the moonlight. Being on the river at night was dangerous, but the guides had insisted it was safer than sleeping on the shore.

Something knocked again against the bottom of the boat. Lizzie held tightly to Esther, who was now awake. Wiping the beads of sweat from her forehead, she tried to convince herself they'd simply gotten too close to the shore and clipped a rock.

She started singing one of the songs her father had taught her. Someone joined her, then another and another until the night was filled with a chorus of voices.

Lizzie felt the sharp smack against the canoe a third time. The boat tipped sharply to the left. Esther screamed. Water rushed over the side. Lizzie sucked in a deep breath as the boat flipped over and she slipped into the darkness of the river.

CHAPTER FIFTEEN

Andrew woke at the sounds of screaming and watched in horror as Lizzie's boat flipped. He heard the ominous splash of bodies plunging beneath the surface and saw the ripples across the water. In an instant, Lizzie and the others disappeared beneath the murky waters.

He shouted at their guide to push hard downstream to catch up with the boat. If a hippo was beneath the dugout canoe, the danger they were in had just multiplied substantially.

He studied the shadows surrounding the boat and searched the tributaries and smaller side channels trying to determine what had caused the accident. While he hadn't seen any of the animals lately, they all knew there were dozens of hippo pods that emerged from the water when darkness came, potentially making the villagers' moonlight trek more dangerous.

The dugout canoe bobbed along the surface upsidedown, its passengers now at the mercy of the river.

And the God she serves.

No. Her God had ignored him. And it would take something other than a miracle to save them. He shoved away the thought and concentrated instead on the situation. How many had been in the boat? Seven? Eight? He couldn't be sure. Without weighing the consequences, he stood up and dove into the river. He opened his eyes and was greeted by darkness. Lizzie's boat had been ten feet ahead of them to the left.

Kicking his feet, he pushed hard to bridge the distance between the two boats. His lungs began to burn as he broke the surface and took in a lungful of air.

The full moon cast an eerie red reflection on the water, giving out barely enough light to illuminate the bobbing dugout. He studied the shadows of the fig and waterberry trees that hung over the banks of the Zambezi for signs of a hippo. Nothing. Which meant the beast could still be in the water.

Something slid past his leg. A chill worked its way up his spine as he searched for the victims and convinced himself it was nothing but a fish or elephant grass.

He could hear Kakoba shouting orders at the other men in the distance. A baby screamed, and someone cried out from one of the boats. There was something ahead. Someone was floating on top of the water. Using every ounce of strength he had left, he swam toward the figure.

He grabbed the child and pulled her head from the water. It was Esther. Treading water, he pulled her small chest to his face and heard the faint sound of air escape her lips. She was still breathing. Holding her head with one hand, he swam for the nearest canoe.

Posha leaned over the edge to take the child, her sobs rising above the nightly chatter of the forest surrounding them.

The guide pounded on the side of his canoe with his paddle. A warning for the hippo, or any other animal that might try to get in the way, that they were here.

He dove back into the water again, searching the surface for Lizzie and the others. Time was running out if they didn't find them soon, and there was still no sign of the hippo. Kakoba had flipped the downed canoe back over and three women sat in it, shivering in the darkness. Four had been found. There had to be at least three more in the water, including Lizzie.

With Kakoba and two other men scanning the surface of the water, Andrew headed for the edge of the bank, which was the natural place for a survivor to swim to. But taking refuge on the bank did not mean that the dangers from the animals had ended.

The moonlight caught the long form of a crocodile, lying still in a sandbank. Andrew pushed away the feeling of panic and quietly moved downstream until there was another opening in the heavy bush lining the river.

With strong strokes, he swam for the shore, wondering if God would hear him if he prayed. It was the second time he'd wanted to pray in the past twenty-four hours, which implied God was either playing a cruel trick or trying to get his attention. And at the moment, he wasn't sure which scared him the most.

His feet touched the ground, his heart pounding more from fear than exertion. He pushed his way through the water toward the sandy shore, watching closely the shadows forming in the water around him.

"Lizzie?" He shouted her name above the competing nightlife. "Lizzie, where are you?"

Silence met him.

Lizzie gasped for breath. Someone—something—was pulling her under. She fought her way to the surface, gasped for air, then was sucked back down again. She'd seen what hippos could do to a boat. The threat of the monstrous beasts far outweighed that of any other animals.

She couldn't feel her legs. Couldn't breathe...

God, save me...

Whatever had been pulling her under suddenly released her. Lizzie kicked her feet as hard as she could and rose to the surface of the black waters. She gasped and let her lungs fill with the perfumed forest air.

She took another gulp and tried to get her bearings. Where were the others? Esther had been sleeping in her lap. Panic wrapped around her like a heavy blanket. Where were they now? Surely God hadn't brought them this far to be lost in the depths of the river?

Her teeth chattered as she scanned her surroundings. Limbs of trees hung in eerie shadows over the Zambezi along the bank. Monkeys howled. Something else cried out in the distance. She had to find Esther.

She looked behind her. The current had pulled her downstream. One of the dugouts bobbed in the distance. She waved her arms and tried to scream, but her voice was little more than a hoarse whisper lost in the night air.

Something moved beside her. Her heart...her head pounded. In the darkness she couldn't tell if it was someone coming to rescue her, or if it was one of the river's deadly animals.

Unwilling to take a chance, she swam as hard as she could toward the shore. Moments later, her feet hit the bottom of the river and she stumbled forward. She could see the bank ahead of her. Nine, maybe ten, feet. All she had to do was reach it. Fatigue from lack of sleep and the exertion of staying afloat in the water began taking over her body.

She stumbled again. This time she was unable to catch her balance. The water engulfed her, flooding her nose and running down her throat. She choked and pushed herself up.

Five feet later, she collapsed against the sand on the shore.

Andrew made his way along the shoreline. Water splashed at his feet, making ripples that sloshed against the riverbank. In the darkness, shadows seemed exaggerated, noises louder, and he was struck with the knowledge that his heart cared more than he wanted to admit.

He watched Kakoba pull a limp body from the water ten feet from where he stood. "She is dead."

Fear coursed through Andrew as Kakoba placed the woman into the back of one of the boats.

But it wasn't Lizzie.

He let out a sharp breath. He shouldn't be glad. Shouldn't allow that feeling of relief that rushed through him. Someone's mother, daughter, who moments ago had expected to find safety on the other side of the journey, was dead.

He pressed back the jumble of thoughts. Lizzie had to be here somewhere. She didn't deserve to let the river swallow her. It could be days before the bodies of victims were found…if ever.

He trudged through the thick elephant grass, still searching in the shallower waters for her. He turned a full 360 degrees then stopped to study the shoreline in front of him, trying to decide if he should continue downriver or turn around. Behind him, Kakoba and the other boats continued slowly down the river. Beside him trees took on the form of men, their gnarled arms grasping at him.

He tried to process what might have happened. Her skirt would have weighed her down and made it difficult for her to swim, but common sense told him that she would have headed for the shore if at all possible. She wouldn't want to struggle against the current or with her weighted-down clothes. With her fatigue, she probably wouldn't have been able to fight either.

If she were alive…

He stopped himself. Not *if* she were alive. She was alive. Which meant she had to be here somewhere along the shore. He decided to continue down river, closer to the shoreline. He made his way to the bank slowly, stopping every few moments to call out her name.

He found her lying face up on the sandy bank. Her limp body didn't move as he knelt beside her. He pulled her toward him and listened for a sign she was still breathing. He felt a whisper of breath against his cheek, faint, but regular.

"Lizzie?"

Andrew rubbed Lizzie's shoulders and tried to bring warmth back into her shivering body.

She jerked up against him and pushed him away.

He held onto her hands. "Lizzie, stop."

"No!" She slammed her hands against his chest, her strength surprising him. Adrenalin had taken over.

"Lizzie, it's Andrew. You need to stay still."

"No!" She pushed against his chest. "It pulled me under. I can't breathe. I can't catch my—"

"Lizzie, stop. You're safe now."

"No. It's still out there. I thought I was going to drown before I could find my way out of the water."

She moaned then finally stopped trying to pull away from him. Smoke from the fire competed with the scent of river water in her tangled hair that tumbled across her shoulders in the moonlight.

Her eyes widened as if she were remembering what happened. "Esther was there. I was holding her. I tried so hard to—"

"She is safe, Lizzie. I promise." He wiped away a tear that had formed in the corner of her eye. "I pulled her from the water myself and gave her to Posha. She is safe. And you too are lucky to be alive."

"Blessed, not lucky."

He laughed. The stubborn Lizzie he knew was back. "All right, blessed."

He studied the river again. The two boats were coming toward them. He waved his hands to catch their attention then helped Lizzie to her feet.

Kakoba met him on the shoreline. "We found them all. Only one did not make it."

"I am sorry."

Kakoba glanced downriver before addressing Andrew. "I am hesitant to continue, but staying ashore will be just as dangerous, if not more so."

Andrew nodded. "I agree that we should take the river."

He glanced at Lizzie. They'd all seen the pods and knew how dangerous such animals were. Adding an imaginary danger to the situation would only cause panic.

Lizzie shivered beside him. Her long skirt was soaked, making it hard for her to move. He wrapped his arm around her waist as they trudged into the water, hoping that if there was a God out there that He was listening.

CHAPTER SIXTEEN

They made it to the mission compound by daybreak. Still wet and cold from the humid air that had not allowed her clothes to dry completely, Lizzie shivered as she walked the last stretch of the familiar dirt path. The silvery glow of the sunrise broke through the early morning mist and led them past the newly built school and medical clinic toward the main house where much of the thick trees and grassy undergrowth on the edges of the compound had been cleared to allow for the needed expansion.

She stopped beside Andrew near the freshly painted white cinder-block house to wait for the rest of the group to catch up. "So much has changed since I was here last."

"Like what?"

"Most of what you see now, besides the main house, the row houses for the workers, and a few of the outbuildings, has been built in the past year, including the school, the chapel, and the clinic. The Carruths have worked hard. They've even enlarged the garden."

"How often do you get to come here?"

A jumble of emotions rose to the surface. "I stayed here for a few weeks after my parents died. Since my return, I've only been back a couple times."

"Doesn't seem near enough."

"That's what Mrs. Carruth tells me. And in truth, they have become like a second family to me—"

"Well, I'll be…" Mrs. Carruth, who spent her days tending to the sick that came to the door and overseeing the work in the gardens, appeared around the corner of the house and welcomed Lizzie with an enthusiastic hug. "Child, you look as if you haven't slept for days. I didn't expect to see you for another couple of months. Come inside, and I'll get you some biscuits and hot tea to warm you up."

"That would be wonderful, but we need your help." Lizzie introduced Andrew then pointed to Kakoba and Posha and the others who stood behind her, all of them as exhausted as she was from the long journey. "They have come seeking temporary shelter and to request that the magistrate return to their village to settle a serious dispute."

With a flap of her hands, Mrs. Carruth was in her element. The two maids that worked in the kitchens were called to prepare breakfast and set up their guests in row houses behind the main house.

"Chela and Fumina will take care of your friends, while the two of you join me in the house for tea. Dr. Carruth is making his morning rounds at the clinic, but he should be back any moment now." Mrs. Carruth bustled them through the front door and into the living room. "I trust you didn't have any problems getting here."

Lizzie sat on a padded chair across from Mrs. Carruth. "A hippo knocked over one of the dugouts on our way here. A women with us died in the accident."

"Oh, Lizzie, how frightening." Mrs. Carruth pressed her hand against her chest. "Did anyone catch a glimpse of the hippo? There have been, from time to time, rogue hippos that can be identified by their scars."

Lizzie shook her head. "I'm afraid it was too dark to see anything."

"That's a shame, for such an animal, unfortunately, needs to be shot."

Dr. Carruth arrived as tea was being served on fine china that had been shipped across the ocean and then by land to the remote mission station.

Lizzie ran her finger across the blue flower pattern and made the introductions to the doctor. "This is Andrew Styles. He is an explorer originally from the United States who has spent time traveling across Africa."

"Then I would say that you and I have a lot to talk about, young man. While the good Lord called me to practice medicine in this country, I long to travel as you do and see the world."

Mrs. Carruth offered Lizzie another biscuit. "It seems clear to me that these two gentlemen will be content to spend the rest of the day talking about frivolous things like hunting and travel, but I'm more interested in how you have been, Lizzie. It's been ages since we've heard anything about how you are doing. But as much as I'd like to sit and talk, you, my dear, need a fresh change of clothes and a good long nap. You look as if you haven't slept for a week. That goes for both of you."

"And Mr. Styles is in need of a doctor for his tooth."

Andrew reached up and touched his jaw. "I certainly don't want to impose."

"Impose?" Mrs. Carruth's boisterous laughter filled the room. "It's been far too long since a visitor from the United States graced us with his presence, and I know for a fact that my husband has a hundred questions he's dying to ask you, which is payment enough for a look at your tooth. Besides, I hardly consider distracting an old man from his rheumatism an imposition."

Lizzie set down her own teacup and tried not to yawn. "I would like to check on Posha and make sure she has everything she needs.

Her baby was born two nights ago, and with the traveling I'm worried that the infant might get sick."

"My wife is right." Dr. Carruth shook his head. "I will be happy to check on your friends as well as your tooth, Mr. Styles. While you, Lizzie, get some much-needed rest."

Andrew set his cup down. "Only if you are sure we are not imposing on your generosity—"

"Nonsense. We are both used to a constant stream of unannounced visitors." Mrs. Carruth grasped Lizzie's hand. "I'll promise to make sure that those from your village are fed and given a temporary place to stay, if you promise to go rest for a while."

Lizzie nodded. There was no use denying the fatigue. "Perhaps a short nap wouldn't hurt."

Lizzie followed Mrs. Carruth down the hall to the guest room, past faded photographs that hung from thick nails on the concrete walls and gave the house a touch of warmth.

Mrs. Carruth stopped in front of one of the wooden doors that lined the passageway. "If I remember correctly, this was always your favorite room. There are fresh linens by the pitcher of water if you'd like to wash your hands and face." Inside, she opened a tall wooden armoire and laid some clothes on the bed. "I think these will fit you, Lizzie, though you look thinner than the last time I saw you. I worry about you living up there by yourself."

"Thank you." Lizzie took the offered navy blue skirt and freshly ironed blouse and set them on the bed. "But I am afraid you worry far too much. I'm happy where I am. Really."

"I hope so." Mrs. Carruth pulled her into a hug. "It's just so good to see you. And I'm afraid I will continue my worrying about you, with hardly a soul for company and you rarely taking the time to come and visit. Seems like it always takes a tragedy to get you to leave that place."

"I'm hardly alone." Lizzie stepped back. "God Himself has always been my source of strength."

"That is true, but the good Lord also commanded a weekly day of rest, and knowing you, you don't keep His Sabbath as you should." Mrs. Carruth stood in the doorway. "But for now, I want you to go to sleep. We'll catch up on everything that has happened since your last visit later this afternoon...including that handsome man sitting out there."

Lizzie pressed the door shut then moved to stand in front of the mirror. She felt her cheeks flush at Mrs. Carruth's last comment. She had no desire to include Andrew among their topics of conversation.

Picking up the cloth, she dipped it into the warm water to wash her face. She'd forgotten how soft the towels could be and how nice soap smelled. Like lilacs in the springtime in New York...

No.

Lizzie closed her eyes and tried to push away thoughts of returning. Africa was her home and nothing Andrew, her aunt and uncle, or even Mrs. Carruth could say would change that.

Pulling off her damp skirt and blouse, she hung them over the back of the chair then slipped on the clean clothes. She looked out the open window across the gardens. Kakoba stood in the distance, talking with one of the workers next to the long row of cinderblock rooms at the bottom of the hill.

Lizzie lay down on the soft mattress with its colorful quilt that brightened up the small room. Mrs. Carruth had been right. She was simply tired. And the lack of sleep and frightening mishap on the Zambezi had done their share in wearing her out.

Fatigue and fear played with her imagination. She pushed away the panic she'd felt in the water and tried to relax. Sunlight poured through the window, illuminating the specks of dust that flittered in the air as she finally closed her eyes and went to sleep.

Andrew followed Dr. Carruth from the row houses toward the main house, feeling out of place in the missionary compound. He rubbed his jaw, thankful for the relief he was already experiencing from the doctor's diagnosis—a sinus infection that wouldn't have to include the extraction of a tooth. At least one positive thing had come out of the trip. "I appreciate your looking at both Kakoba's family and my tooth. I'm feeling better already."

"The medicine should clear up both the pain and the infection. And with Kakoba's family settled in, I'd like to hear more about your journey here."

Andrew clasped his hands behind him. "I don't want to impose. I'm sure your schedule is full, and we've already taken up far too much of your time."

"Nonsense. While our main task is preaching the gospel and ministering to the sick, much of our days are spent visiting with those who drop by unexpectedly like yourself." Dr. Carruth stopped at the edge of the newly planted gardens that spread out before them in neat rows. "We're praying for a large crop this year. And just like these plants will have to be nurtured and cared for as they grow, so do relationships. It's an important part of the culture we've chosen to embrace."

Andrew considered the older man's words. The change of pace from the hustle and bustle of the city was striking, but it wasn't only the imposition that had him feeling uncomfortable. It was the fact that if Dr. Carruth knew who he'd become, he'd probably be classified with the rest of the heathens they were trying to save.

"I appreciate greatly your hospitality," Andrew began. "Our coming here was my idea, which means I feel responsible for what happens to these people."

"It might have been your idea, but knowing Miss MacTavish as I do, I'm quite certain that she agreed with you."

Andrew chuckled. "She does value both her freedom and independence."

Dr. Carruth began walking again toward the house. "She's no different from the handful of other single women we've worked with who have found a freedom on the mission field that enables them to teach and practice medicine. If she were living in America or Europe, her duties would be largely confined to domestic chores, which certainly would not appeal to Lizzie."

And that was clearly why she had no desire to return home. Andrew ignored the guilt that pressed in. What Lizzie wanted was not his concern. His only job was to convince her of the importance of returning with him to New York.

"Have you known Lizzie long?"

"Just a few days, actually. Her grandfather passed away recently and left the bulk of the inheritance to her with the stipulation she remain in New York for one year. I was sent here by her grandfather's solicitors to take her back to New York."

"I'm sorry to hear about her grandfather's death. What was Lizzie's reaction to the idea of returning?"

"Do you have to ask?"

Dr. Carruth chuckled then stopped on the stone path lined with flowering plants and pulled out a handful of weeds. "I can only imagine, but while traveling across the Atlantic ten or fifteen years ago wasn't a luxury one could indulge in, today the trip is much faster. In fact, my wife and I are leaving shortly on a much-needed furlough. We would be happy for her to return with us."

"Unfortunately, with all that's happened, I don't think Lizzie has any plans of returning to New York with me or anyone for that matter, something I have to admit I was not prepared for."

Dr. Carruth turned to face him. "And you would like me to convince her she should return?"

Andrew nodded, hoping Dr. Carruth would turn out to be the ally he was looking for. "May I be honest with you, sir?"

"Of course."

"While it is important that she return home to comply with her grandfather's estate, there is another reason that I fear has become even more pressing."

"And what would that be?"

"Her safety."

"Her safety?" Dr. Carruth shook his head. "While I would be the first to disagree with the wisdom of sending out single women to isolated places, unfortunately that isn't my decision to make, nor has it ever been. But even having said that, I do find it hard to believe that her life might be in danger."

Andrew pressed his lips together before speaking, knowing he must choose his words carefully. "We told you what happened in Kakoba's village, both how several children were stolen from their fields and taken for ransom and how one of the men from the rival clan was killed. I can testify to the fact that his death was an accident, but I fear that won't matter in the eyes of those involved."

"And what exactly is Lizzie's involvement in the situation?"

"There are some in the village who believe that the unfortunate incidents that have happened lately are due to her return to the village. And while you and I both know that such superstitions are not true, we also know how quickly it is possible for such matters to spiral out of control."

"As far as I am concerned, there is no reason then for her not to return immediately and settle her grandfather's estate. I will talk with the others living here and seek out their opinions, but while the missionaries who came before us had little opportunities for furlough and arrived without plans of ever returning home, we can take the train to Cape Town and be on a ship within a matter of days."

"The problem is convincing her of the wisdom of leaving. And due to the added issues facing the village right now..." He clasped his hands in front of him. "I'm quite certain she won't leave without putting up a fight."

"I have known Lizzie since she was a mere child, and while even I have to admit that she can be hardheaded at times, if we decide that her return is in her best interest, I have no doubt that she will willingly go along with the decision."

Andrew doubted the man's optimism but could only hope that he was right.

"In the meantime," the older man continued, "I'd say this is a situation that calls for a heavy amount of prayer."

Lizzie woke to the sound of birds chirping and the warm glow of sunlight on her face. She squeezed her eyes shut and rolled onto her side on the soft mattress. It would be easy to drift back to sleep, but she didn't want Mrs. Carruth to be convinced that she'd become lazy by sleeping away an entire day. And she still needed to check on Posha and the others.

She glanced in the mirror on her way out of the room then hesitated, startled at her pale reflection. Fatigue had taken its toll and brought with it the shadows beneath her eyes, a persistent headache, and aching muscles. She smoothed down the front of her borrowed skirt, thankful for one thing that didn't bear the signs of smoke and river water.

She pinched her cheeks to add some color then left the room in search of Mrs. Carruth. The older woman and one of the kitchen workers sat in the shade snapping beans.

"What are you doing up so soon?" Mrs. Carruth dumped a pile of the green vegetable into the bowl.

"I slept for what seemed like hours."

"Not nearly long enough if you ask me."

"I feel better. Really."

"Good, because it's long past time that we had a good talk." Mrs. Carruth patted the seat beside her. "First you tell me more about this Mr. Styles. He and Dr. Carruth have been talking for hours and are now taking a tour of the clinic and school."

Lizzie sat down and snapped the ends off one of the beans, hoping she could steer the conversation away from Andrew. "I'd like to see what you have done also. The last time I was here they were nothing more than a dream."

"My husband is full of dreams. He wants to expand the clinic and the school and add a home for children. But there will be plenty of time for that. Tell me about this young man of yours."

Lizzie grabbed another handful of beans. "Mr. Styles isn't mine. In fact I hardly know him."

"Strange, as I am quite certain I see something light up in your eyes when you say his name."

Lizzie shifted in her seat. "Mr. Styles is here for one reason only, and that is to take me back to New York."

"My husband told me about that and about the death of your grandfather. I'm so sorry, Lizzie."

"Thank you."

"He also told me that your life could be in danger—"

"I believe that to be an exaggeration." Lizzie let out a sharp humph, wondering just how far Mr. Styles would go to get his way.

"He mentioned that there are those who are blaming you for what is happening in the village."

"Some, not all. I have close friends there who will stand up for me if it becomes necessary."

"I have no doubt of that, but the deeply seated superstitions of the people here cannot be ignored. I think it would be valid to consider Mr. Styles's request."

Lizzie's heart plummeted as she tossed another handful of snapped beans into the bowl. "I believed that you, of all people, would be on my side, but I guess I was wrong."

"Lizzie, I knew your parents before you were born and grieved along with you the day they died. And while they would be proud to know that you are serving the people they were called to, I also know that they would expect you to take care of the family issues that have arisen."

"And I have considered that, but now with the safety of Kakoba's family at risk, I believe my place is here helping them. They listened to me when we went to get the children back and they'll listen to me again."

"Just think about it. No one is forcing your return at this point, but we do want what is best." Mrs. Carruth leaned forward. "And what about Mr. Styles? You never answered about him."

"We don't have the same calling."

"Are you sure?"

"Quite. He has little respect for people like you and me who give our lives to spreading the Good News to those living in darkness. He's here because there's a tidy sum waiting for him in New York if he brings me back."

"That's not what I meant."

"I don't understand."

"Perhaps you are more alike than you think. I sense that you are both searching for something."

"And you believe I will find whatever it is in a man who doesn't share my beliefs?"

"Of course not. But perhaps your need to protect Kakoba and his family is blinding you from what you need to do and even how you see Mr. Styles. You don't have to prove anything to any of us, to the board, to your family...or even to yourself."

Lizzie pressed her lips together. Mrs. Carruth had always been like a second mother to her, and for her to take Andrew's side dug into Lizzie's already raw emotions. It wasn't selfishness that compelled her to stay. And Mrs. Carruth was wrong about something else. She had everything to prove.

CHAPTER SEVENTEEN

Lizzie rocked the crying newborn against her shoulder and tried to absorb Kakoba's words. "You are telling me that the authorities will not help you settle this matter?"

"They did not say that." Kakoba paced in front of them outside the long row of rooms reserved for the mission's workers. "They merely said that it would be some time before they arrived. Which means I must go back to my father's village now. I cannot wait for the authorities, nor can we stay here, as it could be weeks until they have time to deal with the matter."

"Dr. Carruth made it clear to me that anything you needed—"

"We have nothing here, and there are crops to plant and a village to rebuild. I'm sorry, but you know as well as I that we will lose everything if I stay here." He stopped to face her. "I never should have left."

Lizzie took in their surroundings and knew he was right. Two rooms in a row of cinderblock dwellings had been made available to them. Posha knelt in front of the cooking fire preparing a dinner of fish, sauce, and porridge, while the children played in the dirt on the edge of the small compound.

"Just please don't do anything rash. You came here to protect your family." The baby continued crying and Lizzie handed him to Posha, watching as he latched on to his mother's breast and eagerly began to nurse. "Mawela's family will not forget that their son is dead. They will seek revenge on his life."

"Then what would you suggest? I am responsible for the welfare of my family. And it seems clear now that coming here has not solved the problem. Returning is a risk I will have to take."

"Then I will return with you."

He stopped pacing to turn and face her. "I cannot allow that. Not only would you be taking a risk, but you need to return to your own country."

"No." Lizzie pressed her fingers against the back of her neck. Her pulse pounded in her temples, radiating pain down the back of her head and into her achy neck. "This is my country. You are my people, and you know as well as I do that I can help convince the chiefs not to settle for revenge. You need someone who is not only familiar with your people's ways, but one who is respected by both your father and Mawela's father. You need me."

"I don't know." Kakoba shook his head, his torn expression barely visible in the fading light. "My father is stubborn and blames you in part for what has happened. But perhaps there is some truth to what you say. My father has seen how you are willing to risk your life to help our people. Even Mawela's father might find honor in your actions."

The pounding at her temples increased. Lizzie drew in a deep breath and tried to relax her shoulders. "When do you want to leave?"

"In the morning."

"What about Posha and the others?"

"The women and children can stay here for their protection, but only until the matter is settled."

With the decision made, Lizzie said good-bye to the children then made her way up the twisting path toward the main house, her hands clasped behind her back. In front of her, the wild African bush spread out with its endless tufts of brown grass, brush, and scattered acacia trees. She wiped the beads of moisture from her brow. Above them, the orange sun hugged the edge of the horizon below a trail of white clouds, but the heavy heat from the day had yet to lessen.

Andrew appeared on the edge of the trail, carrying his rifle. "Mrs. Carruth asked me to escort you home. She was worried about your walking alone after dark."

"It's not far." Lizzie kicked at a small stone. "What is there to worry about?"

"Apparently there is a lion they have yet to capture that has been hunting men. It was sighted again this afternoon and has already killed several people in the past year."

She shivered at the thought of meeting one of the beasts on the dusky path. She'd seen the scars left on men from lion attacks. Few survived, and those who did would forever bear proof of their encounter.

Andrew pointed his chin back toward the row houses. "Am I right to assume that something has been decided?"

Until tonight, she had considered agreeing to Andrew's request, but her conversation with Kakoba confirmed her fervent prayers of the past few days as to what she should do. There was no reason to prolong things any longer.

"I am going to return with Kakoba and his people to help negotiate a solution with the chiefs." She stopped beneath the shade of a giant tree and drew in a deep breath, wishing she could shake off the growing fatigue.

"He asked you?"

She avoided answering directly. "He agrees that I'm in a unique position to help bring resolution to the situation."

"When does he want to leave?"

"Early in the morning. Posha and the other women and children will stay here until things are safe, then he will return for them."

"I could come with you or wait for you…"

She caught the glimmer of hope in his eyes and dropped her gaze as guilt tried to worm its way into her heart. She shoved it aside. "I think you know as well as I do that I cannot return to New York at this time."

He leaned against the rough bark of the tree's trunk and set the rifle next to him.

"You don't look surprised."

"I think deep down inside, maybe even from the very moment I first saw you, I knew you wouldn't leave."

"Then you understand my decision to stay and help Kakoba and his family?"

"It doesn't really matter what I think."

"But you do understand?" She pressed her lips together, wanting to take back the question. It shouldn't matter so much to her what he thought. But it did.

Andrew stared at the orange color of the sunset trailing across the sky, surprised that money, his one motivation for coming, suddenly didn't seem to matter anymore. "So what happens now?"

She looked up at him, her expression unwavering and determined. "You take the train to Cape Town then sail across the ocean and tell my grandfather's solicitors that my uncle is welcome to the money."

"While you return with Kakoba and his family."

She nodded. "I meant it when I said I don't belong there, and

I won't go back and pretend to be something that I'm not. I have everything I need here."

"So this isn't really about Kakoba, is it? This is really about what is best for you."

"Of course not. I'm staying because Kakoba and his family need me."

He caught the frustration in her voice but wasn't ready to let the conversation drop. "Did they ask, or did you insist on helping?"

"They need someone who is not only familiar with Kakoba's people, but one who is respected by both of the chiefs."

"Is that what you said to convince him that you needed to go with him?"

She started walking toward the house. "Does it matter?"

"I think you are staying because you're afraid."

"Afraid? Of what?"

"Of going back to a place where you don't fit in. Of being out of your element in a world that is completely different from this one. You're comfortable here because you grew up here and know these people, but that still doesn't make you one of them."

"You're wrong." She stopped and faced him. "And you know as well as I do that the timing isn't right for me to leave. They need me here. And I need them."

"Exactly. You need them. And there's nothing wrong with that, but when are you going to stop hiding? Because it will never be the right time for you to return, will it?"

"I'm not hiding." She held up her hand and started walking again, determination in every step. "And please don't say anything else. I'm sure my grandfather's solicitors will pay you the money you deserve for trying to get me to come. I'll even write a letter telling them to pay you whatever is owed."

Andrew closed his eyes for a moment, trying to sort through his turbulent thoughts. Maybe it was those intense eyes of hers or the intoxicating night air, but all he could think about at the moment was how Lizzie MacTavish, temper and all, was unlike anyone he'd ever met before. And how he wasn't ready to walk away from her.

"Wait a minute." He ran to catch up with her. "I'm sorry. I shouldn't have questioned your motives. It's none of my business. I was sent to bring you back to New York. It was a job, plain and simple, and I never should have let my emotions get involved."

"No, you shouldn't have."

"But don't question my motives either. This isn't just about the money anymore." He grasped her shoulder lightly and pulled her around so she was facing him. "Somehow it's become much more than that."

"Is this your way of trying to convince me that I'm making a foolish mistake?"

"I think you're making a crazy, foolish mistake, but that's not what I'm talking about right now."

"Then what is it?"

"It's you."

Lizzie's eyes widened and she stared up at him. "I don't understand."

He studied her full lips, wondering if she'd ever let a man kiss her or hold her in his arms. Wondering if *he'd* ever get the chance to hold her in his arms.

He pushed the thought away for the moment. "I don't think I ever thought you'd return with me. For one, you're the most difficult woman

I've ever met." He cleared his throat. "But that's exactly why I don't want to leave without you."

"I don't understand."

He'd foolishly gone this far, he might as well tell her the truth. "I've never met a woman who is not only fascinated by the world, but full of kindness and compassion for the people around her. Who will risk her life to talk to a chief or even put her own life at risk to save another. I didn't expect to feel this way, but no one has affected me quite like you do, Lizzie MacTavish."

"What are you saying?"

He brushed her check with the back of his hand, stopping himself from pulling her into his arms and kissing her. "That I'm falling in love with you."

She stumbled backward. "What?"

"I know. I know it must sound crazy, but I can't help it. You're different from the other women I know. Most of them would far rather be drinking tea and gossiping about their friends than traveling to the other side of the world. They're fascinated by my stories, but they have no desire to experience the thrill of the unknown firsthand. I've spent a long time waiting for a woman who sees the world as a place to explore."

"I'm no explorer." She shook her head and took another step away from him. "I chose this life because of what I believe, not for what I can gain or experience, something you'll never understand."

"There is so much you still don't know about me, but what I know about you is that you have a rare courage, which is enough to make me want to understand you better."

"You have confused your feelings. You're not in love with me."

She shook her head. "Or perhaps it's your way of trying to convince me that I need to return with you to—"

Andrew winced at the expected comment. "No. I meant it when I said this has nothing to do with money and everything to do with you. If you want to stay here, I'm finished trying to stop you."

"Then, please. Please don't say anything else. Beside the fact that we have nothing in common and our motivations for being here are completely opposite, the decision has been made. In the morning, I'm leaving with Kakoba for the village. You can return with your guides to Cape Town."

Andrew started toward the house with the rifle slung over his shoulder, wondering how much she was willing to let her stubbornness cost her. A chance at love? An inheritance? "Maybe you don't feel the way I do, but I'm not sure I'll ever understand the reason behind your turning down your grandfather's fortune."

"Sometimes what a person believes in is more important than money." She quickened her steps.

"So you say, but missionaries need money to cover expenses and take furloughs. You wouldn't be gone for much more than a year...." He hurried to keep up with her, convinced his reasons were falling on deaf ears. But what did he have to lose? "And there's something else. Staying here won't solve all of their problems. Tomorrow it will be another Mawela and another problem."

"But I can help now. Today. With this problem."

Andrew suddenly regretted putting his heart on the line. "Then I suppose the bottom line is that it doesn't really matter what I think."

Lizzie started running down the path that led to the house, her tears making it hard to see in the quickly fading light of dusk.

This isn't how it was supposed to be, God.

How many times had she lain awake at night, dreaming of one day falling in love with a man who shared her passion for the people here? Praying that God would bring her someone who understood her and her desires. But while she and Andrew might both have a passion for Africa, their motivations were completely different.

Why couldn't he see that? Why did he have to play with her heart?

Holding up her skirt, she ran faster across the uneven terrain, now lit only by the soft glow of the moon. At the top of the rise, she could see the lights of the main house. The familiar noises of the veld at night, the crickets, frogs, and other insects, filled her senses as she breathed in the smoke-tinged air.

She listened for Andrew's footsteps behind her, and was thankful she couldn't hear anything, because she wasn't going to fall for a man who didn't hold her beliefs. He saw the African people as an opportunity for exploitation through photos and stories that could bring him fame and fortune. She saw them as individuals who needed help to make their lives better through the Good News of God's love for them.

Which was why she was here. And why she had to stay.

Fury burned inside her like a live coal. He'd accused her of staying out of fear. How could he interpret her desire to stay as selfishness? But that was exactly what he had done. She wasn't staying to avoid leaving. She was staying because Kakoba needed her to convince the chiefs to settle the dispute in a peaceful manner. There was no fear in her motives.

Or was there?

This is really about what is best for you, isn't it?

She tried to push away Andrew's accusation, but like one of Chuma's arrows, it struck its mark. She slowed down to catch her breath. Maybe she hadn't chosen to be caught in the middle of two worlds, while never truly belonging to either. But this was where she was born, and what she knew. It was who she was.

And no amount of fancy clothes and hefty bank accounts would change that. She'd tried before. Dressing like the other girls...talking like the other girls...while all she'd really wanted to do was run barefoot across the veld through the tall elephant grass and forget that she would never be like any of them.

Lungs burning, she stopped to catch her breath, hoping Andrew hadn't followed her. She brushed the tears away from her cheeks, wondering why the evening still seemed so unbearably hot.

She heard a twig snap by the edge of the trees.

"Andrew?" She peered into the shadows but saw nothing. "Andrew?"

A sliver of fear crawled up her spine. Mrs. Carruth had been right. It wasn't safe to be out here at night. While the threat of man-eating lions was probably exaggerated, there were plenty of dangers in being alone at night, none of which she cared to encounter.

Something grabbed her from behind.

"Andrew!"

A hand closed over her mouth, stopping her screams, and dragged her to the ground. Someone was pulling her toward the thicker forest away from the house. She couldn't breathe. Couldn't see the face of her attacker.

She struggled against the figure as the brambles scratched her arms. Digging her boots into the ground, she tried to pull away.

God help me...

A shot rang out.

Startled, her attacker dropped her to the ground and started running. Lizzie lay still on the ground, unable to move.

"Lizzie?"

"Andrew!"

The silvery light of the moon lit his face as he reached down to pull her into his arms. Her heart pounded. He was close enough that she could feel his breath on her face and see the concern in his eyes.

"I'm sorry...I shouldn't have run."

"It's okay now." He pulled her closer. "Tell me what happened."

"I was running...someone grabbed me...he put his hand over my mouth and..."

"It's okay." Andrew's hand cupped her chin. "Who was it?"

She closed her eyes and tried to see the face of her attacker, but all she could feel were his hands pressing against her face and arms. Black...white...tall...short...she had no idea. Her attacker had been nothing more than a shadowy figure in the dark.

A shiver rushed through her. Had someone seen her walk to Kakoba's and waited for her to return alone, not knowing Andrew had been with her?

Andrew helped her sit up. "You're burning up with fever."

"No. I'm fine." She took a step then stumbled as the world grew dark around her. "I have to leave tomorrow. I have to..."

She couldn't think. The trees were spinning. She was being pulled under again, somewhere dark and hot...so hot.

And then there was nothing.

CHAPTER EIGHTEEN

Lizzie collapsed in his arms. Andrew set the rifle against the trunk of a thick tree then picked up her limp body and started for the house. With only the light from the moon, he couldn't tell if she'd been injured by her attacker—or if the faceless man had been nothing more than a hallucination connected with her fever.

Guilt wrapped around his heart. He never should have let her go off on her own. Never should have let his emotions get involved and admitted he was falling in love with her. Never should have accused her of making a foolish mistake in staying.

The lights from the house flickered in the distance. Her face had paled and her breathing became more rapid as he hurried down the gentle slope. Her damp hair tumbled over his arm like a soft caress, reminding him of everything he'd lost.

God, I'm asking You to save her. Please.

He might not deserve God's mercy, but she did.

All she wants to do is serve You. And if You let her die now…

The familiar plea opened up old wounds he'd thought had been healed long ago. His chest constricted as memories flashed through his mind like exposures from his camera. Mary laughing, with her long dark hair and freckles sprinkled across the tip of her nose…kissing him in the rain near Central Park…and the last time he'd seen her alive.

Andrew shoved the memories away. He wasn't going to lose her all over again. He stumbled onto the porch then hollered for help as he kicked open the door with his foot. He stopped over the threshold. Half a dozen pairs of eyes stared back at him from the long dining room table. He swallowed hard. Dinner had been served promptly at seven for boarders working at the hospital and school. He'd forgotten.

A clattering of silverware hit the table, and chairs scooted backward at his unannounced intrusion.

"I'm sorry." Andrew still froze. "I...she needs a doctor."

Dr. Carruth rose from the table and met him at the door. "Tell me what happened."

"I'm not sure." Andrew studied Lizzie's thin frame. In the dull light of the room, he couldn't see any sign of blood on her dress or face, but there was no way to be certain.

The doctor pressed his hand against her forehead. "She's burning up with fever. Take her quickly into the back bedroom where she is staying. I'll examine her there."

Andrew rushed through the dining room past the sea of startled faces and down the narrow hallway.

I'm not going to lose you again, Mary. Not this time...

The doctor helped him lay her on the bed. "I need you to tell me exactly what happened."

Andrew looked down at the mass of blond hair and Lizzie's face and felt himself jerked back to the present. "I don't know. We were talking on our way back to the house. She was upset and we argued. She ran off toward the house. I know I should have followed her, but she needed to cool off and was close enough to the house that I thought she'd be okay. I'm sorry. I never should have let her go."

He felt Dr. Carruth's firm grip on his arm. "It's all right. Just try to slow down and tell me what happened next."

"I was following behind her a short distance and heard her scream." Andrew gulped a deep breath of air. "I fired a shot to scare off any predator that might be lurking in the bush. When I found her, she was rambling about some man who had attacked her."

"Did you see anyone?"

"No. I didn't see anything."

Lizzie moaned. Her eyes flickered open and she tried to sit up.

The doctor pressed on her shoulder. "I want you to lie back down, and try to tell me what happened."

She pressed her hand against her forehead. "My head…it hurts so bad…"

"I can give you something that will help you in just a minute, but I need you to tell me what happened."

"I don't know."

"Try to remember." Andrew took her hand and squeezed it. "You had gone to speak to Kakoba. I said some things that upset you and you started running toward the house."

Her eyes widened. "Someone grabbed me and pulled me toward the woods. I tried to fight, but he was so—so strong."

"Did he hurt you?"

"I couldn't breathe. I couldn't stop him."

Dr. Carruth turned her gently to one side, then the other. "I don't see any sign of external injury. It could be nothing more than exhaustion, except she's burning up with fever, which signifies an infection. And could account for the hallucination."

Lizzie gripped Andrew's hand. "I wasn't hallucinating. Someone grabbed me. They tried to pull me into the bush."

"And I believe you, but you have to admit that you've been through a lot the past few days, with little sleep."

"The time you spent in the Zambezi River alone would be enough to weaken anyone's constitution," Dr. Carruth added. "How long have you felt sick, Lizzie?"

"I don't know. My head started hurting on the boat. I just thought it was the sun."

"I want to run some tests to see if I can determine what she has. Andrew, if you will wait for me in the living room, I'll let you know as soon as I have an answer."

Andrew paced the small living room while he waited for the doctor to come out and tell him what was wrong. He should have noticed she was sick. Should have insisted she stay in bed and rest. He rubbed the tight muscles in his neck with the tips of his fingers, wishing he could take back some of the things he'd said to her.

This is really about what is best for you.

What had he been thinking when he'd spouted off to her like a pompous pig?

He hadn't been thinking.

Instead, he'd stood in judgment and questioned her motives. He shook his head as guilt slid through the recesses of his mind. Whether his comments were valid or not, he'd been out of place to confront her.

"Are you hungry?"

Andrew stopped pacing. Mrs. Carruth stood at the entrance of the kitchen, pointing to the covered plate sitting on the table. The rest of the dishes, except for teapot and cups, had already been cleared, and the other missionaries had gone home for the evening.

Food was the last thing on his mind. "No, thank you, I'm not."

"Pacing this room isn't going to do anything for Lizzie, and you're liable to wear a hole in my floor. And not eating will have you needing to see the doctor."

He hesitated then sat down and uncovered the plate. Fish, rice, and a boiled egg. His stomach turned, but he managed a smile. "Thank you."

She sat across from him, letting her fingers tap against the wooden table. "You look like a man carrying a big burden."

He picked up his fork and poked at the fried fish head. "I'm worried."

"About Lizzie?"

Andrew tapped his fork against the plate. "We said some things… I said some things I shouldn't have. And I feel guilty for not noticing that she was sick."

"As for whatever is wrong with her, I can assure you that she's in capable hands. Both God's and my husband's."

Her gaze seemed to penetrate all the way through him and made him uneasy. The last thing he wanted to hear was a sermon.

"You haven't known Lizzie for long, but she's a strong woman. I have no doubt that she'll be fine."

He shifted his weight in the chair. "I've known her long enough to know that she fights for what she believes in, no matter the consequences."

He'd been that way once. Before the realities of life and war had torn his world apart and taught him differently.

Mrs. Carruth leaned back. "She's a lot like her mother."

He pushed around a bite of rice on the plate. There was so much he didn't know about Lizzie. So much he wanted to know. And if he read Mrs. Carruth correctly, she was more than willing to pass the time telling stories. Maybe this was his chance. "Tell me about her parents."

She smiled and leaned forward. Clearly he'd read her correctly. "Lizzie's father had already been working in Northern Rhodesia for four or five years as a single missionary when Caroline arrived on the field. The first time I saw them together, I thought they were the perfect match. And I was right. They seemed to have everything in common. A love for adventure and for the people here, the same faith, a sense of humor…"

The perfect match. Funny how he'd once thought he found that.

"Lawrence proposed a month later, and I believe they were truly happy here."

"And Lizzie." She was the one he really wanted to know more about…and to understand. "You knew her growing up?"

"Everyone always loved it when she visited here. She was the kind of child that brightened up the room with her laughter and smile. And she was smart. She soaked up knowledge like a sponge, could speak both English and the native language fluently, and played with the other children like she was one of them."

He felt the tension in his shoulders begin to subside. "I've seen the way she relates to the people here. It is amazing."

"Her faith, though, is what has held her steady through so many difficulties. She's come to me on several occasions needing advice, but in the end, it's always her calling—and her God—that keeps her here."

"I've seen that."

"And what about your faith?"

He shoved a bite of food into his mouth. Talking about his faith had become one of the subjects he'd learned to avoid. "I once was a lot like Lizzie. Eager, innocent, naïve—"

"I'd hardly label Lizzie as innocent or naïve. She's seen more at twenty-five than most people do in a lifetime."

"Naïve then, about her faith."

And God.

"What happened to your faith, Andrew?"

He shoved his plate back, his appetite gone. He had no plans of sharing his darkened soul with a God-fearing missionary.

She, though, seemed to have other ideas. "I've found that talking can be extremely healing."

He folded his arms across his chest and shook his head, unwilling to take the bait. "It was all a long time ago. I'm a different person today."

"Different from the person you want to be?"

Her words hit their target. Emotions, long buried, shot their way to the surface. Anger, hurt, loss, betrayal…

"I've seen the way you look at Lizzie," she continued. "It's the same way her father used to look at her mother."

Andrew combed his fingers through his hair. "Tonight I told her I was falling in love with her. I know it sounds crazy, because I barely know her, but there is something about her that reminds me of how I used to be. And of things I haven't felt for years." Andrew shook his head. "I don't know. I thought my heart had healed years ago. But being here, being with her…"

Andrew pressed his lips together. He'd already said too much.

"Would you like some tea?"

"No. Thank you."

Mrs. Carruth pulled the handmade cozy from the flowered teapot and poured herself a cup of tea. "I lost my first husband when I was twenty-nine. I'm not sure we ever completely get over the loss of someone close to us. Harry will always be a part of who I am and nothing will change that. And that's the way it should be."

"The thing is, none of this really matters. Lizzie sees me as a heathen who's after fame and fortune at the expense of the African people."

"And are you?"

"A heathen or after fame and fortune?"

"Either one, I suppose."

"During the war I was in England as a correspondent and saw things there that I'll never forget. Horrible things that will haunt me the rest of my life."

He still saw them when he closed his eyes. Men he knew who'd been killed on the frontlines. Others who'd lost limbs. But even worse had been those who'd returned having lost their minds.

"So the things you saw changed the way you see God?"

"I don't understand how God could allow such atrocities to happen."

"So the evil in this world is God's fault?"

"No… Yes… I don't know. It just doesn't seem right. Those men didn't deserve to die."

"Nor did Jesus Christ deserve to die, but He did. The truth is that there are no easy answers, Andrew. Just as in Christ's death on the cross, there are times when God doesn't change the circumstances. But He always has a purpose in the circumstances, which is why Christ's redemption from the cross is our only hope. And it's a price He paid with His own life."

Andrew traced a narrow grain of wood on the table, wishing the doctor would hurry.

Mrs. Carruth took another sip of her tea. "How does Lizzie fit into all of this?"

"I don't know. This was supposed to be simple. I was paid to find her and take her back to New York. That was all. But now...I don't know how I feel."

"I guess that's something you're going to have to figure out yourself."

Part of him hoped Lizzie would forget everything he'd said. He'd foolishly allowed emotions to surface that he'd long ago buried. Nothing could change what had happened in the past.

"Somehow I have this feeling that your meeting wasn't an accident." Mrs. Carruth's voice interrupted his thoughts. "Have you ever thought that God is pulling you back to Him?"

Andrew stifled the urge to bolt. Hadn't he felt the tug a thousand times? And dismissed it just as many times out of anger? A door slammed down the hallway. Dr. Carruth entered the living room, saving him from answering her pointed question—for now.

CHAPTER NINETEEN

Andrew shoved back his chair and stood to greet the doctor. "How is she?"

Dr. Carruth set his medical bag on the edge of the table. "I will want to keep a close eye on her for the next few days, but I've given her a dose of quinine to treat the malaria. She should be back on her feet in a day or two."

Andrew gripped the back of his chair. "So she's going to be all right?"

Dr. Carruth nodded and sat beside his wife. "While I don't expect her to suffer any side effects of the illness, Lizzie needs rest. She's physically exhausted, which could be what triggered a relapse of the malaria she contracted several years ago."

Mrs. Carruth poured her husband a cup of tea and handed it to him. "She's not the only one who's tired. You've been working too hard lately."

Dr. Carruth took the offered drink from his wife then started adding sugar.

On the third spoonful his wife stopped him. "Abram."

Dr. Carruth dropped the spoon back into the sugar bowl, frowning at his wife's correction. "My wife worries far too much about me."

Mrs. Carruth grasped her husband's hand and smiled. "With the way you take care of everyone from here to the Zimbabwe boarder, someone's got to take care of you."

He chuckled and patted her hand. "Truth be told, there's nothing like a good wife, Andrew—even when she's determined to knock out my sweet tooth. But back to Lizzie. There is one issue I wonder if you can clarify. She kept mumbling about needing to return to the village in the morning."

Andrew let out a quick breath of relief and sat down. Neither marriage nor spiritual matters were subjects he felt inclined to discuss. "Lizzie was planning to leave in the morning with Kakoba to go back to his village."

"Why would she do that?" the doctor broke in.

"From what she told me, the authorities aren't able to take care of the matter immediately, so she convinced Kakoba she could help in the negotiations between the chiefs."

The concern in Mrs. Carruth's expression mirrored his own. "And what was your response?"

That he was falling in love with her.

Andrew bit back the thought and cleared his throat. "I told her I believed she was making a foolish choice."

"I have to say I agree." Dr. Carruth eyed the sugar bowl before setting down his half-empty cup of tea. "I thought the reason they came here was because it was too dangerous to return."

"It is." Andrew nodded. "At least I believe it is. They were hoping to bring in the authorities, but with the villages as isolated as they are, it will take time to take care of the matter. But I think her returning to the village would be a mistake for another reason as well."

"Which is?"

Andrew debated his next statement. While he might regret the way he'd spoken to her, he still believed he was correct. And while it might not be any of his business, it didn't seem that Lizzie was able to make a rational decision at the moment. "May I be perfectly frank with both of you?"

Mrs. Carruth nodded. "Of course."

"I think there is more behind her insistence on staying."

"What do you mean?" Dr. Carruth asked.

"What did she tell you about her grandfather?"

Mrs. Carruth's thumb traced the rim of the teacup. "She told me he had left her some money in his will on the stipulation she remained in New York for a year."

"*Some* money is quite an understatement. Except for a monthly stipend that will go to her uncle, she was left his entire estate."

"Then why the hesitation to return?" Dr. Carruth asked. "What she receives could help fund the mission for years to come, something I'm sure she's considered."

Andrew measured the impact of his words then went ahead. "I believe she's afraid to return."

"Afraid?" Mrs. Carruth chuckled then added a dollop of cream to her tea. "Lizzie has never let fear stop her from doing anything. She's a single woman, working among a fairly primitive people group. Fear is not one of her vices."

"Which is exactly the issue."

Mrs. Carruth set down the creamer and frowned. "I'm not sure I understand."

"While it's true that she's worked here as a single missionary for many years, she also grew up here. This world, the African veld and its people, is what she knows."

Mrs. Carruth shook her head. "She has spent time in New York. Not a lot perhaps, but once as a young child, then later after her parents died."

"I know, but she never fit in."

Mrs. Carruth shook her head again. "She spoke to me some about her three years in New York, but even though I never could get her to say much, I still find that hard to believe."

"She's afraid to go back, Mrs. Carruth. Afraid she won't fit in. But even if that wasn't an issue, I still think she needs to go back. After what happened in Kakoba's village, it isn't safe for her to return at this point. I'm not saying that she can't ever return, but going to New York now would give her time to rest, to take care of the business concerning her grandfather's estate, and to let the situation here defuse."

"I believe you have a point." Dr. Carruth nodded. "The people's suspicions here run deep, and blame must always be placed at the foot of someone."

"She could go to New York and return later next year—"

"But I know Lizzie. She's stubborn when she gets an idea in her head. With all that's happened, I'm not sure she'll agree to go." Mrs. Carruth interrupted him.

Andrew pulled out his last card. "Even if her life is in danger?"

Mrs. Carruth leaned forward. "What do you mean?"

"The attack tonight might not have been random. It could have a connection with what happened in the village."

Andrew wanted to dismiss the idea that there could be any connection between the attack tonight and what happened in the village. The only evidence he had were Kakoba's convictions that they had been followed on the river, but at the moment it was enough to have him worried.

His fingers gripped the edge of the table. "What if someone doesn't want her to return to the village alive?"

"Surely you don't think someone is trying to kill her."

"Someone just tried to attack her."

"If you are correct, then I don't see that we have a choice." Mrs. Carruth looked to Andrew and then her husband. "We're going to have to send Lizzie back to New York."

Lizzie felt her world shatter. "I can't go back now."

The older woman sat on the side of the bed and grasped Lizzie's hand. "I understand that you had hoped to return with Kakoba in the morning to go back to the village, but we believe that in the light of what has happened the past few days that it is wiser for you to leave for the time being."

"You don't understand—"

"Yes, I do, sweetie. I know how important your work is to you, but because you're a single woman, it is the mission's responsibility to ensure your safety."

"I'm not in any danger, and Kakoba needs my help." Lizzie forced herself up with her elbows. "I'll be fine in the morning. I'm sure of it."

"And I'm quite certain that my husband will not agree with that diagnosis." Mrs. Carruth chuckled. "The problem with malaria is that you start feeling better, then you have a relapse when you push too hard. Trust me. I know firsthand. You have to rest."

A wave of dizziness struck and Lizzie dropped back down onto the pillow. "I'll be gone over a year."

"Which will give you plenty of time to take care of your grandfather's estate, rest, and think about your future before planning your return. And in the meantime, you might as well enjoy yourself some. Unlike most missionaries returning on furlough, it would seem that you won't have to worry about raising funds."

"My father taught me to trust in God for what I need."

"Maybe this is God's way of answering that prayer."

Or perhaps it was the result of one man's determination. "I was afraid this would happen."

"What do you mean?"

A chill from the fever washed over her. "Mr. Styles is determined to make sure I return, and now, because of this ridiculous belief that my life is in danger, I have been given no choice in the matter."

"He's not the one who made the decision."

Lizzie wasn't convinced. "So nothing he said influenced your decision?"

"He—"

"Mrs. Carruth, my life is not in danger. Tonight was nothing more than someone who'd been out drinking too much."

Mrs. Carruth didn't look convinced. "While there might not be a way for us to know for sure, I don't see how we can dismiss the possibility that someone wants to hurt you."

"And my leaving will solve the problem?"

"Maybe not Kakoba's problems, but it will give time for things to settle down and to be worked out among the two villages."

Lizzie balled the sheet in her fists, grasping for something... anything that might convince Mrs. Carruth to change her mind. "I know these people. They will not harm me. They respected my father, and despite the suspicion they've placed on me, they respect me."

"I know that." Mrs. Carruth brushed a strand of loose hair from Lizzie's forehead. "You don't have to prove that to me. I've always been amazed at what you have accomplished."

"But Andrew still gets his way. I return to New York, he gets his money, and everyone is happy."

Everyone but herself.

"Don't be too quick to judge the man. I believe there is much more to Mr. Styles that is hovering below the surface that he doesn't want you to see."

Lizzie rubbed her fingertips against the piercing pain radiating from her neck and tried to clear her head. "He told me I was afraid of returning to New York."

"Is that true?"

Lizzie closed her eyes and drew in a deep breath. All the fears that Andrew had confronted her with rose to the surface. How had he been right? "Sometimes it's easier to believe I'd be nobler if I refused my inheritance so I could trust in God for my support instead of storing up treasures here on earth."

"Money itself isn't evil. It's only what the evil man does with it that hardens people's hearts and turns them from God."

"Maybe."

"And what about your grandfather's wishes? I never met the man, but it seems clear that he believed that you were the one best suited to inherit his money. And he must have had a reason for you to stay in New York for a period of time."

"I knew he never approved of my decision to stay here, but his solicitors wrote of his continued growing concern for my safety in the last few weeks of his life. I suppose he saw his death as a chance to require me to return. And if I remained long enough in New York, I was more likely to decide to stay permanently."

"You might not agree with his actions, but it's clear he loved you."

"I know. I spent as much time with him as I could after my parents' deaths. He might not have always agreed with me, but he always listened to me. We used to go to the ocean on my days off, and he'd have me tell him stories of life along the Zambezi. I never expected to have to deal with his money and his estate."

"He left his fortune to you because he loved you and knew you'd be wise in how you spent it."

"I suppose." The now familiar fear dug deeper. "Have you ever felt as if you don't belong anywhere?"

Mrs. Carruth chuckled. "I'm not sure there's a person alive who hasn't felt left out at one time or another."

Lizzie shook her head. "I'm not talking about being chosen last for a game at school, or feeling like a wallflower at a party because you're shy. I'm talking about not understanding new words, or fashion, or the way people think."

"Oh, sweetie, what you have to understand is that what you are feeling is natural, but I know you. You have a way of bringing out the best in people. You break down barriers so that it doesn't matter what differences lie between you. Look at how you were able to negotiate with the chief for the children's release. You'll be fine. I promise."

Lizzie relaxed her tight grip on the sheet, realizing that no matter how much her heart wanted to stay, there was nothing she could do or say to change the situation.

CHAPTER 20

The dining room was abuzz with chatter the next morning as Andrew sat down at the end of the table with his bowl of porridge and mug of hot coffee. He added a couple spoonfuls of sugar and some cream to the drink and studied the assortment of men and women who called this mission their home.

All of them had welcomed him, but even their warm reception couldn't stop him from feeling out of place. He looked up as laughter erupted on the far side of the table. He smiled at the joke he'd missed but couldn't shake his unease. Sitting in the midst of a room full of missionaries was the last place he wanted to be. Their presence only managed to resurrect a piece of his past better left buried.

He pushed away the turbulent emotions that had hounded him throughout the night. Now that his plans had finally come together, he just had to get through the next few days. The doctor and his wife had already made arrangements to leave on furlough, which meant that by the end of the week, the four of them would take the train to South Africa where they could set sail for New York via England. The thought brought with it a measure of relief. The sooner he returned to New York, the sooner he could arrange his next exploration party—and forget Lizzie MacTavish.

He finished his last bite of porridge. He never should have gotten involved emotionally. Finding Lizzie shouldn't have been any different from tracking down information for an article in a newspaper. He'd spent a lifetime trying to pen his work without including his own biased emotions.

Then why did guilt lie so heavily on his mind this time?

"How long do you plan to stay in Northern Rhodesia, Mr. Styles?"

Andrew set down his coffee mug and turned to the lanky Brit sitting beside him. "I'll be leaving by the end of the week with the Carruths for Southampton and New York."

"Ahh..." The man's smile broadened. "Say hello to my motherland for me while you're in port, will you? I haven't seen England's shores for a good long time."

Andrew chuckled. "I can do that for you."

"The name's Kent Hickling by the way." Kent held out his hand and shook Andrew's.

"Nice to meet you."

"We're always happy to see a new face around here." Kent grabbed a slice of bread from the basket in front of him and started spreading on a thick layer of butter. "Though I hope you have more knowledge of the bush than the typical foreigner."

"What do you mean?"

"I met a chap yesterday morning when I was in town. He was an avid game hunter traveling through the district."

"Did something happen to him?"

"He was mauled to death by our infamous lion last night."

Andrew leaned forward, uncertain he'd heard him correctly. "Mauled to death?"

"It's horrible, isn't it?" Kent folded his slice of bread in half then took a bite. "None of us knows which day will actually be our last. Gives one something to think about."

Andrew dismissed the spiritual implications. "Who found him?"

"One of the workers on his way here. Unfortunately, by the time they got him to the clinic, it was too late for the doctor to do anything."

Andrew shook his head then downed the rest of his coffee. "Mrs. Carruth told me there was a rogue lion on the loose."

"This chap's death brings the body count to seven over the past year."

Mrs. Carruth entered the dining room with a tray of food and headed for the rooms in the back of the house.

"I'm sorry. If you'll excuse me, Kent." Andrew crossed the room, intercepting the older woman before she headed down the hall. "Is that for Lizzie?"

"Yes. She asked for something to eat, which is a good sign."

"How is she feeling?"

"To be honest, I believe she's more concerned about the decision to return to New York than being sick. But given some time, she'll not only recover completely physically, but also come to realize that leaving, for now, is for the best."

"No doubt she is furious at me for her having to return."

"Maybe, but Abram and I also believe it's the right decision. Don't worry about her, Andrew. She's a strong woman, and she'll be fine."

Andrew nodded at the tray. "May I take her breakfast to her? I'd really like to speak to her."

Mrs. Carruth hesitated. "My husband is insisting that she rest so she can be ready for the trip."

"I promise that I will only stay a few minutes. Please."

"All right. But only a few minutes."

Steadying the tray in one hand, Andrew knocked lightly on Lizzie's door then waited for her soft "come in."

"Andrew? I thought Mrs. Carruth—"

"I'm sorry. Mrs. Carruth said I could bring you your breakfast." He set the tray beside her on the small wooden bedside table and ignored her frown. "Did you sleep well?"

"The medicine Dr. Carruth gave me helped, though I believe I could still sleep another week."

"I've had malaria twice." He handed her the cloth napkin, then sat on the edge of the bed. "Once in West Africa and then later a relapse in Europe during the war."

She plucked the spoon from between his fingers. "Thank you, but I'm quite capable of feeding myself."

He gave in and handed her the bowl of cereal. "You can't stay mad at me forever, you know. We'll be staying in rather close quarters aboard ship while crossing the Atlantic."

"Mrs. Carruth assured me that the SS *Arundel Castle* is quite large."

"It is. At over six hundred feet long, she weighs nineteen tons, and has steam turbines, two masts, and four funnels, so she can make the trip from Cape Town to Southampton in less than three weeks."

Lizzie yawned. He clearly wasn't impressing her.

He decided to take another approach. "The accommodations are quite spectacular. Not only is there airconditioning in the rooms, there is an electric lift that takes the passengers from deck to deck."

He studied her expression and thought he caught a spark of interest beneath her scowl.

She pushed her spoon through the porridge. "How much money are they paying you to bring me back?"

He let out a low humph. Apparently not. "What do you mean?"

"What do I mean? It's a simple question. How much money are they paying you to bring me back?"

He swallowed hard. Perhaps the grand expanse of the ship wasn't going to be big enough for the two of them after all. "They paid a percentage of my fee up front to make the trip, and offered a bonus if I brought you back."

She looked up at him. Eyes wide, expression sharp. "Which is enough for what? To fund a six-month expedition for you, or even a year. I suppose if I were you, I would have done whatever it took to bring me back as well."

He shook his head. "You're wrong, Lizzie."

"Wrong that this wasn't all about the money for you? Please. Don't take me for a fool."

Tears welled in her eyes. If she really didn't care, she wasn't doing a good job at making him believe it.

"You came here," she continued, "believing that all you had to do was wave the inheritance in front of me, and I would follow you back to New York. Then when I didn't agree right away, you went as far as trying to convince me that you were in love with me. Like I am some weak-willed woman whose life is not complete without you."

But my life isn't complete without you.

Andrew drew in a deep breath then slowly let it out. The pain from the truth of her harsh words registered. "I didn't tell you I was falling in love with you to trick you into returning with me like some con man working a sting. You have to believe me."

Lizzie shook her head and set her uneaten bowl of porridge on the side table. "You're not in love with me any more than I'm in love with you. But it doesn't matter anymore. I can't return to Kakoba's village with him, which means I can't try to mediate with the chief. I know that you see all of this as trivial, but to me it was important. Not only was I being given the chance to prove my worth among my people, but I might have been able to stop someone else from getting hurt. Now I can't do any of that...because of you."

"You're wrong, Lizzie. I simply told the Carruths that I was concerned about what had happened over the past few days."

"Because I was attacked?"

"Yes, and do you blame me? Try to look at things from my point of view. There is conflict in the village which you are being blamed for, and two people have already died. Kakoba believes we were being followed, then you're attacked—"

"Please." Her fingers gripped the edge of the sheet. "Stop trying to convince me that what you are doing is right. I don't need your conclusions or your persuasions or your help. I can take care of myself without your interference."

"I never meant for this to hurt you. You have to believe me."

"I guess it doesn't really matter, does it, because you got what you want. I'll go back to New York, sign whatever papers my grandfather's solicitors tell me to sign and deal with the rest of his estate, then follow the wishes of my aunt and uncle until the year is over or the mission board allows me to return."

"Time will pass quickly."

"But what about Kakoba and his family? Have you thought about them? The authorities will come eventually, but I could have helped them now."

Andrew combed his fingers through his hair. He was second guessing his actions. What if she were right and more people died because she wasn't there to help defuse the situation?

"Maybe there is still something we can do for Kakoba. I'll go with the doctor in the morning and talk to the British authorities. Explain to them the urgency of the matter and try to convince them to send someone to handle the situation right away."

"They know me and trust me."

"I'm sorry, Lizzie."

"It doesn't really matter anymore. I've faced plenty of roadblocks in my life. And I'll get over this too."

Perhaps, but he wasn't so sure he was going to be able to get over her.

CHAPTER 21

Sunlight spilled across the second-class deck of the RMS *Berengaria*. Andrew had been right about the grandness of the ships. The cramped quarters Lizzie remembered aboard the vessels she'd traveled on with her parents had been transformed by shipping line owners competing to create both the fastest and most luxurious ocean liners to cross the Atlantic.

Lizzie stared at her book from the wooden deckchair and reread the last sentence on the page, but even with the warm ocean breeze playing across the deck and the relaxing view of the sea beyond that, her mind refused to focus.

She flipped the book shut and dropped it onto the steamer rug resting across her lap, admitting defeat. Their departure from Northern Rhodesia nearly a month ago had already become a faint memory. After the long train ride to Cape Town, they'd followed the African coastline aboard the SS *Arundel Castle* beneath clear skies and quiet seas until reaching Southampton, where they'd boarded the RMS *Berengaria* for the week-long voyage from England to the United States.

The frustration that had settled over her from the decision to leave Africa had mellowed during the trip, first due to the malaria, then from bouts of the same seasickness that had plagued thousands of emigrants on their quest to arrive in the United States. The queasiness had hit Lizzie with a vengeance the first few days of the trip then tapered off as her body adjusted to the movement of the massive ship.

But leaving Africa wasn't what had her mind reeling and her heart feeling as if it might explode. In less than twenty-four hours, they would be sailing into the New York Harbor. And along with the approaching arrival in the grand metropolis came a renewed sense of grief as dozens of memories fluttered to the surface—memories of the lonely girl who'd been thrust into a strange, confusing new world after losing her parents.

Lizzie bit back the flow of tears. She'd worked to busy herself with the numerous activities offered on board in order to avoid thinking about her impending arrival at her aunt and uncle's, but the reality of her situation had been impossible to ignore.

Just like Andrew.

Her fingers pulled at the edges of the thick blanket. While she was still convalescing during the first couple weeks of the voyage, Andrew and Mrs. Carruth had taken turns reading to her. Once she had regained her strength, Andrew had insisted on escorting her, first to dinner then later on walks along the promenade and to the endless selection of activities on board like miniature golf, shuffleboard, and bowling—while she'd managed to avoid involving her heart.

Because you care for him more than you want to admit?

She shoved away the errant thought. With only a day left before their arrival, she'd become a jumble of emotions that refused to set-tle—something that had nothing to do with Andrew or his declarations of love.

There had been no more mentions of falling in love, something she'd ensured by refusing to talk about anything personal. That had helped dissolve the anger she'd projected toward him during the first few days of their journey. Blaming him was fruitless. He'd simply had a job to do.

A young girl skipped across the deck, clutching a cloth bag in her hands while her long red hair trailed behind her like a handful of ribbons. For a moment, Lizzie's hurt was replaced by a small tug of desire. Chuma and Esther had become like family to her, but there was still a part of her that wanted her own children, family—and a husband.

The girl turned the corner around the end of Lizzie's deck chair too quickly as she ran toward her mother and slipped. A handful of beads scattered across the deck. Lizzie jumped from her chair to chase the butterscotch and honey-colored amber beads.

The girl's mother knelt beside Lizzie where the colorful beads now pooled along the edge of the railing. "I'm so sorry to have disturbed you. I had hoped the beads would keep her quiet and occupied on the trip."

Lizzie tried to reassure her. "I think a bead project is a wonderful idea, and helping is not a problem at all."

"Frances can be a bit…energetic."

Frances held open her bag, lips pressed together.

"What do you say, Frances?"

"Thank you, miss."

"You're welcome." Lizzie poured her handful of beads into the bag. "Did you hurt yourself?"

Frances pointed to a mark on her knee. "Just a small scratch."

Lizzie found one more bead that had rolled under one of the life preservers hanging against the wall. "What are you making, Frances?"

"A necklace for my grandmother."

"I am quite certain that she will love anything you make."

"Can I help?" Andrew appeared beside Lizzie, camera in hand as the breeze off the water tussled his hair.

Lizzie stood and brushed off her dress. "I believe we've found most if not all of the missing beads, but thank you."

She said good-bye to the pair, then made her way back to her chair.

Andrew sat beside her. "I looked for you in your cabin, and when I didn't find you there, assumed you would be here."

She shot him a half smile. If she wasn't engaged in one of the activities on deck or eating in the dining room, she was curled up, reading a book on the deck chair she'd rented for the duration of the trip. "Am I that predictable?"

"Perhaps more so here than amongst the velds of Africa. There you have dozens of places to explore, illnesses to treat, and villagers to save."

"I don't know about that." She ignored the familiar tug of homesickness. "I've discovered what is offered on board to be quite extensive."

And distracting. Which was exactly what she had needed.

He scooted his chair closer until she could smell his subtle cologne above the sea breeze. He snapped a photo.

She ducked. "Andrew."

"Stop." He snapped a second photo. "This way you won't ever forget this trip."

"How could I? You've been snapping photos for the past month. Enough to fill a dozen books."

"Not quite, but I am on my last roll of film, so you won't have to put up with me much longer."

She smiled. That was what she wanted. Wasn't it?

"Are you hungry?" he asked.

"Yes."

"Good, because there is color in your cheeks for the first time in weeks and, in case you've forgotten, we've been invited to eat with the *higher class* again later this evening. I'm sure your aunt will be quite impressed with your stories of joining them for some of the first-class events."

Lizzie's gaze flicked downward at the reminder of New York.

Andrew's ability to procure invitations to some of the first-class events from a group of friends he'd made had given them a taste of the luxurious accommodations of the upper decks with their expensive murals, lush draperies, and carved wood panels. All things that made their surroundings seem more like a lavish hotel than the bowels of a ship. But such elegance had left her with mixed feelings of the future. And an intense longing for the Africa she'd left behind.

"Lizzie? Are you all right?"

"It's nothing." She waved off his verbal show of concern. "I'm just nervous. It's been so long since I was in New York."

"Surely there's something you're looking forward to about coming back."

Lizzie fiddled with the beads on her dress. "I have a few old friends I'd like to see again."

"See? You do have something to look forward to. How many times have I told you to stop worrying? Besides, all you have to think about tonight is enjoying our little excursion to the upper deck."

He caught her gaze and she managed a smile. He was right. There was no need to worry about tomorrow…until tomorrow. "I am looking forward to tonight, actually. I find Mr. Windham's stories of India most amusing."

"Good, because you look beautiful."

Her heart fluttered as she tugged on one of the ivory beaded fringes of her new dress. "Mrs. Carruth insisted I buy a few dresses before arriving in New York. It's not formal, but as it's our last night, I thought I should dress up a bit for the occasion."

"Then why the frown? Don't you like it?"

She brushed her fingers against the hem that stopped midway against her calf—a far cry from the familiar long skirts, blouses, and boots she was used to wearing in the bush. "All the dresses seem so...short."

"It's not too short, it's perfect. I'll take your photo on the grand staircase just to prove it to you." He leaned forward and caught her gaze. "Trust me. You're going to be the belle of New York when you arrive."

She felt a blush rise to her cheeks and began folding up the steamer rug. "I'm afraid your prediction is exaggerated."

"Perhaps." He smiled then leaned against the back of the deck chair, his arms folded across his chest. "But I still believe that the dress—and its owner—are beautiful."

Lizzie looked away and quickly changed the subject. "Have you started planning your next expedition? I imagine there are dozens of details that must be dealt with, like who to take with you and where you will go."

"It will naturally take time."

"Where do you think you might go first?"

"My problem is not finding a place to go, but rather narrowing it down so I do not choose too many places."

"One day, I'd love to visit Egypt, though I'm not sure why. It seems so..."

"Romantic?"

"Romantic? No. More...exotic."

"Perhaps." He sat up and swung his feet back onto the deck. "But for now I was thinking that perhaps you might want to join me on one last walk around the deck, even though I've been told that it is rather romantic. This is our last night on board."

Lizzie paused at the intensity in his voice and the blueness of his eyes...and at how quickly he was able to sweep her away. But even that wasn't enough to make her drop her defenses. How many times had she reminded herself over the past couple weeks that as charming as Mr. Styles might be, nothing could change the fact that he had traveled to Africa to deliver her back to New York? Even his declarations of love had simply been a ploy to convince her to return. Nothing more.

It was something she'd willed herself not to forget. He'd remained charming and attentive while she'd erected a wall, avoiding any conversation that might include her heart.

She finished folding the blanket. "A walk around the deck would be nice. The weather is perfect out tonight."

Andrew's smile faded. "I find it interesting how all our conversations somehow manage to make it back to the weather. I suppose this is how it's going to end between us. With nothing more than talks of the weather, who's eating what for dinner, and maybe a few stories of Africa thrown in. I had hoped that by now we might have been able to delve a bit deeper into each other's lives."

"I'm sure you are mistaken."

"You haven't noticed? We talk, but never about anything personal, and if conversation veers that direction, you quickly change the subject."

"Like I said, I'm sure you are mistaken. We've talked about your travels in northern Africa and your experiences as a journalist. In fact, I was just talking to Mrs. Carruth regarding the photo you sold—"

"See? You're the master at switching topics to avoid anything personal."

"Does it really matter?" She dipped her chin. She wouldn't allow herself to dwell on the questions her heart kept asking about Andrew. "When we get to New York, I don't imagine that we will see each other again. I'll be living with my aunt and uncle while you, no doubt, will soon return to Africa."

"I suppose you're right."

He shook his head then crossed the deck, stopping at the rail.

She wasn't ready to admit aloud that he was right, but he was. She'd consciously veered their conversations toward anything from last night's dinner menu to who'd won the latest skeet shooting contest. All in order to avoid getting too personal with a man who'd already managed to turn her entire world upside down.

She dropped the blanket onto her chair, wishing for her warmer coat as the temperature began to drop, and joined him at the railing. "I'm sorry."

Andrew stared out across the choppy waters, hands in his pockets, and said nothing.

"Ask me something personal," she said.

"Excuse me?"

"Ask me a question of a personal nature, and I'll prove to you that I'm perfectly capable of handling an intelligent yet personal conversation."

"And you will answer it?"

"Yes."

"Honestly?"

She swallowed hard but kept her chin level. "Yes."

He studied her face, giving her time to wonder what she'd just done. In trying to prove she wasn't afraid of delving into the personal, she'd no doubt just managed to make a complete fool of herself. What had she been thinking?

"Okay." His lips curled into a tight smile. She'd put her heart on the line—and he thought it was humorous. "Are there any suitors waiting in the wings for your return?"

"Suitors?" His question caught her off guard.

"Suitors."

"Of course not." She squirmed at the question, while he seemed as perfectly content to meddle in her personal life as she had been to avoid it. "I had little time for romance while I was there before, due to my school schedule. And besides that, I've been gone far too long for anyone to wait for me."

"I'm not sure that is true." He caught her gaze. "There are some things I believe worth waiting for."

Lizzie turned away from him and let the cool breeze numb her senses. If she could only do the same thing with her heart. "So you've been in love before?"

The amused expression on his face hardened. Apparently her question had been too personal.

She shivered. "Andrew?"

"I didn't say that."

"You didn't say that you weren't, either."

"This was my chance to ask you a question."

"You did and I answered it."

"There was someone...once."

She studied his expression and caught the flicker of loss in his eyes.

Had the woman he'd proposed to left him because of his dreams to explore, or had he found a reason to walk out of her life? She shook her head. Wanting to avoid it herself, she'd given him little chance to talk about such personal matters. Maybe she should have taken the time to understand the man standing before her.

"Tell me about her."

CHAPTER 22

Andrew pulled his leather trench coat tighter around his shoulders, wondering how she'd managed to box him into a corner so quickly. "I thought you preferred non-personal discussions. Ones that deal solely with the mundane and unimportant."

Discussions that don't play games with your heart.

But for once he agreed. He wasn't going to talk to Lizzie about Mary.

Lizzie cocked her head. "You were in love with her, weren't you?"

"It was a long time ago." Andrew closed his eyes for a moment. It was as if she could see right into his past…and into his heart.

"And you lost her?"

He cleared his throat, wishing she'd stop prying. "I'm not sure this is a story you will want to hear."

Or understand.

"Why not?"

"Like I said, there are things you don't know about me."

"Then maybe you were right after all. Maybe it is time we stepped beyond discussions of trivial things, and I took the time to listen to you."

He shook his head. "An easy statement to make when we're talking about my past."

Determination set in her chin. "I didn't think the past was a subject you feared."

He leaned against the rail and watched the white caps breaking on the deep-blue waves, wondering how one woman had managed to tie his heart into such a tight bundle. It had been so much easier with Mary. She'd waltzed into his life one day with that long brown hair, wide smile, and a heart half the size of New York City, and captured his own heart from the first moment they'd met. And he'd let her in totally and completely. Losing his heart a second time couldn't be worth the pain he'd gone through when he'd lost Mary.

Or could it? He couldn't ignore Lizzie's probing questions. She stood beside him with those wide brown eyes, asking him to divulge intimate secrets better left buried in the past. But he couldn't get past how many times he had tried to forget that moment when he'd told her he was falling in love with her. No matter how much he wanted to ignore the fact that being with her made him want to love again...and made him want to tell her.

It was too late to stop.

He swallowed hard, feeling as if the dam inside him had just burst. "I—I always longed to go to Africa, but it wasn't as an explorer."

She brushed a strand of hair from her eyes and looked up at him. "As a writer and photographer?"

"No." He turned away from her probing gaze. "As a missionary to North Africa."

"A missionary?" Lizzie's fingers gripped the railing beside him. "I don't understand. I thought—"

"Like I said, there are a lot of things you don't know about me."

She stared at him as if she were trying to wrap her mind around the information he'd just thrown her way. While he regretted giving it to her. He started down the deck, past the row of wooden deckchairs and life preservers, toward the door leading inside. He'd spent the past month playing the role of the perfect gentleman, attentive and dutiful, in an attempt to prove to her that his feelings for her had nothing to do with the money waiting for him on the other side of the ocean, and everything to do with her.

But any attempt to win Lizzie MacTavish had become as impossible as trying to walk across North Africa's Sahara Desert.

"Andrew, stop." He felt a tug on his coat sleeve. "Please. What happened?"

Stopping, he mulled over her question. He'd made a mistake by telling her what he already had, and he had no desire to bare his heart further. He turned to look at her. Sympathy shone in her eyes. There was no use trying to pretend that the rift between them would vanish with the truth, but perhaps the ache inside his heart would manage to lessen.

He started walking the deck. "My mother's parents were strong Christians and I grew up hearing stories of David and Goliath and Daniel and the lions' den."

Lizzie hurried to keep up with his long strides.

"As a nine-year-old, I heard about Africa from a visiting missionary. It sounded exotic and exciting, and even at that age, I wanted to go there." He paused along the railing. "But it was more than that. I felt the call to go to Africa as a missionary. I wanted to serve God."

And save the world.

But he hadn't even been able to save Mary.

"By the summer I turned twenty-two, I was getting ready to leave for Africa when I met this tenacious single woman who was being sent to Africa by one of the women's societies. We fell in love and planned to go together."

There had never been a question in his mind that they wouldn't spend the rest of their lives together serving God. But God had other plans.

"What was her name?"

"Her name was Mary Franklin, and the first time we met, I knew she was the one God had prepared for me." He stared out across the water shimmering beneath the setting sun. "I suppose the very idea of my wanting to be a missionary must be a bit shocking."

"It's just that from everything you've ever told me—"

"People change because they experience both tragedy and pleasure. And sometimes events happen that are not a part of our plans." Events he still couldn't believe were a part of God's plan. "A few days before we were to marry, she came down with a serious case of influenza after volunteering in one of the local hospitals. She died two weeks later."

Lizzie pressed her hand against her month. The sympathy that had hung in her gaze was now replaced by pity. Something he didn't want. "Oh, Andrew, I'm sorry. What a horrible loss."

"I was numb at first. Not only was Mary suddenly gone, but everything we'd dreamed of doing together was over. People sent me their condolences, but most of them expected me to leave for Africa as scheduled, even if it meant going alone. Who was I to argue with the call of God?"

Reverend Kemper had sat him down in an empty corner of the funeral home on the day of Mary's service. Her wooden coffin sat in the front of the cold building, waiting to be buried.

God's call in your life hasn't changed because of Mary's death. If anything, this situation will strengthen you, because God always works situations together for good.

But there had been nothing good about losing Mary. He'd tuned out the man as he'd rambled on about suffering for Jesus. He hadn't been foolish enough to believe that life in Africa would be without its difficulties, but losing Mary...that wasn't what he'd signed up to do.

Andrew blew out a sharp sigh. "I decided that I couldn't go by myself. Leaving for Africa had been something we had planned to do together. But in the end, life has a way of going on whether you want it to or not."

"So you found another way to go."

He ignored her inquisitive look and wished he could take back his confession. His life with Mary, his dreams of working in North Africa, and the devastation he'd felt in losing them both...these were things he never planned to tell her. Most were things he'd never spoken about with anyone.

"Tell me about her."

The image of Mary brought an involuntary smile to his lips that managed to push away some of the lingering pain. "You would have liked her. She was a lot like you in many ways."

"How?"

"She was dedicated, passionate...and beautiful."

And from what he remembered, far less complicated.

The wind tugged at Lizzie's hair. "I'm afraid I've spent all this time judging you unfairly."

He caught the flicker of guilt registering in her eyes. "It was a long time ago, Lizzie."

"Not so long that the thought of her doesn't bring both joy and sadness to your eyes. What happened after she died?"

"It wasn't long after that the war started. With her gone, I didn't know what to do. All the plans we'd made together were over, so I signed up and served my country."

"But it didn't help you forget."

Her response wasn't a question, as if she knew that forgetting had been the impossible part. He'd never forgotten Mary's face that winter he'd lost her, or while he stood in the trenches halfway around the world, or any moment in between.

He shoved his hands into his pockets again and resumed walking. "The war brought with it a different kind of pain. I lost friends in the throes of battle as I tried to report what was happening."

Death and pain had swirled around him, compounding the pain of losing Mary. There had been a moment, standing on the frontlines, when he decided he'd welcome the chance to slide into oblivion. No pain. No memories of everything he'd lost. Somehow, though, he'd made it back to New York in one piece.

"What you saw there must have been horrific."

As horrible as what he'd lost spiritually.

"Mrs. Carruth asked me if God was using this situation as a way to pull me back to Him."

"How did you respond?"

"I didn't know how. I've felt the tug, but never stopped running. And why should I? Mary and I dedicated our lives to serving God. I'm not sure I'll ever understand why He let her die." The muddled mess running through his thoughts seemed to clear. "Maybe you and I are not so different after all."

"In what way?"

"I ran, and you hid."

Her eyes narrowed. "What do you mean?"

"You've spent the past few years hiding in the middle of the African savannah. Away from your aunt and uncle in New York, even the Carruths, who complain about never seeing you."

Lizzie shook her head. "That is hardly a fair comparison."

"Isn't it?"

"I—I admit that for a time I was angry at God for taking my parents, but I have not been hiding. I have been fulfilling my calling."

"And a noble calling at that." He'd thrown the guilt back at her, but he didn't care. He wasn't the only one wanting to forget his past.

"What is that supposed to mean?"

"You live in a world that's not real. Your parents raised you between two cultures, and you've spent your entire life trying to figure out which one you belong in, while never really belonging to either one."

"At least I didn't turn my back on everything I believed in."

"Passing guilt on to me isn't going to help you come to terms with who you really are."

"That makes a lot of sense, coming from you. Tell me, why is this all of a sudden about me? You're the one who, like Jonah, decided to run away."

Andrew's jaw tensed. "There's a big difference between Jonah and me. I wanted to go. I studied and prepared then found a woman who wanted to share that life with me."

"Then maybe, for whatever reason, your going to Africa with Mary wasn't a part of God's plan."

"But why wouldn't it be a part of God's plan?" It was the same question he'd asked himself over and over the past seven years. "It's not as if there were thousands of people lined up to take my place. He could have saved Mary. He could have sent us together as we planned."

"But He didn't."

Memories of Mary encircled him. Andrew felt the ship rock beneath his feet and the salty spray brush against his lips. Band music floated across the breeze from the upper deck, playing out the moment like a silent film. Waves crashed. People walked behind them in slow motion.

He'd wanted answers but had only found more questions. Mary was gone, but in losing her had he thrown away everything worth keeping?

"Jonah didn't want the direction God had chosen for him," he said finally. "I did."

"And what about now?"

Andrew forced himself not to run this time. "I don't know."

"Then maybe it's time you decided."

CHAPTER TWENTY-THREE

Andrew tossed and turned until early the next morning before finally giving up on trying to sleep. Between turbulent dreams that had included both Mary and Lizzie, he'd stared at the ceiling of the small, single-berth room, grieving for all he had lost—and regretting how far his anger and resentment had taken him.

Nothing would change the fact that Mary was gone. And just like the soldiers he'd watched die on the English coastline, who would never return to their wives and sweethearts, the life he'd planned to have with Mary would never be.

He swung his legs off the edge of the metal bed, flipped on the light, and searched for his clothes. Guilt over the blame he'd placed on Lizzie last night surfaced. He'd accused her of avoiding the truth then done everything he could to shift any blame back onto her in the very same way he'd dismissed the persistent tugging of God. Instead of following His call, he'd jumped into the belly of a smelly whale and blamed God for the outcome.

O God, what have I done?

He reached up and wiped away the beads of sweat from the back of his neck, then finished dressing. He needed time to think...and time to pray.

The sky was still dark and the air cold as he stepped onto the deck where a handful of people had gathered to witness the first signs of land.

Maybe He's pulling you back to Him…. Maybe it's time you decided.

He drew in a deep breath of the salty air and watched as his breath materialized in front of him, unable to repress the jumble of words he'd replayed in his mind a thousand times. He'd felt the tug of conscience as Jonah must have experienced during his escape from Nineveh. He'd felt it and ignored it, but today the voice called louder, and he could no longer disregard it.

Funny how he'd never thought of himself like that legendary wayward character. Fresh out of Bible college, he'd been ready to take on the world. He'd planned to sail to Africa and convert the masses of heathens across the Dark Continent. Except things hadn't turned out the way he'd planned. Mary had died. And he'd run.

Andrew stared across the choppy waters. In the silvery mist of the new day, lights flickered in the distance. New York City hung on the horizon, nestled against miles and miles of the Eastern seaboard that stretched from Florida to Maine. He should be rejoicing over the fact that with the money he received he'd be able to fund another expedition, allowing him to return to Africa. Instead he felt the heavy sting of emptiness and regret. Regret for turning his back on his Savior. And for losing Lizzie.

Stopping beside the rail, he tried to rub away the tension from the back of his neck as guilt pressed against him. Despite her stubbornness, Lizzie had been right in so many ways. He'd done everything in his power to ensure she made the return trip with him, even to the point of persuading Mrs. Carruth that returning to New York was what was best for Lizzie. He'd forced her hand so she would return and claim her fortune.

So he could in turn claim his.

They're right, God. I've been running from You for far too long.
And he was tired of running.

He continued his prayer, something that had once been the lifeline that had kept his dreams and plans focused on God's call—until he'd turned his back and tried to do things his own way. Which had turned his life into a jumbled mess with no direction.

But like a camera lens coming into focus, things were finally becoming clearer. Taking the job of finding Lizzie had been nothing more than another escape route. He knew that now. Just as he'd finally seen how far he'd traveled away from his heavenly Father.

Thankful for the quiet of the early hour, Andrew began pouring out his heart like the prodigal son who'd spent far too long away from his father's presence. Regret grew, then transformed into a wave of confession that started with his response to Mary's death and ended with his recent trip across the Atlantic.

And in the midst of his confessions, a peace began to settle over him that he never thought he'd find again.

An hour later, he headed for the stairway then stopped. Lizzie stood beside the rail, staring out across the dark waters as the engines churned beneath them. Blond hair whipped in the wind as she gathered her coat closer around her.

He couldn't help but smile. Somehow it had taken a spunky, stubborn woman to get him to realize that in all this time he'd been heading in the wrong direction. But despite the manipulating he'd done, there was one thing he'd told her that had been true. No matter how hard he'd tried to fight it, he had fallen in love with her.

Those words had been from his heart. But there was something else he had to do before making any attempts at declaring his feelings toward her. He might never have the chance to make Lizzie a part of his life, but he still needed to confess to her that he'd been wrong.

Walking along the rail, he slowly bridged the distance between them. A group of young men passed by, the anticipation of their impending arrival clear on their clean-shaven faces. Behind them, a couple strolled, hand in hand, then stopped to gaze out across the sea now sparkling like millions of diamonds from the sun that crested the eastern horizon.

He stopped halfway, suddenly unsure of what he wanted to say, and studied her profile. She had yet to see him. The wind played with the ends of her hair that had escaped her hat, but he couldn't see her face or read her expression. He did not deserve her, but that thought did little to lessen his desire for her. He reined in his thoughts. He would first apologize, and after that—maybe—she'd find a way to consider the request his heart longed to make.

But no matter what his heart desired, he held no illusions of Lizzie welcoming him home like the prodigal son and letting him become a part of her life. And for him, time had just run out. After today, there would be no more excuses to see her. No more reasons to convince her to return with him. He'd already done that. By tomorrow he'd have delivered Lizzie to her aunt and uncle and shown up at the solicitors' office to pick up his bonus that would have him heading back to explore the wonders of Africa so he could forget her.

Something he wasn't sure he could ever do.

He shoved his hands into his coat pockets. What he wanted at the moment didn't matter. Lizzie deserved someone who could come into her life and sweep her off her feet without the cumbersome baggage of a scarred past that had hardened his heart. Which meant that what he should do was walk away and forget everything that had happened between them—along with any dreams he might have foolishly grasped on to.

He turned away then stopped as she looked up and caught his gaze. A faint smile played across her lips.

His heart pounded. His feet wouldn't move. He'd meant it when he said he didn't want to run anymore. He tried to read her expression as she walked toward him. Some of the tension from last night appeared to have lessened, but he didn't miss the caution in her gaze.

Lizzie was the first to break the silence between them. "Good morning."

"Good morning." He bridged the final few feet between them. "Couldn't sleep?"

Lizzie felt her lungs expand and her heart quicken, despite the dozen times she'd had to remind her heart that she didn't care. "I—I wanted a first glimpse of the New York City skyline, and the porter told me that this would be the best time, before the deck became filled with excited passengers waiting to disembark."

While her words were true, she had no intention of telling him the rest of the truth. That she'd spent half the night praying she could find a way to forget him. But instead of the peace she'd longed for, her dreams had been filled with haunting scenes from Kakoba's village, the terror she'd felt on the Zambezi...and of Andrew.

Still, she watched him, trying to determine whether or not his hopeful expression had something to do with her. Andrew was clearly a man who'd spent his life getting what he wanted. Hadn't he made that clear with her?

No. Today was the last day she had to see Andrew. And while she still harbored a measure of resentment over what had happened between them, it was time to say good-bye and forget Andrew Styles.

The feeling of relief she'd prayed for in the wee hours of the night didn't come. Instead, Andrew's nearness left her with feelings of regret and loss. As if a small part of her wished that today wasn't the last time she'd see him. Wishing she could believe his claims that he'd fallen in love with her.

She shook her head and tried to chase away the longing flooding her heart. Theirs was a love that could never—would never—be.

"It's the perfect time to be out here, isn't it?" His smile melted a layer of the coolness she'd erected around her heart. "It will get quite crowded before long, but for the moment it's worth being out here just to see the sunlight sparkling like jewels across the water. And if you look to the west, you can see a hint of the skyline coming into view."

"It's beautiful. The water's so endless, like the savannah." Lizzie pulled her coat closer around her to block the chill that colored her breath white. She tried to ignore his blue eyes that seemed to see right through her, and searched for a distraction. "I remember the first time we sailed back to the United States. I was nine, and I'd never stepped foot off the African soil. I was terrified yet fascinated at the same time."

She'd stood among the other second-class passengers, secretly thankful that they hadn't sailed in the third class like those who would have to endure the time-consuming process of being ferried to Ellis Island and questioned by doctors and immigration.

"It seems so long ago, but I still remember the magic of that first arrival. Can you imagine a young girl, who'd never been out of Northern Rhodesia, suddenly thrust into a world with automobiles, skyscrapers, and people everywhere? I was enthralled and terrified all at the same moment."

"I would love to have seen your reaction."

"My father stood beside me along the rail with the spray of the surf below us and the city of New York ahead of us. Through the Ambrose channel, then to Pier 90. Passengers lined up against the railing for their chance to catch a glimpse of the Long Island coastline. And then the skyline came into view. It was like a giant sea wall and unlike anything I'd ever seen."

Andrew's smile broadened. "The first time I saw the harbor come into view after my first trip to Africa, I remember clearly the familiar tug of Africa that had not yet let me go, clashing with the familiar pull of home."

"I suppose that describes how I feel. I miss Kakoba and his family so much it hurts, and yet I suppose, if I were completely honest, there is a part of me that is excited to be back. My parents loved New York, and my grandfather wanted me to return. Now it makes me wonder if I shouldn't have returned sooner. Before he died."

"You'll never be able to change the past. Just the future."

She mulled over his words. "I suppose you're right."

"Which is why I need to speak to you. Lizzie…I'm sorry about last night. I never should have accused you of hiding. What you do with your life is not for me to judge. Unlike me, you've obeyed God's calling. Can you forgive me?"

Forgiveness came easier than she'd thought. "I forgive you. I realize now that you were simply following through with a commitment you'd made to my grandfather's solicitors."

"That is where you are wrong. Finding you was never simply a job,

Lizzie. Or rather, that isn't what it became after I met you. What happened between us these past few weeks made my job personal. I'm not ready to just walk away."

She considered the implications of his words. Was there a chance that he really did care for her? She studied his face, the shape of his lips, the strength of his jawline, and the unspoken words in his gaze, and felt her heart tremble. Maybe if the situation had been different she'd be able to consider a life together with him, but the situation wasn't different. She held a calling by God she intended to follow. Andrew, on the other hand, had clearly rejected his. "Andrew, I don't think—"

"Lizzie, wait. Before you say anything else, there is also something I want you to know. I've had almost a month to grapple with a number of things, and you were right about one."

She shot him a coy smile. "Only one?"

Andrew chuckled. "I'm sure between the two of us we could come up with a dozen more things I need to get right, but there's only one that really matters right now. It's a scary thing to realize that you've spent the last few years running and don't like where you've ended up."

She studied his handsome profile, welcoming his honesty. "Where do you want to be?"

"At a place where I don't have to run anymore."

Her mind refused to hope. "Where is that?"

"I don't know. Africa is one of those places that gets in your blood, holds on tight, and refuses to let you go. I still have this dream to return and explore the interior. Much of its beauty has already been found, but there is still so much more to be discovered."

"I'm sure you'll be successful in your quest."

"But it's not just about success anymore. Unless—"

"Unless what?"

"God has finally led me to the point where I realize the foolishness of shoving Him out of my life. I want—need—Him to be the center of my plans once again, but there is something else. Something that affects you. I want you in my life, Lizzie. I'm not ready to lose you."

She felt her heart explode. These were the words she'd feared, yet at the same time the ones she'd longed to hear.

She pressed her hands against her chest and tried to calm her tangled emotions. "I don't know."

She'd spent the night praying that God would take away her desire. Doubts over his sincerity clashed with her longing to believe him. They were like two floundering, wounded hearts that had crossed paths, but were never meant to be together.

"I won't press you into giving me any answers today, but neither can I walk away without telling you how I feel."

She searched his gaze. "Please don't. We're an ocean apart in who we are, how we look at life, as well as in our hopes and dreams for the future."

"Because I ran and you didn't?" he asked.

"Yes... No." She didn't know how to search through her muddled thoughts.

"I'm not so sure that we're really that different, but what I do know is that I can't just walk away, ignoring these feelings I have for you. When we first met, you were unlike anyone I'd ever known before. Passionate and adventurous, yet at the same time feminine and charming."

While her heart worked to grasp his words, there was a burning question she had to ask. "Like Mary?"

"No." Andrew shook his head. "Not like Mary. I loved Mary, and will probably always miss her, but she's gone. And nothing I do or think or wish will bring her back. She's a part of my past. You're a part of right now."

Someone jostled against her as the deck began to fill with passengers, anxious for their arrival. "When you came to Africa it was all about the money and what you planned to do with it."

"It was, at the beginning. But now, there is no reason for me to pursue you any longer unless my feelings are true. I meant what I said to you that night in Africa. I didn't expect to fall in love with you, but I have."

"Andrew, I…"

He tilted her chin until she had to look up at him. "Don't say anything. Not yet. I know you see me as some heathen who's searching for fame and fortune, but in the past couple weeks I've been forced to grapple with who I really am. And all that I thought would make me happy suddenly isn't enough anymore."

"It would never work between us."

"How do you know that?"

"Because once I've taken care of my grandfather's estate and fulfilled his wishes of staying, I plan to return to Northern Rhodesia. And I believe I know you enough to see that you'd be restless living the isolated life I lead."

He pressed his hands against her shoulders then brushed his lips across hers. "Tell me you don't feel anything, and I'll walk away."

She pulled back and touched her mouth with the back of her hand. "What I feel right now doesn't matter."

"Of course it does. I believe that I know you enough to see that you want a family and children one day, and that you've imagined that life with me. All I'm asking is for you to give me a chance. Give us a chance. I'd like to see you again once you get settled in at your aunt and uncle's home and see if we can't make something work between us."

Her mind swam as the grand skyline came into view before them on the now crowded deck. She wanted him to kiss her again, to tell her that he loved her and that everything was going to be okay because he wasn't going to leave her.

"I'm through running, Lizzie. What about you? Are you through hiding?"

Tears pooled in her eyes. "I don't know."

"Don't let your fear cost you something you'll later regret. If I come by your aunt's house would you see me?"

Her hands gripped the railing as she grappled with his words. "It's not that simple."

"Why not?"

"Because no matter what either of us might feel or even want in this situation, we don't share the same dreams."

"What if that weren't true anymore?"

"Andrew—"

"Maybe now it's time *you* decided." Andrew pulled her against his chest and kissed her again, this time lingering for a long breathless moment before turning away and disappearing into the crowd.

NEW YORK CITY, NEW YORK

———————

1921

CHAPTER TWENTY-FOUR

Living in Northern Rhodesia for most of her twenty-five years had made the endless African savannah her home and New York the foreign country. Lizzie gripped the seat of the taxi as they left the pink granite facades of the Chelsea Piers and headed toward the east side of Manhattan. She peered out the fingerprint-smudged window as their driver maneuvered through the six narrow lanes of heavy traffic that were flanked by massive high-rise buildings, elegant brownstone row houses, and the occasional cathedral.

Her fingers clutched the seat tighter. Even though her parents grew up and eventually fell in love here, the looming structures and masses of pedestrians rushing past were as unfamiliar as fetching water in a large calabash would be to her aunt Ella.

"Are you all right?"

Lizzie turned from the chaotic scene outside to Andrew's questioning look. When the Carruths left for Maine after the RMS *Berengaria*'s arrival at the pier, Andrew had insisted on delivering her to her aunt and uncle's home, something she was grateful for despite the unfinished conversation hanging between them. She dropped her gaze from his face that served as a reminder of their kiss and focused instead on the stain on his collar.

Maybe it's time you decide.

A deep longing for what could be between them clashed with the reality of the situation. She'd meant it when she told him that a relationship between them wouldn't be simple. Even if he had found his way home spiritually, their dreams encompassed too great a span.

The blast of a car horn and the sudden right turn of the taxi jerked her back to the present—and to Andrew's question.

Was she all right? She pondered her answer. "I'm nervous, excited... and everything seems so different. It's as if I stepped through a long tunnel and emerged into another world."

"Which is pretty much exactly what you have done. Africa is a world away from New York City."

"I remember the crowds of pedestrians and the noise and long rows of buildings that seem to touch the sky, but it seems even more crowded now."

"That's because it is. Time doesn't stand still just because you're not here. With a population of around six million, New York has already been hailed as a center for manufacturing, commerce, and, of course, the growing music scene. I don't see things slowing down anytime soon."

"There are just so many automobiles, and people, and buildings."

He shot her a smile. "We could have taken the subway."

"Thank you, but no." The thought of being enclosed in the underground transport system, no matter how safe it was said to be, had to be far worse than crossing the city by taxi.

Andrew leaned back in the seat, looking perfectly relaxed. "Don't worry. We're almost there."

He was right. Five minutes later, the taxi came to a stop along Thirty-sixth Street. Lizzie looked out from the yellow cab to the narrow, four-story townhouse that sat nestled in one of Manhattan's networks of neighborhoods. "I'd forgotten how grand the house is."

Andrew helped her from the cab then paid the fare and helped the cabbie with their pile of luggage.

Lizzie waited on the sidewalk and was still staring up at the towering structure when he'd finished.

"Lizzie?"

"I'm sorry." She breathed in the exhaust fumes from the idling car and tried to gather her frayed nerves. "I appreciate your escorting me here."

"Do you want me to come inside?"

She nodded. She wasn't ready to make the entrance on her own. "I'm sure my aunt would like to thank you."

Holding her small handbag, she made her way up the narrow steps to the ground floor, wishing foolishly she could vanish like the morning mist that hung across the veld. If she closed her eyes, she was back in Kakoba's windowless hut. The faint scent of smoke rose from the clay fireplace that sat on the hard clay floor. Esther sat playing with her doll in the corner of the room, Chuma in another with one of his spears.

I threw a spear, threw a spear, in the east, in the east...

The large door with its thick leaded glass swung open, revealing a uniformed maid.

"Welcome home, Miss MacTavish. Your aunt is expecting you in the garden."

Lizzie stepped inside the high-ceilinged foyer. The house smelled of spiced apples and cinnamon and reminded her of teatime in the parlor with her aunt's friends—and of their probing questions about life in the Dark Continent. She pushed aside the memories and walked past the wood-burning fireplace, with its marble mantel and the curved staircase leading to the second floor, toward the large, private garden in the back of the house.

"Aunt Ella?"

Her aunt sat in the corner of the patio in a wheelchair wearing a dull green dress and covered with a thick blanket around her legs. Her once long brown hair, now thin and prematurely gray, was pulled back into a long braid that hung over her shoulder.

"Lizzie." Her aunt's smile broadened as she wheeled across the stone patio in her wooden chair with its wire wheels and caned seat. "You'll have to excuse the sparse garden. I wish you could have seen it in the spring. We planted every color of flower you can imagine, but now with winter upon us it's sorely lacking in color."

"There's no need to worry about that. I didn't come all this way to see your garden."

Lizzie swallowed the lump of grief swelling inside her chest. Five years ago, her aunt had been the belle of New York City, enchanting her audiences with popular renditions of "By the Light of the Silvery Moon" and "Let Me Call You Sweetheart." Today, she'd become a gaunt shadow of the past.

She forced a smile. "It's good to see you, Aunt Ella."

"Let me look at you, Lizzie." Her aunt's hands trembled as she grasped Lizzie's. "You've grown into quite a beautiful young woman, though I was afraid you might return with one of those heathens at your side."

Lizzie bit back a harsh response as she pulled away. Her aunt had never understood the reason her parents had left.

She motioned toward Andrew. "The only person with me is Mr. Styles, who graciously accompanied me from the ship. I believe you've already met."

"Ah, Mr. Styles. It's quite good to see you again." Her aunt's smile brightened. "You must say you'll stay for dinner. I'm sure my husband will want to thank you personally for bringing Lizzie home to us. It's been far too long since we've been together and so tragic that it took my failing health and a death in the family to bring my niece home."

"I…" Lizzie searched for something to say.

Her aunt laughed. "I'm teasing you, you know. The few times I saw your mother after she moved away, she always managed to glow despite Africa's harsh conditions, and you, it seems, are no different."

"I consider it a compliment to be compared to my mother."

"She was a wonderful woman, but I don't want to talk about the past right now." She waved them toward the wrought-iron table that had been covered with a linen tablecloth and her aunt's silver tea service. "Dinner won't be ready for a while, so come sit down and have some tea with me. I have so many questions for you, Lizzie. About your trip across the Atlantic, but in particular, about your future."

"My future?" Lizzie sat down at the table between Andrew and her aunt.

"There's so much to discuss and plan."

"I don't understand." The only plan she had for her future was returning home as soon as she fulfilled her grandfather's wishes.

"Please, help yourself. I had Maria prepare something light for your arrival in case you were hungry." Her aunt uncovered a plate of small tea sandwiches and sweetbreads then set one of each on her small plate. "Now, back to your future. To begin with, I've arranged a large party for your homecoming this Friday. You know I've never felt comfortable with your overseas commission. Because as much as your parents loved Africa, I'm quite certain that they would agree with me that living among the heathens is no place for a young single woman of your status."

Lizzie blinked. "But I have no intention of staying permanently—"

"Your grandfather in particular knew you thought that way. He worried about you. We all do. Which means if that is how you are thinking, then it is up to me to convince you otherwise." Aunt Ella gripped

Lizzie's hand. "I've always seen you as the daughter I never had, especially after your mother died. We need each other. And you need me to find you a rich young man who will marry you and give you a passel of babies that I can call my grandchildren. That should be enough to curb your desire to return."

Andrew choked on his sandwich.

Lizzie ignored his amused stare. "But—"

"Before you say anything else, there is one other pressing matter to discuss. Where in the world did you get this dress?" Aunt Ella tugged on the sleeve of Lizzie's dress, her frown deepening.

"My dress…I…" Lizzie glanced at Andrew, who had just taken a bite of sandwich and was clearly not going to help. "Before setting sail in Cape Town, Mrs. Carruth thought it would be appropriate to use a small portion of my allowance to buy some clothes that were more— more suitable for New York."

Lizzie pressed her lips together. Apparently she'd been wrong.

Aunt Ella shot her a disapproving look. "While her intentions might have been good, Mrs. Carruth clearly has no sense of fashion. You will soon have enough money now to have an entire wardrobe many times over. You must think about your future and the image you want to portray."

"But I—"

"Don't worry." Aunt Ella reached for another sweetbread. "It's something we can remedy tomorrow, as I already have a seamstress scheduled to come in. She's incredible with design and will have an entire wardrobe made for you by the end of the month."

Lizzie didn't comment. Instead she took a sandwich from the plate and contemplated booking passage on the next ship across the Atlantic.

CHAPTER TWENTY-FIVE

"How is your dessert, Mr. Styles?"

Andrew held out his cup while Mrs. MacTavish refilled his coffee. "Excellent. Thank you. I appreciate your invitation to stay and eat dinner with you."

Mr. MacTavish took another helping of the raspberry mousse. "I'd love to hear about your plans, Mr. Styles. I'm sure you remember that I was quite enthralled with the stories you told us last time, though I hope, for the sake of my niece, that this recent trip was considerably less eventful."

Andrew glanced at Lizzie, who had spoken little throughout the meal of roast lamb and potatoes. "It was, for the most part, rather uneventful."

"Now I find that hard to believe." Mr. MacTavish took a long sip of his coffee and looked at Lizzie. "I don't remember your parents ever coming back without at least one or two stories that would terrify most people, isn't that true, Lizzie? Stories of savages, tribal wars, and those dreaded diseases they're all dying from."

Lizzie remained focused on her dessert, no doubt irritated at the implication that men like Kakoba were savages. "We did have several interesting encounters that included a snake and a hippo, but no dreaded diseases or war, or attacks by savages for that matter."

"Ah, then I was right. Which must give you, Mr. Styles, plenty of fodder for your writing."

Andrew vacillated between Mr. MacTavish's enthusiasm and Lizzie's certain disgust. "I have several newspapers interested in my writing features on what I experienced."

"Then I will look forward to reading them. Where will you be staying while you're here?"

"With my brother." Andrew noted the tinge of relief in Lizzie's expression. "He lives on the Lower East Side of Manhattan."

Mr. MacTavish nodded. "Ah...yes. I remember you telling me that the last time we met, though I suppose that before long you'll be heading back to Africa with the funds you procured for bringing Lizzie back to us."

"That was the plan, yes."

"Was the plan?"

Andrew took the last bite of his dessert then set his spoon on his plate and avoided Lizzie's gaze. "A lot happened on the trip to make me reconsider my future. And I haven't had time to fully explore what those new options might be."

"Well, Lizzie's future is certainly full of options and opportunities. With the Christmas season upon us, her schedule is going to be full of parties and—"

"Would you mind if I stepped out into the garden for a few moments?" Lizzie pressed her napkin to her lips then pushed back her chair. "I need some fresh air."

Mrs. MacTavish shook her head. "Of course not, but don't you think it's a bit too chilly this time of night? I've heard we should expect the first snow of the season any day now."

"I'll be fine. I have the coat I brought with me."

"But are you sure you're feeling all right, Lizzie?" Mrs. MacTavish set her napkin onto her lap. "I know with such a long trip across the Atlantic and with you still recovering from being sick—"

"I'm fine, really." Her smile was forced. "I've fully recovered from my bout with malaria. I just need some fresh air."

Andrew watched her leave then pushed back his chair. "If you'll excuse me, I think I'll go with her."

He left before the older couple had a chance to reply and followed Lizzie out of the house and into the large, private garden.

"Are you all right?"

"I can't breathe in there." Lizzie pulled off her shoes and tossed them onto the ground before digging her feet into the patch of grass in the middle of the garden.

"Your aunt was right." He handed her the coat she'd left in the house. "You're going to catch something far worse than malaria being out here without shoes and a coat."

"I don't care. Besides, you looked as if you needed to be rescued as much as I did."

"From what?"

"From a future of formal dinners, invitations, stuffy conversation, and people who have no idea why I do what I do." She plopped down on the grass, lay back, and stared up at the sky. "I miss the thousands of stars hanging overhead at night and the smell of smoke in the air from the cooking fires."

"There's always the smell of fumes from passing cars."

She laughed. "That is not the same, and you know it. The noise here is unbearable with the crowded streets and rows and rows of automobiles."

"You're right." He smiled as he lay down beside her on the

manicured lawn, disappointed that the lights of the city obscured all but a handful of stars. "There are no sounds of the young men ringing bells to call in the cows at dusk."

"Or women stamping corn for their dinner."

"Or blacksmiths hammering out a hoe."

"Or children singing while playing *kulea miumba*." Lizzie giggled. "I miss them, Andrew. I miss Esther's sweet smile, Chuma's attempts to be a man, and Posha's new baby. I'm so worried about them."

"I know. Tonight I even missed Posha's porridge, though the dessert was delicious. What was that brown gelled appetizer?"

"My aunt called it a jellied anchovy mould."

"It was horrid."

"It was…cultured. That's how my aunt has always lived. Appearances are everything. Which is why I'm scheduled for dress fittings tomorrow, and shopping for shoes and accessories."

He rolled over onto his side and leaned up on his elbow. "If we were holding Friday's party in Kakoba's village, your aunt would have to shave her head and cover it with butter."

"Oh, I know dozens of men who would find that quite fashionable," she said.

"And we would have to ensure that your uncle's front teeth were missing."

Her giggle was contagious. He started laughing, unable to stop until his chest hurt and he couldn't breathe. He lay back down, listening to her breathe beside him.

She reached over and brushed her fingers across his hand before pulling away. "Thank you for being here with me tonight."

"I can't imagine being anywhere else right now."

He hesitated, not wanting to ruin the moment. There was so much he wanted to say. To remind her that he loved her and that he didn't want to lose her. To tell her that he'd travel anywhere, live anywhere just to be with her... But this was not a moment he wanted lost because he rushed her. Instead he savored the feel of the grass beneath him, the whisper of her breath beside him, and the knowledge that at this moment she wanted him to be with her.

"Give yourself some time," he said finally. "You'll get used to things here."

"I'm not sure I want to get used to the constant talk of food and clothes and parties."

"And a future husband for yourself."

"Don't forget he must be rich."

"Which excludes me, I suppose."

He waited for her laughter, but this time there was none.

"She is determined to run my life, isn't she?"

"She cares about you. But knowing you, I'm quite certain that getting you to do anything you don't want to do is going to be quite impossible."

"You're right. I have no interest in marrying someone for prestige or because they come from a wealthy family. All I want to do right now is settle my grandfather's estate, get through the next year, and return home."

"And until then?"

"I suppose I'll have to put up with my aunt's antics." She sat up and wrapped her arms around her knees. "Will you be at the party on Friday?"

"Do you want me to come?"

"Yes." She nodded. "And I want to go home."

"You will."

His heart fought with whatever common sense he still had. Pressuring her to give him an answer as to how she felt would only push her away. But try to tell that to his heart. "Lizzie, I—"

"I need to go back inside." She started to get up. "They will wonder what has become of me."

He helped her to her feet. Their fingers entwined, but he didn't move away. The moon hung above them, spilling its rays across her face and capturing the moment. "I probably should leave."

She looked up at him with those big brown eyes. "Promise you'll be here on Friday?"

He nodded.

Until Friday.

He slipped out the front door of the house without another word and without looking back.

Lizzie stood in the middle of the lawn as Andrew left the garden. It had felt good to laugh until her sides ached and tears had trickled down her cheeks—not from sorrow, but from an unexpected sense of joy.

And it was all because of him.

But if that were true, then what was stopping her from admitting what her heart felt? What if they could find a way to span the distance between their two worlds? She shivered in the chilly night breeze, but the warmth of his hand on hers remained. She couldn't deny that his presence had become like a salve on her spirit as he'd become the bridge between their two worlds.

Maybe it was time to decide.

She bent down and picked up her shoes, savoring the notion like an unopened gift.

"Lizzie?" Her uncle appeared at the edge of the patio. "I was worried about you when you didn't return. Aren't you cold out here?"

"I'm sorry." She finished slipping on her shoes as her uncle crossed the open space between them. "I'm still trying to get used to the feeling of being so confined."

"I suppose New York isn't anything like Northern Rhodesia."

"The two worlds hold little in common and unfortunately for me right now, this is the foreign one."

Her uncle started walking with her back to the house. "I'm not so sure that it's as unfortunate as you imply. I've envied your situation at times. Sometimes I long for the simplicity of life that I imagine you've found on the other side of the Atlantic." The lines around his eyes deepened. "It seems that the older I get, the more I dislike the complications opportunity often brings."

"It isn't always easy, but there is something comforting in the simple things of life—growing your own food, harvesting its bounty, gazing up at the canopy of stars at night."

"Perhaps it will be my turn one day to cross the Atlantic and visit your home."

"I would like that." She paused at the edge of the patio. "Before we go in, I wanted to talk to you about Aunt Ella. I'm worried about her."

"I've watched her deteriorate in front of me the past few months, and some days even I can't believe it. There are mornings when I wake up hoping to find the woman I married, but in her place is someone I hardly recognize."

"What do the doctors say?"

Her uncle sat down on the wooden bench beside the stone wall of the house and clutched his hands in front of him. "They can't find anything wrong with her. At first she simply grew tired. She started taking naps in the afternoon and retiring early in the evening. Then she stopped hosting the dinner parties and luncheons she'd always enjoyed and began canceling performances…until one day, she wasn't singing anymore."

Lizzie sat next to him. "I'm so sorry. If I had known her health had deteriorated and that my grandfather was dying…I would have come."

"There is no need for you to blame yourself. I might not be one for religion, but I understand that one needs to follow one's own heart."

As with Andrew?

She pushed away the thought. This moment was not about her.

"Can I be perfectly honest with you, Lizzie?"

"Of course."

"I can understand how you've never been completely comfortable here, but we would like you to consider remaining here with us in New York."

"Permanently?"

Even though her aunt had expressed the same desire, everything within her revolted at her uncle's words. Unbridled emotions she'd tried to hold on to resurfaced. Fear if she stayed. Guilt if she left.

"I can't stay—"

"You belong here. That was what your grandfather hoped you would come to see. And there is something else. I don't know if your aunt's deterioration is something physical or emotional, but when she found out you were coming, it was as if I had my Ella back again."

"I don't understand."

"You've given her a reason to get up in the morning. Ever since we received the telegram with the news that you were returning, she's been planning your welcome home party, luncheons and teas, and arranging to have a seamstress design a new wardrobe for you."

All the things she'd hoped to escape.

"She even started playing the piano again," he continued. "She needs you here. I need you here. This is where you belong."

"I don't know if I can."

"Please, Lizzie. Just think about it. I know your father and I never saw eye to eye on much of anything, and the same could be said about my father and me. But Ella and I can be the family you lost. Just think about it. You have money to do whatever you want now. With Ella's contacts you'll be able to meet and marry a man who is well established in the community. I know you've spent your entire life living in a different world, but give it some time; you'll fit into this one."

Lizzie shook her head. She'd never fit in here.

"Just think about what I'm saying, Lizzie. Perhaps it's time for a new season in your life."

CHAPTER TWENTY-SIX

Andrew followed his brother Charlie down the short flight of stairs to the narrow sidewalk below. His sister-in-law needed both a half-dozen eggs for supper and a break from Leo, their energetic four-year-old. Andrew needed some time to clear his head after being cooped up inside the tight quarters of the apartment for the past three days. There was clearly something to Lizzie's preference for open spaces and fresh air.

A few steps down the sidewalk lining the long row of tenement buildings made him momentarily second-guess his desire to get out. Neither openness nor fresh air were available as they dodged pedestrians and breathed in the thick fumes from the heavy traffic.

"Remind me again why you insist on living in the city?" Andrew spoke above the noisy scene.

"Because I've lived here my entire life."

Andrew laughed. If it weren't for some innate desire to see beyond the East River, he'd never have left either. He'd grown up exploring the city with its elevated trains, surface trolleys, and subways. In the Lower East End, he could feast on onion rolls as he strolled down the crowded streets, past soap sellers, barbershops, and butchers, while the subtle smells of garlic and cheese, cabbage and fish surrounded him.

New York City to him was like the African savannah was to Lizzie. A part of him never wanted to completely leave it behind. But as he thrived on the chaotic scene around him, he tried to imagine the city through Lizzie's eyes.

Instead of open plains with their occasional outcropping of trees and sprawling villages, tenement buildings rose from the ground like giants that cast gray shadows across the neighborhoods. Here, Germans, Italians, Jews, and Irish had converged on the city, along with his own immigrant grandparents, looking for better lives for their families.

The never-ending noise from the gasoline cars filled the morning air along with the musical inflections of dozens of languages. Double-decker buses passed children playing jump rope on the sidewalk. Pushcarts, full of fruit and baked goods, pretzels and cigars lined the streets, competing with merchants who sold from ground floor storefronts with canvas awnings covering sidewalk displays.

"So how long are you staying this time?"

Andrew considered his brother's question. Even the timbre of the English language must sound foreign to Lizzie.

"Is Pearl ready for me to leave?"

His brother chuckled. "No. You're lucky she likes you. I'm the one asking."

"Thanks for the vote of confidence, big brother." Constant sparring as children had evolved into comfortable banter once they'd become adults. "Now that I have the money that was due me, I suppose it's time to decide. I need to finish up a number of articles for some magazines and get my photos developed."

Charlie lifted Leo, who clutched his small rubber ball in his hands, onto his shoulders then picked up his pace as they headed north toward Hamilton Fish Park.

"You haven't forgotten the reason you left for Africa this last time, have you? To make enough money to fund an exploration party?"

"Of course not. But it's going to take time to organize the trip. I've only been back three days."

A car roared down the street, blaring its horn as they started to cross. Andrew stepped back onto the edge of the curb beside his brother and waited for it to pass. He was stalling and he knew it, but if he left now, he'd lose Lizzie. On the other hand, she had yet to reveal her feelings to him. If he stayed, there was no guarantee things would work out between them.

Leo squealed atop his father's shoulders as they crossed the busy street. "Sounds to me as if there's more to your bringing a woman half-way around the world than simply fulfilling your part of a business deal."

"That's all it was supposed to be." Until he'd fallen in love. "Remember how we used to listen to stories of Grandpa's travels and dream about setting sail across the ocean for Africa, China, and Australia? We were going to explore the world and discover hidden treasure like King Solomon's Mines."

"I remember."

He studied his brother's tall, lanky frame and the crop of red hair his sons had all inherited. "Then you met Pearl and lost your head."

"I can't say I ever thought about it that way."

"Maybe not, but as much as I like Pearl, I used to resent your leaving me to go alone." Andrew breathed in the savory smell of steak, *kishka*, and hot fries as they passed one of the eateries, and felt his stomach growl. "I don't think I've ever seen a guy fall so hard for a woman."

"And I've never been quite the same since."

"How could you be with three boys and another baby on the way? I remember a time when marriage and the thought of having kids was as foreign as places we planned to explore."

"Maybe so, but you won't see me complaining. They, along with Pearl, are the best things that ever happened to me."

Andrew reached up and tickled his nephew. Leo giggled as he clutched a handful of his father's hair in one hand and his ball in the other. "'You know I'm happy for you, Charlie. I really am."

Charlie stopped to face Andrew in front of a family-owned butchery, with Leo's feet dangling against his chest. "I know you still miss Mary."

Andrew shrugged off the concern and started walking again. "A part of me misses what we were to have, but it was a long time ago, and a lot has happened between then and now."

The war…Africa…Lizzie…

"When are you going to stop running, little brother?"

A flash of anger surfaced. "You too?"

"What do you mean?"

"You're not the only person who's asked me that lately."

"It's because I know you so well. You ran off to war, then when the troops all came home you couldn't stay around to celebrate. No, you were off on some crazy quest to Africa, and now this time you went there to bring back a woman, of all the crazy things."

Andrew stopped in front of a vender selling flowers and picked up a colorful mixture.

"And spiritually?"

He pushed back another wave of anger. "I'm slowly finding my way back."

"I'm glad to hear that. I don't think there's a night that goes by when Pearl doesn't pray for you over the dinner table."

Andrew scribbled an address and note on a piece of paper then handed it to the seller along with enough money to cover both the flowers and the delivery.

"Sending flowers?"

"I just thought I'd...cheer someone up."

"Who is she?"

Andrew frowned. His brother had always been able to read him. It had been a curse growing up that had kept him from getting away with anything.

"Lizzie MacTavish. The girl I brought back from Africa."

"Or should you say dragged back against her will, if I understood your story correctly over dinner last night. She doesn't exactly sound like a woman wanting to be wooed."

"I was just doing a job." He thanked the seller and continued up the busy street. "From what I've already heard, it sounds like this became more than a job," Charlie said.

Andrew remained silent as they finally entered the park where he and Charlie had played as children. Asphalt walks, basketball and tennis courts, and outdoor landscaping had all been built to bring a sense of the countryside to a crowded urban population.

Leo tugged on the collar of his father's jacket and squealed when he saw the playground.

"Nothing has changed," Charlie said. "I remember your asking mom one day if you could set up a tent and camp here for the summer."

Andrew swung Leo off his father's shoulders. "Every kid needs a wide open space where they can run and play."

"Tell me what else happened over there that's got my carefree brother so pensive."

Andrew sat on one of the benches beside his brother and watched Leo play catch with another little boy. "It's hard to explain."

Charlie folded his arms across his chest, his gaze on Leo. "While you fascinated Pearl and me last night with your tales of floating down the Zambezi and inter-tribal conflicts, I found it quite interesting that you included very few mentions of Miss MacTavish. Is she in love with you? Or is it the other way around?"

Andrew dropped his gaze. "I never said I was in love with her."

"Ah, but you just did. You answered too quickly. You always were easy to read."

"So you've said."

"All I know is that if she's the one, grab her while you can, because it's worth it, Andrew. Settle down, marry the girl, have babies, and forget about everything else that used to be important to you."

"That's not so easy. I'm still waiting for her to figure out what she wants."

"You think she'll go back to Africa?"

"Considering the fact she didn't want to come in the first place? Definitely."

"Can you see yourself living there? Permanently?"

"I'm not sure."

"Did you mention your hesitancy when you told her you loved her?"

Charlie's question burned through Andrew's conscience. Returning to New York had brought with it a sense of reality. He loved the travel and adventure but wasn't sure he could see himself spending the rest of his life in a thatched hut and hunting his dinner.

"Maybe you don't have to worry about that question." Charlie caught the ball Leo threw, then tossed it back to him. "If she falls in love with you, she'll start thinking of a family and having children. Do you really think she'll want to trudge through the heart of Africa with a bunch of children in tow?" Charlie caught the ball Leo threw him. "Trust me, no matter what they say, women want stability, and she's not going to find that there."

Andrew wasn't so sure. "You've never met Lizzie."

"You've never been married." Charlie tossed the ball back to Leo. "My list of priorities changed to making sure I had enough money for diapers, bottles, and clothes, which means you can forget exploring the Dark Continent. Give her a couple months and she'll change her mind and want to settle down right here in some posh Manhattan neighborhood with her family fortune."

Andrew shook his head. Lizzie would never be happy here.

"There's something else you need to know about Lizzie's family," Charlie continued.

"What's that?"

Charlie tossed the ball back to his son. "Go play on the playground for a few minutes, Leo. I need to talk to your uncle Andrew."

Leo scampered off to play and Charlie leaned forward on the bench and faced Andrew. "Everyone's heard the rumors of Mr. MacTavish's extensive gambling debts. How he manages to live the way he does, I have no idea, because the rumors have been circulating for as long as I can remember. But now there's talk that he's in trouble with one of the mob bosses."

Andrew sat back and clasped his hands in front of him. Finding yourself in trouble with the mob was worse than being on the wrong side of the law. "What did he do?"

"According to the rumors, he borrowed a large amount of money from a friend in order to produce illegal liquor that would in turn be sold to and distributed by the mob."

An uneasy feeling settled over Andrew. "Another one of his get-rich-quick schemes?"

"Yes, but the problem this time was that the liquor was stolen before he was able to deliver the final product. Now, not only can he not pay back his loan, but he can't even go to the police and claim the goods stolen."

"Because the goods in question were illegally produced." Andrew tried to play out different scenarios in his mind, but each one ended in calamity. "If this is true, he's in a lot of trouble."

And Lizzie—and her fortune—had just become a possible target.

"How reliable are these rumors?" Andrew asked.

"Considering my source, reliable enough for me to believe them."

Andrew shivered. Lizzie's inheritance might be a solution to her uncle's financial problems, but that fact alone didn't mean he was desperate enough to want to harm her.

"What is it?" Charlie asked.

Andrew shook his head. "I don't know."

Surely it wasn't possible. Her uncle might be a womanizer who foolishly gambled away the profits from his business, but even that didn't make him a murderer. No. Which meant the incidents in Africa couldn't have had anything to do with Lizzie's uncle or any financial trouble he might be facing.

Andrew stood and began pacing in front of the bench. That was what he wanted to believe. But no matter how hard he tried, he couldn't dismiss the feeling that what had happened in Africa hadn't been a coincidence. Thomas MacTavish wouldn't be the first man who gambled on success no matter what the cost. And if that were true, Lizzie's life could be in danger.

Andrew shivered then shoved his hands into the pockets of his coat. The temperature was dropping and the wind had picked up a notch since they'd left the apartment. Maybe Mrs. MacTavish had been correct about the coming cold spell. "I'll keep my eye on things to ensure she's not in any kind of trouble."

"So the prodigal son returns to save the day?"

Andrew ignored the comment. "Just tell me what else you know about her uncle."

"Not too much. Pearl's sister works at his candy factory, which is why I know what I do. What are you thinking?"

"That my imagination is working overtime. Or at least I hope it is."

"What do you mean?"

He sat back down beside his brother and tried to find perspective on the situation. In the first five chapters of the adventure novel he was penning, the heroine had already escaped the clutches of death twice, but this was not a situation where he had control over the final outcome.

"Lizzie and I both assumed that if the attack in Africa wasn't random, then it had to have something to do with the conflict that was brewing between the tribes where she lived."

"Which makes sense," Charlie said.

"So if that is true, then by being here, she should be out of danger."

Unless those incidents had something to do with her uncle wanting her fortune—and her dead. Connections with the mob gave MacTavish connections to hit men. For a ticket across the Atlantic and a couple hundred bucks, any problem—even one in Northern Rhodesia—could be eliminated.

"When do you see her again?" Charlie asked.

"Her aunt is holding a big welcome home party tomorrow night, and I was invited."

"From the way you describe her, I would assume that a big party wasn't her idea?"

"Hardly. I think she wants me there as a distraction more than anything else."

"And your reason for going?"

"I think you already know the first reason. Now you've just given me a second one."

CHAPTER TWENTY-SEVEN

Lizzie stood in front of the three-way mirror and studied her reflection. Even she had to admit that the silky rose-colored dress with its knife-pleated skirt was stunning. She ran her fingers across the smooth fabric of the scooped neckline. Helen, the seamstress her aunt had hired, had added a narrow row of lace around the hemline and sleeves with her perfectly even stitches as finishing touches.

"The dress is beautiful on you." Helen readjusted the shoulders then tugged gently on the dropped waistline. "If I take in the shoulders another half an inch, I believe it will be perfect for tomorrow night's party."

"Don't forget the shoes and the hat, Lizzie," Aunt Ella added. "Both are sitting on the bed. I want to see what they look like with the dress."

Lizzie slipped on the embroidered satin evening shoes then tugged the close-fitting hat over her hair that was loosely knotted at the base of her neck. She studied the ensemble. The pale mauve velvet fabric with its large fabric rose matched the dress to perfection, but she felt as if she were staring in the mirror at a stranger. "I'm not sure about the hat."

"If you cut your hair, it would be so much easier to wear the tight-fitting cloche hats that are so popular—" her aunt began.

"It's not the hair. It's just…everything, I suppose. It is so very different from what I'm used to wearing."

She caught her aunt's frown in the mirror. "There is nothing wrong with your practical attire while you're tramping through the bush, but while you are living here, you can afford to dress fashionably. You must trust me, Lizzie. You're going to be the belle of the party."

Lizzie swallowed her frustration. Andrew had said the same thing, yet she had no desire to be the belle of the party, or to even go to the party for that matter. The only reason she'd agreed was because she wanted to make her aunt happy—and at times she wondered if she'd achieved even that.

"Helen, I believe that will be all for today. I will need you to finish the alterations on this dress and on the other four she just tried on. We'll worry about some more casual outfits next week."

"Yes ma'am." Helen gathered up her supplies in the small trunk she'd brought, then closed the door behind her, leaving Lizzie and her aunt alone in the room.

Lizzie slipped back into her *practical* skirt and blouse, as her aunt called them—thankful that the fitting session was over. She'd spent the past three days sorting through dress patterns, enduring fittings, and planning the menu for Friday night's party. While her aunt had raved over recipes of oyster toast and stuffed pimientos, her mind had kept wandering to Kakoba's family...and Andrew.

She sat on the edge of the bed and put on her well-worn boots that would, no doubt, be replaced shortly with something more stylish. "I do appreciate all that you are doing, Aunt Ella, but none of it is necessary. I would be content to celebrate my arrival with just you and Uncle Thomas and a simple meal."

"Of course it's necessary." Aunt Ella rolled her chair across the room. "Your life will never be the same, Lizzie, because of your inheritance. Your new status in life will open doors for you, and as your aunt, I intend to ensure you know which ones to walk through."

"But I—"

"Now, as soon as you're ready, we'll go downstairs and work with Maria on the menu. I want you to have the final say, as this is your party."

Lizzie sighed, wishing her aunt was as intent on listening to her questions as she was on planning her life. She finished pulling on the other boot, overwhelmed by the amount of choices. Two or three outfits had always been adequate, and the long list of menu items her aunt had suggested made her head spin. All she needed was something simple and nourishing—like fish cooked over a fire. Instead, she'd been served hearty dishes with rich sauces three times a day that had left her feeling bloated and disagreeable.

"Whatever you choose is fine with me, Aunt Ella."

"Nonsense. Planning the menu is half the fun."

There was a knock on the door. "I'm sorry to bother you, ma'am. These flowers just came for Miss MacTavish. Someone paid a pretty penny to send such a stunning bouquet this time of year."

Lizzie felt her heart quiver as she took the bouquet. "Thank you, Maria."

Aunt Ella rolled her wheelchair across the room to examine the flowers. "You've been in New York barely three days and you already have an admirer?"

Lizzie clutched the handwritten card. "They're from Andrew Styles."

"Ah, Mr. Styles. He seems to be quite the ambitious man. I know your uncle was quite caught up in his tales of Africa the other night over dinner. And from his gift, he's clearly a gentleman as well."

"He is." Lizzie felt her breath catch. She inhaled the flowers' sweet scent, wondering when she'd gone from trying to avoid Andrew's presence to missing him like crazy.

"He's from the Lower East Side, I understand?"

"Yes." Lizzie caught the disapproval in her aunt's voice. "His father's parents immigrated three decades ago and eventually opened a butcher shop. His mother's father was an explorer, which is where he got his thirst to travel."

"It sounds as if you spent quite a lot of time together on your trip here."

"It was…unavoidable." Lizzie searched for a way to end the conversation. She still had to figure out exactly what her heart wanted before she could voice her feelings aloud. "It's been a long morning, and I know you're tired. Maybe you should go lie down, and we can work on the menu after lunch."

"I'm fine. Really. In fact it's been months since I felt so good." Aunt Ella took her hand. "You don't know how good it is to have you here. So much has changed in my life these past few months, but having you here is like a breath of fresh air that gives me something to look forward to every day."

"I'm glad you feel that way, but I'm still worried about you."

"I'm getting old, Lizzie. That happens to everyone, you know."

"But what about your music? You've given up so much that has always been important to you."

Her aunt turned to stare into the mirror at her reflection as if she hoped to catch a glimpse of the woman she used to be. "The world is changing. Young people want to listen to jazz and blues, not a sixty-year-old woman singing outdated songs from the past."

"Is that all it is?"

Aunt Ella hesitated then picked up the hairbrush from the dressing table. "Sit down on the stool next to me, and I'll brush your hair."

Lizzie complied. The gentle strokes brought back memories of her mother brushing her hair before bedtime. Andrew wasn't the only person she missed.

"The doctors haven't been able to give me any answers," Aunt Ella began. "Which means that I've had to accept that the fast-paced life I've been used to is something I have to leave behind."

"I still remember the concert of yours I went to with my parents. I was so amazed at the beautiful music." After living her entire life in the bush, watching her aunt had been an experience she'd never forgotten. Her aunt had a voice that sounded to Lizzie like that of an angel. "I'd love to hear you perform again. You will sing at the party, won't you?"

"I hadn't planned to. I haven't played much for months, and besides, I'm sure the guests would prefer something more upbeat and current."

"I wouldn't. I love the old songs. They are what I remember."

"You sound like Thomas. I complain at how he spends most of his time at the factory working, but at heart he's still very old-fashioned."

"Is his business going well?"

"That is a matter of opinion. Thomas has good intentions, but he also has a habit of spending freely and gambling." Her aunt resumed brushing her hair again. "But we have an arrangement, I suppose you could call it. He doesn't expect me to be concerned with the factory and financial matters, and I don't ask questions."

"Aren't you interested?"

"I never needed to be. I've always had my music to keep me busy."

"And now?"

"Though I have had no interest in the business side of things, I have recently considered asking Thomas for a consulting job in his company just to keep me busy. If nothing else I believe Maria and I could come up with a new chocolate bar for the market."

"Then why didn't you?"

"Thomas is a good man, and he doesn't need me underfoot." She set the brush in her lap and caught Lizzie's gaze in the mirror. "And there are things that I'd prefer not knowing about."

"I don't understand." Lizzie turned to face her aunt.

"Times have changed since you were here, Lizzie. The war changed people, and prohibition, which might have started out as a way to stop husbands from spending the family income on liquor, has done little to stop its actual consumption. Nothing can stop evil. It always finds a way of raising its ugly head."

"That's why the world needs the hope and forgiveness of a Savior."

"I believe there is a God, but that doesn't make evil any less real. Or stop people from participating in it."

Lizzie searched her aunt's eyes. "Do you think he's involved with something illegal?"

Aunt Ella dropped her gaze. "I have my suspicions. Alcohol may be illegal, but that doesn't mean our society doesn't have access to it, or that there aren't those making a fortune to make it available."

"Where do they get the alcohol?"

"If it's not homemade, the major importing comes from Mexico... Canada...even the West Indies. Or it's produced right here in the city."

"And you think Uncle Thomas is involved?"

"While I have always been behind prohibition, no one can deny that bootlegging can be profitable. Thomas wouldn't be the first man who decided it was a quick way to make money to ease his debt and raise his financial stability."

Her aunt had emphasized more than once how her inheritance would change Lizzie's life. The obvious flickered on the edges of her conscience. What if bootlegging liquor hadn't made enough to cover her uncle's debts? With her out of the way, her fortune—the one he no doubt believed was rightfully his—would solve everything for him.

"I think you're right, Lizzie."

Lizzie turned her attention back to her aunt. "About what?"

"I think I will take a nap before lunch."

"And I think that is a very wise decision." Lizzie kissed her aunt on her forehead then helped her onto the bed before stepping from the room.

The blurred image of a face appeared in her mind. She worked to bring it into focus. Someone had been there that night outside the missionary compound. Someone wanted her out of the way.

The question that remained unanswered was, "who?"

CHAPTER TWENTY-EIGHT

Lizzie started down the narrow third-floor hallway toward the upstairs library, trying to erase the unease her aunt's comments had brought with them. It wasn't the first time she'd heard about her uncle's unscrupulous habits. According to her father, Thomas MacTavish had always been the black sheep of the family. And according to her grandfather's solicitors, it was the reason her grandfather had left his fortune to her and not his son. It had been the way, she feared, for her grandfather's disapproval of Thomas's gratuitous lifestyle to follow Thomas even after his father's death.

She paused alongside the wooden banister where the skylight scattered sunshine along the staircase, and studied the first-floor landing two stories below. According to her father, Uncle Thomas wouldn't save a penny if he thought he could make a nickel out of it. And if he couldn't find a way to make a profit, he'd gamble it away. But despite the rift that had risen between the two brothers, then lingered on long after his move to Africa, her father had most often spoken of another side of the man.

Uncle Thomas had been the one who had arranged care for their mother when doctors diagnosed her with tuberculosis, then had donated money to the hospital after her death. Which in turn fueled the desire in her father to make things right between them—until his untimely death had taken away that chance.

"Lizzie?"

Uncle Thomas hurried down the staircase from the fourth floor, dressed in one of his smart suits, with its narrow lapels and cuffed trousers. Lizzie glanced again at the first floor landing, two stories below. If it was her inheritance he was after, eliminating her from the equation would be easy. One calculated push and she would plunge to certain death. No. She took the thought captive as her imagination tried to turn him from Dr. Jekyll into Mr. Hyde.

Just because her uncle had always been eager to turn a profit didn't mean he would stoop to harm her in order to get his hands on her fortune. Their family ties ran deeper than greed. No. Nothing had happened since her return. And nothing was going to happen.

"Uncle Thomas." She shoved her faulty suspicions aside. "I didn't know you'd returned from the factory."

"I needed to pick up some papers. Is Ella awake?"

"I hope not." Lizzie glanced back to the couple's bedroom. "I convinced her that she needed to rest until lunch time. She seemed tired."

His expression softened. "See why we need you here? If I were to have suggested a nap, she would have thrown me out of the room."

"I doubt that."

"Then you don't know her the way I do. She's persistent, and for the most part always gets her way. I've seen how she has kept you busy with dressmaking and party plans even though you've barely just returned. I told her it might be wiser to wait until you'd adjusted somewhat to life here, but she was quite insistent."

Some of the apprehension she'd had began to scatter. "She is rather…enthusiastic."

"That she is." He tugged on the collar of his suit jacket. "I'm glad I saw you before I left for the factory. I had a meeting with an investor this morning and I wanted to show you some of our ideas. I left the paperwork upstairs in the library if you have a few minutes to look over it."

He was already halfway up the stairs before she could nod her approval. Her aunt wasn't the only persistent member of this household. She entered the fourth-floor library that he used as an office when he was away from the factory. Two walls of floor-to-ceiling walnut bookshelves stood on either side of the windows that overlooked the street below.

Uncle Thomas slid into the seat behind the large oak desk. "Have you had time to consider our conversation from the other night?"

She crossed the light-brown carpet of his office and sat down on the leather chair across from him, shoving her suspicions aside. "Your offer for me to stay is…tempting, but to be honest, while it might have been my grandfather's wishes as well, I'm not ready to commit to remaining in New York. There is still much I wish to accomplish back in Northern Rhodesia. And it is my home."

He pulled a handful of wrapped caramel pieces from his pocket and offered her one.

She shook her head. "No, thank you."

He unwrapped one and popped it into his mouth. "I understand your hesitancy to stay, but while you consider the idea, there is another thing I've been concerned about, the primary one being your inheritance."

It was the topic she'd hoped to avoid discussing. "If this is regarding the fact that your father left me the majority of his estate instead of—"

"Please." Her uncle held up his hand. "My father leaving me nothing more than a modest monthly allowance came as no surprise. It was no secret that we never got along. But I still feel responsible for your well-being, and quite frankly, as you might well imagine, a large fortune is going to drastically change your situation."

"Aunt Ella has told me the same thing, and while I understand your concern, to be honest, I don't foresee anything changing in my case. When I return to Africa I will live exactly how I've always lived. My financial needs are small, which will allow me to help support my fellow mission workers and the board I work for."

He rested his elbows on the black leather desktop and steepled his fingers. "Which is exactly my point. You might think that the amount your grandfather left you is enough to last you a dozen lifetimes, but money has a way of quickly slipping through one's fingers. You need to think about investing your money in something that will give you a high return while allowing you to be flexible in—in donating it the way you want."

"I know very little about investments—"

"And that's why I want to help. You have to understand that between a growing list of con men and the Mafia, there are people in this world who would be more than happy to take your money. Have you ever heard of a man named Charles Ponzi?"

"No."

"He swindled close to ten million dollars from investors in a money-trading program that never existed. And he's not the only one. There are dozens of men and even women who spend their life working one con after another. They're smart, quick, and able to leave with everything you have before you're aware of what happened."

"While I appreciate your concern, I spoke briefly to Grandfather's solicitors about this while I was at their offices yesterday, and on their advice, I plan to keep Grandfather's investments. He trusted his solicitors, and so do I."

Uncle Thomas unwrapped a second piece of caramel. "And while their conservative investments will bring you steady growth, I'd like to offer you an opportunity to double your grandfather's fortune."

"My father often told me that if anything in life seems too good to be true, then it probably is. I'm perfectly content to err on the side of caution."

"Which is a valid concern—and why your father was always broke. He never invested or planned for his future, perhaps in anticipation of our father's fortune. But family squabbles aside, I'd like you to consider a guaranteed money-making business opportunity."

Lizzie frowned. Her aunt's commentary on her uncle's spending and gambling habits had done nothing to gain her confidence in her uncle's investment expertise. "What exactly do you mean?"

"It's a chance to expand my business. It's going quite well, and I have four new products ready to hit the market next year. I already have one investor who is quite enthusiastic. With you on board, the possibilities are endless."

How did she tell him she had little confidence in his financial advice? "You know I want to help in any way I can, but to be honest I'm not sure I'm ready to reinvest my inheritance."

"I have specifics of the planned expansion for you to study. Just promise me that you will consider my offer, and when you're ready I can answer any questions you have." He slid a folder across the desk then stood. "We would do well as business partners, Lizzie. I have twenty years of experience behind me, which means I know a sure deal when I see one."

And she was the one with the capital. "I promise to read through this and consider your offer."

"That's all I ask." He grabbed his coat off the back of the chair and walked her to the door. "There is one other thing. Please don't mention any of this to your aunt Ella. With her health as fragile as it is, I'm trying to protect her. She doesn't have to concern herself with such trivial matters."

She stopped on the landing to face him. "I hardly see investing the bulk of my inheritance as a trivial matter."

"Of course not. I'm sorry if I implied that. But I still don't want to do anything that would cause a strain on her emotionally." He dumped his candy wrappers in the trash bin by the door. "I realize that New York is not where your heart is. I can see it in your eyes. But I truly believe if you'd give it some time you would come to enjoy living here."

She grasped the banister and started down the stairs. "I'm sorry if I seem ungrateful."

"No, it's not that. If I had a chance to take the next boat to Africa and someone asked me to remain here, I'd have a thousand reasons why I couldn't stay. I just want you to consider this house as your home. And us as your family."

She paused on the landing below. "I do appreciate your generosity."

"We are family." He pulled on his coat. "Why don't you get out of the house while your aunt sleeps and the sun's out? I realize the city will never compare to Africa's open spaces, but Bryant Park isn't too far from here, and you would enjoy the fresh air."

Her uncle had been right. Despite the chill in the air, there was enough sunshine to make the walk a pleasant change from dress fittings and menu planning. Lizzie followed the sidewalk past the long row of townhouses in her uncle's neighborhood to the high-rise buildings and shops that lined Fifth Avenue. Drug stores, cafés, clothing stores, and tailors vied for her attention with their colorful advertisements while the vibrant sounds and smells of the city pressed in around her.

But even with the congested streets and towering giants looking down on her, a welcome sense of freedom swept over her. Here she could disappear and become nothing more than a face in the crowd. No one stopped her to ask questions about where she was from. Nor did they want to hear stories of the savages from the Dark Continent or what she planned to do with her inheritance. Not the woman carrying the toddler on her hip, or the man sporting a red handkerchief in his suit pocket, or the group of children buying apples from a grocer.

But in her anonymity, neither could they give her answers to her questions.

I don't know what to do, God.

Returning to Africa on the next boat might not be an option, but neither was staying permanently. Because as hard as she tried, she would never be able to picture herself staying and caring for her aunt, working in a hospital, or even raising a family amidst the crowded conditions of the city.

But was Africa the place to raise a family? The question surfaced unexpectedly. She'd spent her life embracing its people and culture, but even she couldn't deny that New York offered the chance for better schooling, churches, and medical care.

And then there was Andrew.

She passed a bakery and breathed in the fresh scent of bread. Just the thought of him made her heart tremble. In the short amount of time she'd known him, he'd somehow become her hero and confidant... and someone she wasn't ready to let go.

Isn't it time you decided?

The answer to that question remained the most elusive of all. While she'd allowed herself to dream of the two of them together, circumstances had placed them in two different worlds, forcing one impossible choice. There was more to falling in love than simply following her heart. While she couldn't imagine settling in Manhattan, neither could she see Andrew finding contentment in the life she'd chosen in Africa.

An automat caught her attention with its neatly etched sign across its window. Memories surfaced of her father slipping coins into the slots and allowing her to choose her own meal from the wall of small glass doors. Lizzie breathed in the scent of grilled onion and garlic and felt her stomach rumble. Her fingers tightened around her small handbag. With her grandfather's money she could certainly afford a meal out. She started toward the front door then stopped as she caught the reflection of the man with the red handkerchief in the glass.

Smart suit, long mustache, black fedora… She'd seen him only moments before. Was he following her? She turned around and scanned the bustling crowd behind her. The man had vanished.

Lizzie tried to shake the sensation. Her imagination had been stretched to the breaking point these past few weeks. Being followed along the river, attacks in the bush. Even if those incidents had been made by someone from Mawela's village, she was now almost ten thousand miles away from any danger. There was nothing for her to worry about here other than the con men her uncle had warned her of.

She quickened her steps. The sidewalks teemed with shoppers and businessmen, but no one noticed the concern in her eyes or her suspicions that something could be wrong. But that didn't matter. Surely her fears were based on nothing more than her vivid imagination playing tricks on her.

Lizzie glanced back. Or maybe it wasn't a trick at all. He was there, less than twenty feet behind her on the crowded thoroughfare. She stumbled on a crack in the sidewalk and scraped the palm of her hand across the rough edge of a wooden display of fruit. Her heart pounded. The intersection loomed ahead. In the middle of the street, an officer regulated traffic from his booth high above the roadway, allowing pedestrians and vehicles to traverse beneath him.

She ran toward the busy intersection and crossed behind the flood of pedestrians. A car honked as she stepped onto the sidewalk on the opposite side of the street. The electric lamp overhead turned green, allowing cars to go. Brakes squealed. A woman screamed.

Lizzie dared a quick glance back. A man had been struck by an automobile from the line of traffic that now roared by. He lay on the far side of the street, a red handkerchief in his pocket, and less than two feet from his fedora hat.

A policeman was already on the scene, but Lizzie didn't stop. Two blocks away, a bell jingled on the door as she slipped inside a lunchroom and tried to catch her breath. A long counter ran down one side of the narrow restaurant with a line of stools. The remainder of the room was filled with tables and chairs.

A woman standing at the front handed her a ticket. "They will stamp this so you can pay before you leave."

Lizzie glanced around the restaurant that had already begun filling up for the lunchtime meal. Food no longer seemed tempting, but she needed a crowd to lose herself in.

"Are you all right, miss?"

She started for the back of the room, ignoring the young woman's curious stare. "I need to make a phone call."

"I'm sorry, but we don't allow—"

"Please. This is urgent." Lizzie fumbled for her purse. "I'll pay for the call."

"Are you all right?" The waitress nodded at Lizzie's hand.

A patch of blood oozed on the spot where she'd scraped it against the cart.

"Please. There was a man following me." Lizzie dumped the contents of her purse onto the wooden counter. She picked up a white handkerchief and pressed it against the wound, then searched for the number Andrew had given her.

"You poor thing. My ol' man never did treat me right either." The woman's demeanor changed from wariness to sympathy. She pointed to the phone hanging on the back wall. "Don't you worry. Sunny's working behind the rear counter today. He'll take care of anyone who tries to bother you."

Lizzie nodded her thanks. Her fingers shook as she dialed the number. She couldn't help but wonder if modern society might turn out to be more treacherous than the hazards of the African bush.

CHAPTER TWENTY-NINE

The bell on the front door of the lunchroom jingled again. Lizzie flinched. A couple strode into the restaurant and took a seat at the lunch counter while Lizzie waited on one of the stools in the back of the room. If it weren't for the two gentlemen sitting at a nearby table eating grilled sandwiches, she'd still be wondering if she hadn't imagined the entire situation. The older of the two gentlemen had told his friend in great detail about an accident he'd just witnessed in the nearby inter-section. Which verified two things in Lizzie's mind. One, that the accident had really taken place, and two, that the man wasn't still coming after her. But it didn't answer the question of why the man had been following her.

The bell jingled again. This time, Andrew entered the restaurant.

She signaled to him from the back of the lunchroom, studying his lean form as he made his way down the narrow room. His long trench coat hung over neatly pressed grey slacks and polished shoes, and his hair had been recently trimmed. Her pulse faltered. It had only been three days since she'd seen him, but to the ache in her heart it seemed so much longer.

He spoke briefly to the man behind the counter then stopped in front of her. Before she could say anything, he grabbed her hands and pulled her against his chest. She could hear the soft thud of his heart and feel the warmth of his arms around her.

"I've been worried about you. Are you okay?"

"Just a little shook up."

He took a step back then turned over her hand, which was still wrapped in the handkerchief. "What is this?"

She pulled off the cloth. The bleeding had stopped and all that was left was a long, jagged scrape. "It's nothing. I scraped it against a wooden display box."

"I hardly think any of this is nothing. You told me a man was following you." He nodded at the other side of the room. "Do you mind if we move to one of the tables?"

"Of course not."

He took her hand and led her to the table farthest back then sat down, facing the front of the restaurant. "I want you to tell me exactly what happened. You look as if you've tangled with the Mafia."

"Funny you should say that."

Except it wasn't funny.

"Why do you say that?"

"My uncle warned me earlier today about con men and the Mafia."

"You think this has something to do with your inheritance?"

She shrugged a shoulder. "I don't know. For all I know it was nothing more than a coincidence."

"Like what happened in Africa?" Andrew looked anything but convinced. "I don't think so. Besides, if it were nothing you wouldn't be sitting across from me with your voice shaking and your hands trembling."

The waitress set two tall glasses in front of them. "Anything else?"

Andrew shook his head. "Not right now. Thank you."

Lizzie cocked her head. "What is this?"

"What does it look like?" He shot her a smile. "It's a chocolate milkshake."

Lizzie dabbed at the whipped cream with her finger then tasted it.

"You do know what a milkshake is, don't you?"

"Of course." She nodded and sipped the milk, chocolate syrup, and malt powder combination and felt herself relaxing slightly. There were clearly a few things missing from the African bush. "It's been forever since I had one, but it's delicious."

"I thought you might say that. If I've learned anything from my sister-in-law about women," Andrew continued, "it's that chocolate can ease at least some of the strain from most situations. She's raising three boys and is married to my brother, so I figure she has to know something about stress."

Lizzie couldn't help but laugh. Leave it to a chocolaty fountain drink and handsome explorer to make her smile again.

"I was right. I've got you laughing."

She ignored his stare. "You're incorrigible."

"No, just smart. Now, start from the beginning and tell me what happened."

Lizzie drew in a deep breath as she shifted her thoughts back to reality. "My uncle suggested I go for a walk. It sounded good after hours of dress fittings and menu planning. And while I would have preferred less traffic and more open spaces, it was still nice. Coming up Fifth Avenue, I noticed a man wearing a nice suit and fedora."

"Along with every other man on the street."

Her fingers wrapped around the tall, cold glass. "This man's red handkerchief and long mustache made him stand out. But I didn't think anything about it at first. Not until after several blocks, and he was still following close behind me, looking as if he didn't want me to notice."

Andrew worked to put the pieces of the puzzle together. With her uncle's connections to the mob and his outstanding debt, today's incident had to be related. It wouldn't have been the first time a drive-by shooting had been planned in broad daylight, and neither were kidnappings unheard of. "You're sure he was following you?"

"I was sure at the time."

He tried to read her expression. "And you're hesitant now."

"I've faced situations that on the surface have appeared far more serious than this, but I panicked today because I believed some—some Mafia figure was after me." She jutted her chin toward the busy street outside the restaurant. "There are hundreds of people out there all going different places perhaps, but moving in the same direction. There's a chance I was wrong."

"And a bigger chance that you're right. How did you lose him?"

"I crossed the street. The light must have turned green for the oncoming traffic right behind me. I heard the squeal of brakes and looked back... he was lying in the street. There was a policeman who must have seen the accident. I slipped into the crowd, disappeared, and called you."

"Has anything else strange happened since your arrival?"

"No, nothing. I've been helping my aunt prepare for the party she's throwing for me on Friday. Menus, dress fittings, music, but nothing strange."

"What about your uncle?"

Her gaze dropped. "He spoke to me earlier today about my inheritance."

Andrew's suspicions mounted. "Specifically?"

"He was concerned that with such a fortune, I might be vulnerable to any number of scams and encouraged me to consider an investment opportunity with his company."

"What was your response?"

"I told him that I had to think about it. Though when I spoke to my grandfather's solicitors, I agreed with them to keep the money invested the way my grandfather did."

"Which I believe is a wise decision. Did your uncle mention how business is at the factory?"

"According to him, things have never been better."

Andrew didn't believe it. The image of a doting relative that had been presented to him when they'd first met had been replaced by a man who apparently would go to any lengths to get what he wanted. Perhaps even murder? "Do you believe him?"

Lizzie played with the straw in her drink. "My aunt has hinted at the fact that he might be involved in some…illegal ventures. But that doesn't mean he is after my money."

"Lizzie, your uncle has a—a reputation."

"What kind of reputation?"

"One for being a ladies' man, a gambler, and—"

"And a murderer? Is that what the rumors say?"

Despite her own questions regarding her uncle's moral standards, his comments clearly infuriated her. "I didn't say that."

"You're wrong." She shoved her half-empty glass to the center of the table. "I won't say that the thought didn't cross my mind, because it has, but if my uncle wanted me out of the way, he's had numerous chances."

"Maybe, but my brother's sister-in-law works for your uncle in his factory. She's heard that he's gotten himself into deep financial debt with money owed to the mob."

Lizzie shook her head. "I know that my uncle isn't perfect, but I can't believe he wants to kill me."

Andrew leaned forward and took her hands. "Then answer one more question for me, Lizzie. If anything were to happen to you, who gets your inheritance?"

He caught the hesitation reflected in her eyes as she looked away. "My uncle."

CHAPTER THIRTY

Lizzie sipped her too-sweet punch and tried to settle the jumble of nerves stirring in her stomach. While her welcome home party had barely started, her aunt had already introduced her to half a dozen eligible gentlemen who now hovered around her like a swarm of bees, all vying for her attention.

Robert…or was it Ronald…droned on about how the New York Giants had beaten the New York Yankees in the World Series while she tried to smile and laugh in all the right places. But all she could really think about was how she longed to escape her own welcome home party.

She teetered in the heels her aunt had bought her. A month ago she'd been nothing more than a single missionary woman, content to spend her days teaching, nursing sick patients, and hoeing her field so she'd have enough to eat in the coming months. Today she was a New York heiress, worthy of the admiration of dozens of wealthy men she had little interest in.

All because of an inheritance she didn't even want.

She glanced around the room decorated with twinkling strings of lights, candles, and paper lanterns. A small band played live music in the background, songs she didn't know, by artists she'd never heard of. Along the edges stood long tables laden with everything from baked ham sandwiches to stuffed eggs and smoked salmon along with menu items whose names she'd forgotten—all served by girls in starched uniforms and broad smiles.

She took the last sip of her drink and tried to suppress a wave of homesickness. There was one thing her aunt had yet to understand. While she had aspirations of her niece winning a husband from one of New York City's leading families, Lizzie had no plan to accept advances of any kind from them, let alone a proposal of marriage.

One of the young men who had just joined the swarm grabbed the empty cup from her hand and offered her a full one. "Lemonade?"

She forced a smile. "Thank you."

"I'm Miles Stanton."

She shook the offered hand as Mr. Stanton began a longwinded monologue to impress her—and presumably the other gentlemen— with his newly purchased McFarlan Six Roadster that held two passengers and had cost six thousand rupees.

Her mind clicked off again as she stared past the boisterous group to the open doors that led to the balcony. Outside a full moon hung amid a sky full of stars. Inside, the large living area was filled with tobacco smoke and crowded with the scores of stuffy socialites her aunt had invited to her welcome home party.

The man standing next to her, happily eating from his plate of finger sandwiches, nudged her with his elbow. "Don't listen to him, babe. He's dizzy with all the dames."

Lizzie blinked. "Excuse me?"

"This cat falls in love with every woman he meets."

"I'm sorry, but some of the…lingo…you use is unfamiliar."

Somebody laughed. "Baby, cat means man, and dizzy with all the dames means deeply in love."

Lizzie's head spun. Music pounded in the background. She downed her lemonade in one big gulp. She had to get out of here, but at the moment there was no escape.

"I suppose you don't hear a lot of English living in the bush like you do."

"No. I grew up speaking a tribal language. And in fact until this trip, I only speak English when I am teaching the language."

Another gentleman with dark hair and eyes and dressed in a tailored gray suit—no doubt to impress her and her inheritance—stepped up beside her. "I noticed you hadn't eaten anything and thought you'd enjoy this."

"Oh." She stared at the congealed concoction sitting on a plate of lettuce, and wrinkled her nose. "Thank you."

"Don't you like it?"

Lizzie tried to remember this dish from the piles of menus and cookbooks she'd perused with her aunt. "To be honest, I'm not sure what it is."

The man chuckled. "It's a gelatin salad with chopped tongue and vegetables."

"Of course." Her stomach roiled. She'd do anything for a bowl of fish and sauce.

"I suppose the heathens you work with wouldn't know what to do with gelatin in the heat they live in." The blond leaned forward. "What do they eat?"

Lizzie swallowed her irritation. "The heathens, as you call them—"

"They're cannibals, some of them, aren't they?" someone else interrupted.

Lizzie bit her tongue, praying Andrew would show up and whisk her away. "There are the normal things they enjoy, of course, like wild fruits and buffalo, but it's also not uncommon to eat things like monkey, field rats, and flying termites."

Mr. Stanton set his plate on the edge of the table. "Field rats?"

"And flying termites?"

Perhaps she'd found a way to turn them off. "They're quite nice, actually."

"I've heard they run around without any clothing as well."

"Only the children."

She continued her descriptions, wondering if they saw beauty in the plaited palm-leaf strips worn around the waist, or in the rows of bead and iron bells that jingled as the women walked. She gazed at their expressions. Apparently they found something about her amusing. They flocked around her as if she were the most interesting hostess they'd ever met.

"Lizzie?"

She turned, and her ankle twisted, dropping her hip and sending her gelatin surprise sliding off her plate...and onto a pair of black patent-leather shoes.

Lizzie stared at the gooey mess...and up at Andrew.

"I'm so sorry..." Her eyes widened.

He stood there smiling in his black shirt and black tie, looking utterly handsome and making her wish that the rest of the world would disappear so he could take her in his arms and kiss her as he'd done that one time...

His hand touched her elbow. "Are you all right?"

"Yes...I...your shoe."

Andrew lifted up his shoe and a lump of green gelatin slid onto the floor. "I'm the one who's sorry. I didn't mean to interrupt your conversation."

"It's not a problem at all." She turned back to the group of gentlemen. "If you will excuse me. I need to take care of this—this cat's shoe."

"Certainly." The throng of potential suitors excused her in unison.

Lizzie took Andrew's elbow and steered him out of earshot before signaling one of the servers for a cloth and for him to clean up the mess on the floor. "What took you so long?"

"To come to your rescue?"

Lizzie took the cloth and began wiping the goo from his shoe. "I've never been so bored in my entire life with discussions of sports and movie stars and cars. It's as if they all speak a foreign language. I had no idea things had changed that much."

"Why Lizzie MacTavish." Andrew folded his arms across his chest and shot her a wry grin. "I do believe you're a snob."

"A snob?" She handed the cloth to the server then ushered Andrew into the garden.

"You're clearly too refined to play ball with the hordes of boys grappling for your attention."

Her cheeks flushed and her smile vanished. "I'm not a snob. I'm simply...I'm not used to standing around, talking about...McFarlan Six Roadsters that cost six thousand rupees and—and eating things I've never seen before, all while smiling and wearing shoes with heels the height of the Statue of Liberty."

"Now that would be quite a feat to pull off."

Tears pooled in her eyes.

"I'm sorry." Andrew tilted her chin and caught her gaze. His efforts to lighten the mood had gone too far. "You just looked so completely miserable, and I thought if I could make you laugh you'd feel better. I've been worried about you. Leaving you yesterday was not what I wanted to do."

"I told you I'd be fine, and I am."

"There haven't been any more unusual incidents?"

"None."

He studied the silky rose-colored dress and stylish hat she wore. Her outfit was completely different from the sensible skirt and blouse he'd seen her in when they first met, but she was just as beautiful. "Enough serious talk for the moment. Did I tell you yet how beautiful you look?"

She shot him a half smile. "No, but at least a dozen young men already have."

He breathed in the subtle scent of her flowery perfume. "I should have gotten here earlier."

"Yes, you should have."

"I've heard that your aunt's parties are the cat's meow."

Lizzie's eyes narrowed. "Is that the only reason you decided to come?"

"There is this gorgeous debutante who is supposed to make an appearance tonight—"

"Enough." She smiled. The sparkle was back in her eye. "I suppose I'll have to tell my aunt that all the fussing over what to wear was worth it, since you approve."

"Oh, I approve, and I'm determined to find a way to make you enjoy yourself tonight."

A dab of seriousness in her expression threatened to erase the sparkle. "Even when all the gentlemen inside want to know is what savages wear and eat for dinner, and I'm being served sweet pickles, jellied tongue, and other things I can't identify?"

"You don't have to be like them to have a good time. The setting's romantic, the music's catchy, and the hostess is a looker."

"A looker?"

"Beautiful."

He wanted nothing more than for the party guests to disappear so he could take her in his arms and remind her how much he cared for her. But tonight wasn't about him. "You do have more than just one guest to entertain."

"I'm sure no one will notice my absence."

"Don't be so sure about that. Not only am I quite certain that your aunt isn't particularly fond of me, I saw the way those young men were looking at you."

Her cheeks reddened at the compliment. "Were you able to talk to your brother?"

Lizzie's question brought back everything he wanted to forget. "Changing the subject?"

Her smile lingered, but the apprehension in her expression had returned. "Yes."

"Charlie managed to ask a few subtle questions to a couple of the factory supervisors he knows. In the past six months, over a fourth of his employees have been quietly laid off even though business remains fairly steady. Three more workers, each from different shifts and departments, were let go the end of last week. People are beginning to notice and are getting nervous."

"What does your brother believe is the reason behind the layoffs?"

"That he's cutting corners in order to up his revenue."

"To pay off debt."

"More than likely."

Lizzie swayed slightly to the music. "If he's run out of money, then how does he pay for all of this?"

"More borrowed money. He was spotted with someone from the Mafia recently, which would seem to verify the rumor of his connection with the mob."

"So Uncle Thomas borrows money to make it look as if he's still making good money."

"It would be the perfect way to reel in investors. He's probably talking with several tonight. But if it's true that it's the mob he's borrowing from, he's going to find himself in a lot of trouble if he can't pay it back."

Which would make him desperate.

"So what do we do?"

Andrew glanced up at the glass doors leading into the house. While the party was in full swing inside, the patio was still private. "We need to find out where your uncle's business stands and exactly who he's in debt to."

"He'll never tell me, and I'm certain my aunt doesn't know."

"I'm sure you're right."

"Which means?"

"Does he have an office here at the house?"

"He uses the library upstairs when he works from home."

"Then we need to search that room. It would make sense that he brings home personal papers that he doesn't want anyone to see at the factory."

"What would we be looking for?"

"We need to know if he's left behind a paper trail. Any sign of a loan he's taken out under the table, or anything else that might point to the fact that he's in trouble financially."

"Anything that gives him motivation to come after my inheritance."

"I'm sorry, Lizzie, but yes."

"I don't know if I can do that."

"Do you have any other ideas? Because trust me, if there are other options, I'm open to considering them."

"I do have another idea." She cocked her head and gazed up at him. "Do you know this song?"

He tried to follow her train of thought. "Strauss?"

"It's his Blue Danube. I asked my aunt if the band could play some more classic songs. It's beautiful, isn't it?"

"Yes, but I'm not sure what that has to do with searching your uncle's office."

"It has nothing to do with it. Music is one thing I learned to appreciate while here, and my aunt made sure I learned to dance a few steps."

"Is that a hint?"

Her smile broadened. "It would be a shame to waste such a lovely song."

Andrew leaned forward and bowed. "Then may I have this dance, Miss MacTavish?"

She stepped into his arms, and the urgency of their situation began to slip away. He felt his heart accelerate as he pulled her closer. Soft music played in the background. A hint of starlight twinkled above. The evening breeze teased the wisps of her hair beneath the silky edges of her hat. And the smile on her lips had yet to disappear. For the moment, everything was perfect. For the moment, she was safe and he didn't have to worry about her.

She looked up at him as if they were the only two people in the world. "It's a beautiful night, isn't it?"

"It's perfect now."

They kept dancing, waltzing across the patio in perfect rhythm to the music. There were so many things he wanted to say to her. "Lizzie, I—"

"Why there you are, Lizzie."

Andrew turned back to the entrance of the house. Lizzie's aunt wheeled herself across the patio, the look of disapproval across her face clear. He dropped her hands to her sides. Their perfect moment was over.

"Have you forgotten that you have a house full of guests to entertain?"

Lizzie brushed against his shoulder. "I'll meet you upstairs in twenty minutes."

"They are all wondering where their hostess is." Mrs. MacTavish wheeled herself closer.

"Of course I haven't forgotten." Lizzie stepped away from Andrew. "That's exactly what I was doing. Entertaining—"

"One man?"

"I'm sorry." Andrew clasped his hands behind him. "It's completely my fault. I just wanted a few moments to speak with her alone."

"Though it is nice to see you again, Mr. Styles, my niece's presence is required inside with her guests."

"Of course. I understand."

Mrs. MacTavish pushed her chair back toward the house then paused. "And by the way, Mr. Styles, I almost forgot. My husband is looking for you. He'd like to speak to you."

CHAPTER THIRTY-ONE

Lizzie crept up the staircase of the fourth floor toward her uncle's office. She walked on tiptoes along the hardwood floor so she wouldn't be heard and prayed that she wouldn't be missed. Escaping from the party had not been easy. Downstairs was crowded with guests, and her aunt's goal for the evening was to ensure she met every one of them.

At the top of the stairs, she flipped on the cylinder-shaped flashlight she'd brought and tried the library door handle. It was unlocked. The dim light from the flashlight wasn't ideal for searching the room, but turning on any lights was out of the question. They'd simply have to make do with what they had.

She entered the room and gasped. Someone sat in the leather chair. The figure stood.

"Lizzie?"

She shined the light at his face. "Andrew!"

"Shh..." He held up his hand to block the glare. "We're supposed to be quiet. And put that thing down."

She lowered the light. "I was being quiet until you scared me to death."

"I'm sorry, but I've been waiting..." He flipped on another flashlight and checked his pocket watch. "For almost forty-five minutes."

"I couldn't get away, and I won't be able to stay long. My aunt is going to miss me. And if she notices that you are gone as well..."

"I solved that problem. After speaking with several of the guests, I thanked her for the invitation and bid her good night. She called a taxi for me, and I got in it and paid the man to take me around the block. She'll think you're out on the garden patio with one of your rich suitors who's vying for your attention."

"You sound jealous."

"Maybe I am."

Lizzie smiled. "We'll talk about that later. For now, we have a job to do. Though you know, we could get arrested for this."

"We're not going to get arrested."

"How can you be sure of that? Or that we're even going to find anything? Chances are, even if my uncle is guilty, he's not going to keep anything incriminating in plain sight."

"Then look for something out of plain sight."

She gave up arguing and started sifting through the drawers of the desk, while Andrew looked through the four-drawer wooden file cabinet set against the wall. Her uncle was organized. More so than she would have imagined for a man who never seemed to be able to pick up his coat off the back of a chair or remember to place his hat on the hat rack. She filed through the piles of notes and receipts, careful to leave things exactly as she'd found them.

Nothing.

Ten minutes later, she closed the last drawer. She shone the flashlight against the wall and considered the possibility that her uncle had hidden what they were looking for in one of the books in his vast collection. There was no way they could search the books now. She'd be missed downstairs before they were able to thoroughly search the first shelf.

"Have you found anything?" she whispered.

"Nothing."

She tapped her flashlight against the leather top of the desk and tried to think where else they could look. Her uncle's office at the factory was the next logical place—and would be far more difficult to get into than this room. The beam of light hit the newspaper sitting atop the desk. She started to turn then stopped. The photo on the bottom of the page pictured a man arrested in Manhattan for distributing alcohol.

Her eyes widened. "That's him."

"Who?"

She moved the flashlight closer and pointed to the photo. Long mustache, beady eyes… "Imagine him in a fedora and a suit. This is the man who followed me yesterday."

"Are you sure?"

"Positive." Her heart pounded as she read the article out loud.

"'Samuel Porter was involved in an accident yesterday when he was struck by an automobile while attempting to cross the busy intersection. Ironically, the police officer who arrived first on the scene recognized Porter from a wanted poster and arrested him on the spot. He is wanted on several counts of fraud, burglary, and the distribution of alcohol. Porter was treated for several minor injuries before being taken into police custody.'"

Lizzie tried to run through the possibilities. "Maybe this gives us another explanation for what happened yesterday."

Andrew's light cast an eerie shadow across the wall. "What do you mean?"

"What if yesterday wasn't about me, but about my uncle?"

"Then wouldn't he have gone after your uncle? Why involve you?"

"Because I'm leverage to get him to pay. Except we're pretty sure he's broke."

"Which is something he doesn't want anyone to know." Andrew reached up and ran his hand along the top of the bookshelf, still looking for evidence. "That could put him in deeper trouble with the mob if they found out he couldn't pay it back."

"Exactly. And secondly, I haven't lived here the past few years, but I'm not completely ignorant about everything. Despite the government's attempt to stop the distribution of alcohol, bootlegging and organized crime have taken control of the illegal market."

He moved on to the second bookshelf. "It's common knowledge that there are certain people making hundreds of thousands off the sale of alcohol."

"Like my uncle. The article says Porter was involved in the sale of alcohol. What if he double-crossed Porter or owed him money?"

"It's possible. Nothing but dust here." He stopped in front of the coat rack and checked her uncle's coat pockets. "Porter also might not be anything more than a paid hit man. But either way, it doesn't explain what happened in Africa. Nor why they would be after you."

"Maybe we're searching for answers that don't exist."

He pulled out a folded piece of paper and held it up to his light. "What if we're not?"

"What do you mean?"

"Look at this. It's a telegram from someone in…South Africa."

"What does it say?"

Andrew held the light closer. "It is to your uncle, informing him that one of his employees, a Mr. George Jamieson, was killed in an unfortunate accident while on the continent."

Lizzie shook her head. "I didn't know my uncle had business in South Africa."

"Then why would he send one of his workers?"

She searched for a plausible answer. "He spoke to me of expanding his company. Perhaps he's looking into the possibility of setting up an international site."

"Lizzie, people expand their businesses and set up offices in Chicago and Boston, not halfway around the world. And not when they are broke."

"There has to be another explanation then."

"There is something else that has been bothering me."

She was certain she didn't like the direction the conversation was about to go. "What?"

He held up the telegram. "This potentially ties everything back to you."

"No it doesn't."

"Then let me remind you of the facts. Your uncle is heavily in debt and he sends a man across the ocean where you are—"

"These are rumors, not facts. Every one of them. I can't go in and confront my uncle—or the police for that matter—with a handful of rumors."

Andrew tapped on the paper. "This is not a rumor. And that newspaper article with the photo of the man who followed you yesterday is not a rumor."

She didn't want to go there. Not again. "Andrew."

He held up her hand, where she'd fallen against the wooden cart. The tender spot had turned into a purple bruise. "You still believe you're not the target of this?"

"What exactly are you implying?"

"I'm not implying anything. You stand to inherit a large amount of money and your uncle is in debt. I believe George Jamieson and Samuel Porter were both hired as hit men to kill you."

Andrew counted to thirty after Lizzie left the room then slid out of Mr. MacTavish's office, shutting the door firmly behind him. She'd tried to convince him that his accusations were wrong, but he had seen the doubt in her eyes. Which meant leaving her here was not an option. She'd reluctantly agreed to meet him outside before the party was over. He'd escort her to Charlie and Pearl's, where they'd discuss a plan to expose Mr. MacTavish—and ensure Lizzie's safety.

He paused for a moment to listen for voices on the staircase, but the only sound was the music and laughter drifting up from the party below. All he had to do was make it down three flights of stairs without having to explain what he was doing upstairs in the house of a party he'd already left.

With the dimly lit staircase clear, Andrew headed down the stairs then stopped short of running into Mr. MacTavish on the second-floor landing.

Mr. MacTavish held up a half-empty glass in his hand. "Andrew. Have you come to see for yourself what the rest of us are enjoying so much about tonight's party?"

"Excuse me?"

Mr. MacTavish nodded toward the living room at the end of the narrow hall. Cigar smoke drifted from the space, where no doubt liquor flowed just as freely. "You don't really believe that my niece's role as a missionary would stop me from having some fun at her welcome home party, now do you?"

Clearly his host had already had more than his share of illegal drink.

"You know my wife and I will be forever in your debt for bringing Lizzie back to us. And the additional excuse to celebrate doesn't hurt." Mr. MacTavish clapped Andrew on the shoulder and led him down the hall and into the room. "Why don't you join me and a few of my friends? We have better drinks than they do downstairs and a supply of cigars."

"I was actually planning to leave."

"Leave?"

Andrew fought the temptation to confront MacTavish. The evidence he held wasn't enough to convict the man and would only give him time to cover his tracks. No, a showdown involving his word against MacTavish's needed the police and revenuers involved, with enough compelling evidence to leave no escape.

"Would you like a smell from the barrel, or perhaps a cigar?"

Andrew waved away the offer of the homemade brew that no doubt tasted more like quinine than gin. "I'm fine, thank you."

Mr. MacTavish leaned against the back of the couch that sat in the center of the room. "I understand that everything has been taken care of with the lawyers?"

"I received my rightful pay, if that is what you mean."

"Good. My wife and I want you to know that we appreciate the way you took care of Lizzie. Her return has served to be a motivation for my wife's return to health."

"I'm glad to hear that."

"Did you hear Ella tonight?" Mr. MacTavish's speech slurred. "That canary can sing. She hasn't done that in months. And then there is Lizzie. With the death of her grandfather, her situation has changed considerably. There is now a world of opportunity for her, including a chance to invest in my factory. I'm planning to expand."

"Have you talked to Lizzie about this?"

"About her future?" Mr. MacTavish walked to the bar and refilled his drink. "Of course. She promised to carefully consider the opportunity. Why do you ask?"

"If you really knew her, you would realize that there is little she wants, at least in the way of finances. It was hard for me to see until recently, but I've begun to realize just how perfectly content she was back in Northern Rhodesia. In fact, as you might have discerned by now, it was quite a feat just to get her to return with me."

"That doesn't surprise me at all. Her father was just as stubborn, with his ideas of saving the world. But it's good for her to get away from those savages and see that there is more to the world than just the limited life she's lived."

"I wouldn't want to argue with you, sir, but I'm not certain she would agree with you." Neither the assessment of the savages, nor that her world was limited.

"That doesn't matter. It's a dangerous world she's come from. I had to bring her back in order to keep her safe."

"Is that why you sent Jamieson?" Andrew decided to throw the first punch. "As backup in case something happened to me?"

"Jamieson?" MacTavish's hands trembled, spilling liquid on his suit coat.

"George Jamieson. One of your employees."

MacTavish shook his head. "I don't know what you mean."

Andrew wasn't sure if it was MacTavish or the alcohol talking, but the man looked legitimately confused.

"What happened to Jamieson?" Andrew asked.

"Jamieson told me he needed some time off. That his mother was sick and he had to take care of her. He never came back."

"Because he was killed while in Africa."

"But I didn't know he went to Africa until I got the telegram telling me of his death. I have no idea what he was doing there. He told me he needed to take care of his mother." Mr. MacTavish took another sip of his drink. "I didn't bring you here to talk about Jamieson. I brought you in here because I know of an opportunity I'd like you to consider. Have you heard of Harvey Butler?"

"The explorer? Of course. I've admired his work for years."

"Harvey not only has spent half of his life in Africa tracking, hunting, and studying remote places, but he happens to be a close friend of mine. I spoke to him by telephone only a few hours ago. He has booked passage on a ship bound for West Africa." Mr. MacTavish walked across the room and sat down on one of the empty chairs in the corner. He took another sip of his drink. "Unfortunately, the photographer he hired to help document the book he's planning to write was involved in a serious accident four days ago and will not be able to join him on the trip. I assumed you wouldn't mind my taking the initiative, so I told him about you."

"Me?"

"As you know, Harvey is well-known for his research across the African continent. What I am proposing to you is a once-in-a-lifetime opportunity. If you prove yourself to be a valuable asset to the team, it could open all kinds of doors for you."

Andrew sat across from the older man. There was no denying his interest. While he still wanted to lead up his own expedition, to work with a man like Butler was not an opportunity to simply shrug off.

"You would be wise to consider the offer."

Andrew leaned forward. "I would need some time before I decided."

"I'm thrilled to hear the enthusiasm in your voice." Mr. MacTavish set his empty glass on the end table beside him. "Unfortunately, the opportunity won't be available for long, Mr. Styles. The expedition is leaving immediately. Mr. Butler will need an answer by tomorrow morning."

"Tomorrow?" Andrew shook his head. Leaving now was not an option. Not as long as Lizzie's life was at stake. "I'm sorry, but if that is the case I will have to decline the generous offer."

"I'm sorry to hear that." Mr. MacTavish stood. Apparently their conversation was over. "Because this is a decision I fear you will one day regret, Mr. Styles."

Andrew left the room then hesitated on the landing and tried to process the conversation with Mr. MacTavish. His parting words might have held a threatening tone, but he seemed to have been in the dark regarding Mr. Jamieson's trip to Africa.

Someone called his name. Andrew turned, but not in time to avoid the sharp blow to the back of his head. He staggered against the wall then everything went black.

CHAPTER THIRTY-TWO

Lizzie smiled at Timothy Prince as he handed her a glass of punch and yet another plate of food. She poked at the rich piece of chocolate cake with her fork. If she ate every morsel she'd been offered tonight, she'd never make it up the stairs once the party was over. She glanced across the room at the staircase. Andrew's instructions had been clear.

I'll count to thirty then follow you down the stairs.

She'd agreed that it was safer if they left the library separately. She'd even agreed that the risk was significant enough for her to go with Andrew to his brother's house. But Andrew was supposed to have been right behind her.

Timothy didn't seem to notice her inattentiveness. "The *Adventures of Tarzan* is definitely the best film of the year, though of course you live in Africa, so I suppose you've seen real lions and elephants."

She tried to relax her pasted-on smile. "Yes."

Timothy looked impressed. "Your life must be fascinating. In the film…"

She continued smiling and nodding as he rambled on about the highlights of the silent film. Andrew had been right. She was coming across as a snob, but she knew nothing about the majority of the conversations she'd been forced to hold with eligible gentleman her aunt had invited. What did she think about who won Wimbledon, or the Kentucky Derby, and now, what did she think about Elmo Lincoln who had played Tarzan?

Timothy waited for her to answer.

"Elmo Lincoln?" How could she have an opinion of a man she'd never heard of? "Well, I—"

"You've heard of him, haven't you?"

There was no other option but to confess her ignorance. "I've been back such a short time after being gone for several years."

"You must see it if you enjoy films. Even Tantor the Elephant has become a household name across the country."

She swallowed the rest of her lemonade as Timothy continued his detailed description of the film's highlights. According to Aunt Ella's description, Timothy Prince was heir to his father's hotel empire and was a movie buff.

He took a breath and glanced at her empty glass. "Can I get you some more?"

She handed him the glass. "Yes, thank you."

"I'll be right back then."

She glanced again at the staircase. Uncle Thomas had just entered the room. If he'd caught Andrew in the library...

Uncle Thomas approached her with his arms open. "I haven't had a chance to tell you how lovely you look tonight."

Lizzie hesitated. Alcohol tinged his breath. "Thank you. I believe the guests are having an enjoyable time."

"How could they not with such a beautiful hostess?"

Lizzie decided to take a gamble on her next question. "Uncle Thomas, have you seen Andrew? I needed to speak to him about something."

"I..." Her uncle glanced back at the staircase.

"What's wrong?"

"I hadn't wanted to say anything until the evening was over…"

"I don't understand."

"It's quite good news, actually. I received a message from a close friend of mine who's getting ready to set sail on his tenth—or is it his eleventh expedition to Africa? Anyway, he studies rare fauna and wildlife and is in fact writing a book on his adventures."

"What does that have to do with Andrew?"

"I told him about Andrew, and my friend offered Andrew the job as photographer."

Lizzie felt the surge of relief that Andrew was all right collide with a sense of loss. Surely she hadn't expected his feelings for her to erase his sense of adventure. "It sounds like a wonderful opportunity for him."

"It is. They are scheduled to leave early in the morning."

"Tomorrow?" Lizzie felt her knees weaken.

"You have to understand that a young man like Andrew will come across an opportunity like this only once in a lifetime. I'm sorry, Lizzie. Andrew asked me to tell you good-bye for him, as he feared his leaving would upset you."

"Upset me?" Lizzie's chest heaved. "He would never leave without saying good-bye to me himself."

"I told you, this is a once-in-a-lifetime opportunity, Lizzie. You must understand. He had to make a quick decision."

The room closed in around her. "No. He told me he loved me."

"You barely know him."

"I love him."

She loved him. And her decision had come too late. She had to find him.

Lizzie rushed past her uncle, colliding with Timothy, who stood holding her drink. Red punch spilled down his suit and across the floor. She wiped the drink from her arm. "I'm sorry."

"Are you all right?"

No, she wasn't all right. Couldn't he see that?

"I'm sorry. I can't do this anymore."

She hated the constant questions she couldn't answer, the unfamiliar foods, the rushed pace of the city…and the fact that she'd lost her heart.

"Lizzie?"

She ignored her uncle's voice and ran out the front door of the house and down the steps to the sidewalk. She had to stop Andrew before it was too late. She had to tell him that she'd made her decision, and that no matter what she had said, they'd find a way to work things out between them.

It couldn't be too late.

She ran until her feet throbbed and she couldn't catch her breath. She pulled off her embroidered shoes and stopped in the middle of the sidewalk. A few pedestrians walked along the street. An automobile passed. The sky was dark, but there was no sign of the stars above her. She stared down the row of townhouses spread out before her. She needed to find a taxi, but she had no money and no idea of Andrew's address.

Her uncle's words crept up her spine. This was the world of gangsters, the Mafia, and hired hit men. What had she been thinking?

Someone shouted her name.

A vehicle stopped beside her. The woman's face in the back seat was familiar but she couldn't place it. She'd met so many people tonight. Friends of her aunt. Suitors lined up in a row—all of them eager to befriend New York City's latest heiress.

"Lizzie?" The woman's voice interrupted her thoughts. "Are you all right? I've just come from the party at your aunt's home."

"I'm fine, thank you." Lizzie started walking again.

"I'd be happy to give you a ride back home. You shouldn't be out here alone at night."

"I'm fine."

The automobile came to a stop and the door swung open. A man wearing a dark suit exited the vehicle. "The lady said she wants to give you a ride."

He grabbed Lizzie's arm and pushed her into the back seat. She fought against her attacker, but the man was twice her size. Lights flashed like fireworks behind her eyes. And then she felt nothing.

Andrew woke with a start. The smell of stale cigarette smoke and salt-water filled his lungs. He tried to move, but his hands were tied together. Ignoring the throbbing in his head, he tried to orient himself. The floor was rolling—which either meant he was suffering from vertigo…or he was on a ship.

He sorted through a jumble of memories. What had happened? He'd spoken to Lizzie's uncle at his home. They'd talked about an exploration that was being organized for West Africa. He had to choose between Lizzie and the exploration. But Lizzie's life was in danger. He couldn't leave her. There had been a sharp blow. Stars flashed before his eyes…then darkness.

Voices shouted from above him. Engines roared to life.

Cold reality flushed over him. He was not on this ship as an invited crewmember leaving on an expedition, but as a prisoner. The vessel rumbled beneath him. He had to get off the boat before they headed into the harbor, because what happened tonight had confirmed everything he'd feared. Lizzie's life was in danger, and someone didn't want him around to try to stop them from hurting her.

I need a miracle, Lord. I know I need to give this situation completely to You, but I don't want to lose Lizzie. Not this way.

Pressing against a stack of boxes behind him, he felt the pressure of a handle against the small of his back. Whoever had brought him here hadn't taken his knife.

Two minutes later he finished cutting through the thick rope, freeing his hands and feet. But the vessel had already started moving, which meant time was running out. He ran onto the deck, praying that no one would see him in the shadowy cover of darkness.

He tried to gauge the boat's distance from the dock, but there was no time to second-guess his decision. Climbing onto the rail, he jumped as far as he could and landed on the dock. His foot slipped on impact. His body plummeted over the edge where there was nothing beneath him but air and water. Swallowing the rising panic, he caught the edge of the dock.

Please, God.

His body stopped falling, and he dangled over the edge. Using the last of his strength, he pulled himself onto the dock as the boat motored off into the harbor.

It took over an hour to chase down a taxi and return to the Mac-Tavish home. With the party over and the guests gone, the house sat quiet and dark except for a light shining upstairs. Someone was still awake.

Andrew pounded on the front door, but no one answered. He tried the handle. Unlocked. Opening the door, he made his way through the remains of dirty plates and empty dishes toward the third floor. The maids must have been given the night off.

Andrew burst into the upstairs library. Thomas MacTavish sat behind his desk with a bottle of gin in his hands.

"Andrew Styles." He set the drink down with a thud. "I thought you were on your way to Africa."

"And I thought I was clear when I told you I wasn't interested in your offer."

"You should have been. Then we wouldn't be having this conversation."

Andrew's jaw tensed. "Where is Lizzie?"

"I don't know."

"I don't buy that. If you've done something to hurt her—"

Mr. MacTavish held up the half-empty bottle then took a long drink. "Why would I hurt her? You were the one who got in the way."

"Got in the way of what?"

"My wife. Ella doesn't like you. Of course, she doesn't like me either."

Andrew slammed his hands against the edge of the desk. "I'm tired of playing games. How much did you pay Jamieson so Lizzie wouldn't make it back to New York to collect her inheritance? And who are you paying now?"

"What are you talking about?"

"I suspect you weren't prepared for your father to cut you from his will, but when he did, you still needed that money, didn't you? And you believed that no one would question an accident in the African bush."

"I said I don't know what you're talking about."

"Like you don't know about the telegram telling you that your employee, George Jamieson, is dead?"

"I swear, I had nothing to do with that."

"So you admit to knowing him."

"Of course. He was my employee."

"And the man you sent to kill Lizzie."

MacTavish shook his head. "I've already told you. Why would I try to get rid of Lizzie? She's my niece. She's family. Getting rid of you was Ella's idea."

"What do you mean?"

"Ella had it all planned out. Lizzie would stay and marry some rich man who would give her a name. Status is everything to Ella. Except Lizzie fell in love with you."

"So you tried to ship me off to Africa in the hull of a cargo ship so I wouldn't get involved."

"I had no choice."

"Everyone has a choice."

"I promised I'd get rid of you."

"In exchange for what?"

MacTavish gripped the bottle. "A divorce."

"She asked you for a divorce?"

"No. I asked her for one."

Andrew shook his head. "Why?"

"Because I'm in love with another woman. Clara Jamieson."

"George's—"

"Sister."

The implications rushed through his mind, except at this point, he was no longer certain who'd run the con and who'd been played.

"Where's your wife?"

"I don't know. I came home and she and Lizzie were gone."

"Your wife and niece are both missing, and you're sitting here drinking." Andrew smashed the bottle on the floor and grabbed Mac-Tavish by the collar. "Where are they?"

"I told you, I don't know. I came back from Clara's apartment and the house was empty." MacTavish looked up at him with bloodshot eyes. "She sent George, didn't she?"

"Who did?"

"Clara. She knew about my father's money, but she told me she loved me. Even when my father died and Lizzie received the bulk of the inheritance, she assured me that she loved me. I didn't see it coming, because I thought she truly did love me. Instead she played me."

"By sending her brother to ensure Lizzie didn't make it back to New York, so she could marry you and get your father's inheritance." Andrew took a step back. "She has to have them now. Where would she take them?"

"I don't know."

"Think. You have to have some idea."

"We fought before she left. She mumbled something about the factory and revenge, but I swear I'm telling the truth. I don't know."

Andrew ran down the steps of the townhouse in search of a cab. There was only one other place he knew to check.

CHAPTER THIRTY-THREE

The pounding headache reached from the back of Lizzie's neck to her temples while the pungent smell of gasoline filled her senses. What had happened? A flood of memories engulfed her. Andrew had left without telling her good-bye and she'd run, foolishly trying to find a way to soothe her broken heart.

The room tilted again then came into focus. Two desks, each with a typewriter, a handful of chairs, file cabinets against the wall. Her face pressed against the cold concrete floor as she rolled over in an attempt to sit up. Her vision cleared. It was her uncle's office at the factory with its large posters of MacTavish Candy on the wall.

She blinked. A woman sat at one of the desks. Her hair was short, her face familiar...Lizzie recognized the flashy red dress the woman had worn to her aunt's home last night.

She'd been at her welcome home party.

"Miss MacTavish. You weren't supposed to wake up yet."

Lizzie searched for a name as she finally was able to sit up. "Miss Jamieson?"

"Call me Clara. I so enjoyed our conversation at the party last night. If I had more time I'd love to hear some of your stories. Africa has always intrigued me."

Lizzie tugged on the ropes that secured her hands and feet. "What's going on?"

"Do you mean how did you manage to tangle yourself up in this situation? It is an unfortunate situation for you, I'm afraid, but I need you out of the way." She set down the pen she'd been writing with. "Don't worry. It won't be much longer until all this is over."

"Until what is over?" Lizzie kept tugging at her bonds while studying the layout of the room. The three windows behind the desk were at least six feet up the wall, there were two doors on opposite sides of the room, and a gun sitting in front of Clara. "I would appreciate it if you would untie me now."

The woman's hollow laugh rang out. "You're not exactly in a position to tell me what to do, now are you?"

Clara folded the paper in thirds as if she had all the time in the world. A groan sounded from another corner of the room. Lizzie peered across the dimly lit office. Aunt Ella lay on her side on the hard floor.

Lizzie used her knees to try to scoot across the floor. "Aunt Ella?"

"Leave her alone. She's asleep. For now, anyway."

"Who else is in here?"

"Just the two of you. The last of my loose ends. Of course, it wasn't supposed to get this complicated."

"What was supposed to happen?"

Clara slipped the letter into the envelope and closed the flap. "Let's just say if my brother had carried out his part of the plan, you wouldn't have even crossed the Atlantic."

"He was sent to murder me?"

"Murder seems so…primitive. Dispose of, shall we say? Though I should have known that my brother's feeble attempts would get him killed. And that yesterday's paid hit would fail."

"Samuel Porter?"

"He was another foolish mistake. Porter was more interested in the supply of liquor he was promised in payment. He was supposed to make your death look like a mob hit and ended up getting hit himself. Which proves that if you want to have things done properly, you do have to take care of it yourself."

"Your brother was Uncle Thomas's employee who was killed."

"I was told George was mauled by a lion. A rather unfortunate turn of events for him and for me."

"And all this has to do with my inheritance?"

"You're finally catching on." Clara tapped the envelope against the desk and walked around to the front of it. "Your grandfather was supposed to leave half the estate to Thomas, but apparently he and Thomas never got along well, so in the end, he decided to give it all to you."

"I'll give you the money. Whatever you want. Just let us go."

"It's far too late for that."

"Why?"

"Am I supposed to believe that you would hand over the money and never say a word to anyone? And then there is your uncle, who never had enough guts to go through with a divorce. I will have to make sure he doesn't open his mouth."

"My uncle knows about this?"

"Ah, Thomas. He's such a chump."

Lizzie shook her head. "A what?"

"A chump. Gullible. Though I suppose he'll be innocent, at least of murder, if ignorance counts as a plea—though I could easily pin half a dozen crimes on him if I were the one prosecuting his case. Running a brewery on the premises of the factory, bootlegging, and of course adultery. But I suppose they couldn't throw him into jail for that, now could they? All he needs to know is that his dear wife had enough of his errant ways and decided to end things the easy way. It's horrid, really. A woman slighted by her husband who decides it's better not to live at all than to live without him."

Lizzie tugged harder on the ropes. Andrew might have broken her heart as well, but that didn't mean life wasn't worth living. And she didn't believe her aunt would feel that either. She tried to clear the fog from her mind. Until she could figure a way out of this, perhaps she could find the answers she was looking for.

"Isn't the fortune my uncle has enough for you?"

"What fortune?" Clara laughed again. "It would have been enough until I found out that while Thomas might have his good qualities, his money management leaves much to be desired. Between gambling and other women, the man is completely broke."

So the rumors Andrew heard were true.

Lizzie threw in another baited hook. "What about the liquor he's producing?"

"His entire last shipment was stolen, leaving him in debt and without the capital to continue. That's why he needs me. And this letter from your aunt will explain everything to Thomas and the police."

Lizzie's prayers multiplied. The pieces of the puzzle were falling together, including what happened in Africa, but having answers to her questions wasn't going to be enough to save her and her aunt.

"There's something about these old buildings." Clara picked up a matchbox from the desk and lit one of the matches. The flame burned brightly for a few seconds before she blew it out. "If the circumstances are right, they can burn quite easily."

Panic flared in Lizzie's gut. "You're going to burn the place down?"

"Yes, I will, but everyone will think that Mrs. MacTavish did the dirty deed." Clara leaned against the desk. "She was a heartbroken woman when she found out that not only was her career as a singer washed up, but her husband had been unfaithful."

"Why would anyone believe she did that?"

"Because her husband's been cheating on her and she has no reason left to live. If she's going to die, don't you think she would prefer to take him down with her? Though, of course, it would have been so much easier if Thomas had gone through with the divorce—at least for Mrs. MacTavish."

"You're a foolish woman, Clara Jamieson." Aunt Ella was awake now and had just managed to sit up on the other side of the room. "I granted Thomas the divorce he wanted tonight. Though I never suspected you were the other woman."

Lizzie scooted closer to her aunt on the hard concrete.

"Stay where you are, Lizzie." Clara picked up the gun off the desk.

Lizzie struggled for something else to say. She had to keep the woman talking. "You won't get away with this."

"Says who? The workers aren't due in for hours. Thomas is sound asleep in my bed where I left him. It's the end of the line for both you and your aunt."

The door swung open. Clara turned and aimed her gun at the intruder. Andrew stood in the doorway.

Andrew took in the scene in one panic-filled moment. "Lizzie?"

"Andrew?" Her voice broke. "My uncle told me you were leaving for Africa this morning."

He caught the mixture of hurt and relief in her eyes and took a step toward her. "I turned down his generous offer, but apparently he didn't listen. I woke up in the middle of the night on a ship."

"Don't come any farther." The woman who was apparently in charge of the situation pointed her weapon at him. "You've really put me in an awkward position, Mr. Styles. I'd hoped for one body to dispose of, and now it seems we're up to three."

"Who are you?"

"Clara Jamieson." Lizzie answered the question for her. "George Jamieson's sister. The man who was sent to Africa to murder me."

Andrew studied the room for a way out. "From what I've heard, things didn't turn out so well for your brother."

"No, they didn't."

He'd called Charlie on a public phone on his way to the factory and told him where he was going, but even if his brother arrived with the whole New York City police force, they'd never get here in time. The only obvious solution was to disarm Clara.

Before he could get to *how* he'd do it, the door slammed open behind him. A second later, the door across the room burst open and a dozen federal prohibition officers raided the office. Someone screamed for everyone to get down on the floor. Andrew dropped to his knees. Clara's gun dropped to the ground as one of the men slapped handcuffs on her.

Clara glared at Andrew. "How did you know I would be here?"

Andrew shook his head. "I didn't. Not for sure, anyway."

"I'm the one who called in the tip." Lizzie's aunt stood up slowly. "You didn't really think I'd let my husband go without a fight, did you? I called the police this evening and told them that this factory was being used as a brewery and that there were people working shifts here at night. I wanted him to suffer for what he has done to me. Ironic, isn't it, that this is the place you chose to bring us? Any other place and you might actually have gotten away with murder."

Another uniformed officer entered the office. "The tip was correct. There are barrels in vats in the east wing of the building. It's an entire setup."

"I believe you'll find my husband, Thomas MacTavish—"

"At home." Andrew tried to spare Lizzie's aunt any further embarrassment. "Can we leave?"

"As soon as I get statements from each of you, you'll be free to go."

"You didn't leave me." Lizzie stepped in front of him, still wearing the dress from the party.

"I'd never leave without saying good-bye."

"My uncle told me they offered you a place on an exploration team."

"Did he tell you that I turned it down because I'm in love with you?"

Tears formed in her eyes. "I've never been so terrified. She wanted me dead so she could marry my uncle and get my inheritance."

Andrew brushed his hand across her cheek to wipe away the tears, then he gathered Lizzie into his arms. "It's all over now. You're safe."

CHAPTER THIRTY-FOUR

Lizzie had been mesmerized by the fifty-four-story terra-cotta building with its ornate lobby, glittering mosaics, and glass-walled elevator shaft that had taken them from the lobby to the top-story observation deck. But it was the view from the top of the Woolworth Building that took her breath away.

New York City sprawled beneath them with the twinkling lights of its vast landscape appearing as thousands of stars from the wrap-around cupola where a handful of other visitors had joined them. But she hardly noticed their presence. Andrew nestled against her with his arms wrapped around her waist, seemingly as captivated by the scene as she was. "It might not be as majestic as the African sky framing the savannah, but you can see everything from here. The New York Harbor, Liberty Island, Midtown, Chinatown—"

"It's incredible." She shivered and leaned closer against him.

"You're cold."

"I'm far too content to care."

Lizzie gazed down at the harbor. The scene Frank Woolworth offered to the world made her feel like a child who'd just opened her first package at Christmas.

"Standing here makes Africa seem like a lifetime away." She hadn't come close to forgetting, but neither did she continue to feel haunted by some of the memories.

"Do you still think about going back?"

"Every day. But so much has happened since the moment I stepped off the *Berengaria* a month ago."

Her efforts to fit into life in New York, the frightening attempts on her life, her aunt and uncle's betrayal, and even the telegram she'd received with the news that Kakoba and his family had been able to return home—all of it had forced her to grapple with who she really was. It was something she'd longed to share with Andrew as he'd helped her deal with her uncle's arrest and her aunt's diminishing health, but it had taken her this long to find the words to express how she felt.

She turned around and looked up at him, still close enough that she could feel the warmth of his breath against her face. "I've had to change the way I look at life. My uncle's identity was so wrapped up in worldly possessions that he was determined to do anything to get ahead. And my aunt was no different. She was willing to betray me for a chance to keep her status as a wealthy woman."

He pushed back a strand of hair the wind had blown against her forehead. "It's an easy trap to fall into. I'm just as guilty. When I thought I'd lost everything I was, I ran."

"And I hid. Except who I am isn't based on how much money I have, or what culture I'm from, or where I live. Who I am is based on who God is."

"Those are wise words coming from one so young."

She laughed then laid her head against his chest. She could feel his heartbeat, the warmth of his presence…and the wonder of discovering unexpected love."Before we go back down, I have something to give you."

Lizzie took a step back as he pulled something from his pocket, then she gasped. "It's my mother's necklace."

"I had a replica made for you." His familiar blue eyes gazed down at her, causing her heart to tremble. "I know how much the locket meant to you, and how hard it was for you to give it away."

A well of emotion surfaced. She pressed her hand against her lips and shook her head, trying to stop the tears. "I don't know what to say."

Andrew clasped the locket around her neck. "Say you'll marry me."

Overflowing joy erupted but was quickly tempered by the fears she still hadn't gotten control of. "There are still so many unknowns. I have to find a place for my aunt to live, and you'd never be content living an isolated life like mine—"

"Slow down." He touched his finger against her lips. "You're already worried that God can't triumph through any circumstance."

She pressed her lips together and smiled. Choosing to have her identity with Christ also meant casting all her cares on the One who created her.

"I have an aunt who lives along the oceanfront not far from here," Andrew continued. "She's been looking for a companion and has assured me that your aunt is welcome to live there. She'll be well taken care of and will have the ocean to enjoy, new friends, and a new start."

Some of the anger she'd felt toward the older woman began to dissipate. "I think she'd like that."

"Secondly, I spoke to the Carruths a few days ago. They are looking for a couple to join them at the mission station. You could work with Dr. Carruth in the hospital while I teach in the surrounding towns and villages, including Kakoba's. It would be the fulfillment of a long-lost dream, and one I could fulfill with you by my side." Andrew bent down on one knee. "I want you to be my wife, Lizzie MacTavish."

The small crowd around them began to clap, but all she could see was the one man who'd captured her heart.

"Yes." Her pulse quickened. "Yes, I'll marry you."

The shimmering lights of New York spread out beneath them like the millions of stars in the African night sky. Andrew pulled her to him and drew his arms around her. This time there was no hesitancy in what she wanted as he pressed his lips against hers and sealed their promise with a kiss.

Dear Reader,

Thank you so much for embarking on Lizzie and Andrew's journey with me. In writing their story, I found myself challenged on several levels. Lizzie struggled over belonging, because she didn't feel as if she fit completely into either world. Our identity in Christ, though, is not based on where we live, who we are, or what our culture is. It's based on who He is. We all struggle to fit in, but if we base our identity on Him, we will find true freedom.

Maybe you feel more like Andrew and are running from God because you don't understand why He allowed tragedy to strike your life. In Isaiah chapter 40, Israel felt that God didn't understand what they were going through. Isaiah begins his answer with a question in verse twenty-one. Do you not know? Have you not heard? The Lord is big! He will never grow tired or weary. He is not only the creator of the world who brings out the starry host at night and calls them one by one by name, but He's the creator of you!

He is the everlasting God, the Creator of the ends of the earth who never grows tired or weary. He gives strength to the weary and increases the power of the weak. He comes to those who put their hope in him and renews their strength so they can soar on wings like eagles. God doesn't always change circumstances, but His plan will triumph through any circumstances we face.

So who am I? Who are you?

We are children of the King of kings, the creator of the universe. God has called us to follow Him, to serve others through His strength, to find intimacy with Him, and to discover that who we are is not based on our accomplishments any more than it is based on our regrets and failures.

God, we want to be more like You. Content to dream big, but also to enjoy the ups and downs of the journey while we get there. We want to be content to love family, friends, and those around us. We want to be content to serve others in Your name. Content to cry with those around us when our hearts are breaking, but also to never forget that true contentment cannot be found in our circumstances, but only through You, because You are the one who gives us strength to get through each day.

Be blessed today!
Lisa Harris

∽

FROM MY KITCHEN TO YOURS...

One of the things I loved about writing this book was the research involved, from the endless African savannah to the hustle and bustle of New York City in the early 1920s. Researching about favorite foods from that era turned out to be especially interesting. For example, salads back in the early 1900s had always been a bit...messy. The solution? Pour your fruits, canned and cooked vegetables, and even meats into gelatin. This brought about things like jellied tomato and pimiento salad, sardines in aspic, fruited Jell-O salads, and jellied anchovy molds.

How many of you still love Jell-O? Okay, maybe not with pimientos and sardines, but the yummy fruit and whipped cream kind. My favorite growing up was lime Jell-O with pineapple and shredded cheddar cheese.

While writing the book, I held a contest on my blog to see what kind of gelatin my readers enjoyed by asking them to submit their favorite recipes. Thanks to my wonderful blog readers, I ended up with a great selection from layered Jell-O, to cookies, to cakes. You can visit my blog and read the submitted recipes in the comments of my Crazy Contest post. I had my children vote on their favorites and I've included two of them below. Thanks to Abi and Jackie for submitting your recipes!

Cherry Coke Salad

1 20 oz. can cherry pie filling
1½ cups water
½ cup sugar
1 12 oz. can coke, room temperature
2 small boxes cherry Jell-O

Mix pie filling, water, and sugar. Bring mixture to a boil. Boil until mixture is no longer cloudy (I generally boil 10 minutes). Remove from heat. Add Jell-O, stir, and cool. Add Coke. Pour in bowl or mold and refrigerate until firm ~Abi

My children also unanimously chose this simple recipe idea from Jackie.

"I always liked the strawberry Jell-O with miniature marshmallows in it that my grandmother made...back in those days Jell-O came wrapped in a sort of waxed cream-colored paper that she let my sister and me have so we could lick off the last little grain of Jell-O...oh, the good ole days!"

Enjoy!

summerside
PRESS™

Soul-stirring romance...set against a historical backdrop readers will love!

Summerside Press™ is pleased to present our fresh new line of historical romance fiction—including stories set amid the action-packed eras of the twentieth century.

Watch for a number of new Summerside Press™ historical romance titles to release in 2011.

NOW AVAILABLE IN STORES

Sons of Thunder
BY SUSAN MAY WARREN
ISBN 978-1-935416-67-8

The Crimson Cipher
BY SUSAN PAGE DAVIS
ISBN 978-1-60936-012-2

Songbird Under a German Moon
BY TRICIA GOYER
ISBN 978-1-935416-68-5

Stars in the Night
BY CARA PUTMAN
ISBN 978-1-60936-011-5

The Silent Order
BY MELANIE DOBSON
ISBN 978-1-60936-019-1

Nightingale
BY SUSAN MAY WARREN
ISBN 978-1-60936-025-2

COMING SOON

Exciting New Historical Romance Stories by These Great Authors—
Margaret Daley...DiAnn Mills...Hannah Alexander...and MORE!